A Pacifica Resort Novel

First Loves *and* Last Resorts

DEE ROLLINGS

First Loves and Last Resorts: A Pacifica Resort Novel (Book 3)

First paperback edition May 2025

979-8-9861581-6-7 (Ebook)

979-8-9861581-7-4 (Paperback)

To YOU. For being here with me. Whether this is your first time diving into one of my stories or your fourth, I'm so damn grateful that you exist.

Chapter One

I've only ever slept with one man.

Which wasn't that big of a deal until a year and a half ago when he told me he just wasn't that into me. That maybe he hadn't ever been into me.

Shaking my head to clear that past version of myself, I glanced out the window of the private jet, thankful we'd finally hit a cruising altitude. Unfortunately, I knew I couldn't get through this flight without getting the whole plan out of Zane. I'd been busy at the office trying to make time for this trip, but if I was being honest with myself, I was avoiding this conversation until the last possible minute. We were almost out of time. "Does anyone know what's really going on between us?"

His lips twisted into a frown as he straightened his salmon-colored button-down. For every black outfit I wore, he was the pastel counterpart. "Well, my cousin David knows everything."

"Everything?"

"Mostly everything. He knows about Caleb. And that

I moved out. He thinks we're starting the divorce, but that it's not finalized yet." His fingers tapped against his armrest. He was more nervous than he was letting on.

"I can't fucking believe we're doing this." I rubbed my face with my hands. "Why did we think this would be a good idea?"

For the next two weeks, Zane and I would have to pretend we were still married. Or at least until we could sit his parents down and tell them the truth. For the sake of this family reunion we couldn't get out of.

Zane rolled his eyes at me. "Don't tell me you're having cold feet. You're the most terrifying woman I know." I must have made a face because he added, "I mean that as a compliment."

I had been told my whole life that I was intimidating, and I learned early on to lean into it, so I knew he meant it kindly. I'd never meant to be that woman. At first, I just wanted to be left alone. But when my aloofness started getting me opportunities in the business world, not letting people second-guess me, I let it consume me. "I just hate that I have to look your mom in the eye and tell her we split up."

He lifted an eyebrow. "Do you think she's going to be surprised?"

"It's not like you were obsessed with David Hasselhoff or Burt Reynolds when you were growing up, Zane."

"I mean about the divorce, smartass. Even if I hadn't figured myself out, we'd still be ending like this, and you know it."

I pulled back like I'd been slapped. He never spoke like this during any of our counseling sessions. Not that

I'd gone to very many of them. "I thought we were fine, thank you very much."

I lay against the headrest of my seat, thankful that my ex-husband had followed through with his promise of bringing one of his family's private planes to and from Michigan for this sham of a reunion.

After the lone flight attendant brought us each a glass of wine, I thanked her and turned to him, sitting next to me with his sleep mask perched on his forehead. He really was beautiful. Perfect hair, perfect skin, and a smile that should have broken a thousand hearts before he found me.

When your husband sits you down and tells you it's not you, it's him, usually he's full of shit. And yes, mine followed it up with the cliché that he'd met someone else.

I just didn't expect the other person to be his personal trainer. His very muscular, very *male* personal trainer.

We stayed friends, because no matter how upsetting this new arrangement was, how weird our life had become, I still loved him.

Not that soul-crushing, romantic kind of love, obviously. And maybe I hadn't loved him like I should have for a long time. Maybe I had never loved him in that way that envelops your entire being.

Sure, we weren't married anymore, but despite all the drama we'd kept privately between us, he was still my best friend, and had been since we were twenty years old.

The first thing we had in common when we met the first week of college was our heritage. We were both half white and half Asian, but where I'd tried to blend into both cultures, he was able to shine in any social circle he joined. He was outgoing, but serious about the future. And he loved me, which was the most important thing that lost, lonely Lizette needed at the time.

He put his hand on my knee, bringing me back to the present. "Izzy. We've been married on paper only for years. You know this. Your career is your husband and I'm just the guy who slept in your bed."

"That's not . . ."

"What did your parents say when you told them?" He asked, a sneaky smile shifting his lips to one side.

I leaned forward, reaching for my drink, mumbling my response.

"What was that? I couldn't hear you." He cupped his hand over his ear dramatically.

I straightened, glaring at him. "I haven't told them."

"Oh, okay then." He nodded, but the smile crept further across his face.

"You know how different it is for me, Zane. Your family cares about you. They want to spend time with you."

"Reece likes spending time with you when he's in town. Or do you not remember being the officiant at his wedding last month?" My brother had just made all of his dreams come true, despite his personal issues. I hadn't had the heart to spring our divorce on him on the best day of his life.

"Reece is different." It was my dad I didn't want to deal with, but I didn't want to admit it. I took a large gulp of my wine. If I was going to revisit my family history, I needed some liquid courage.

"Come here." Zane pulled me into his arms, which

was awkward with the armrest between us. "Fuck anyone who doesn't love you." I started to pull away, but he squeezed me tighter. "No, Izzy. You're perfect just the way you are."

I set my glass back on the table in front of us, scooting to the edge of my seat so I could wrap my arms around him. "Camilla and Blake know. That's what matters for now." My two best friends knew everything. Even though they'd had to pry it out of me.

This trip to Michigan could work. It was private enough in the Upper Peninsula that we could share the news and move on with our lives without it ending up all over the internet. Zane's family owned one of the oldest banks in China. They had pull that was even stronger than mine.

And I was ready to move on. My two friends made me promise to start dating as soon as this trip was over, and a little part of me was almost excited about it. Almost. I wasn't looking for anything serious, but it might be nice to have sex again. It had been a very, very long time. Which, I also had to admit, was a big sign that I had a gay husband.

He released our hug, pulling away and lying back against his seat. "I just hope my brother doesn't make this whole thing about him."

Ah yes, Bradley. The real reason I was on this trip. "We'll just avoid him until we can talk to your parents. Maybe you could even fly Caleb in after?"

"Why are you so confident that my parents will be okay with all of this?" he asked. I shrugged, but didn't answer, so he went on, "I'm the first person in our family that's ever been divorced. Ever. Hundreds of years of traditional family values, and I'm the one to throw it all down the drain."

"That's not something your mom and dad are going to worry about. They're very open-minded." It was one of the reasons I had loved him so easily when we were young.

"But Bradley's running for senate. Any change to his platform has the possibility of destroying his campaign." This was easily the tenth time I'd heard these exact words. The panic in his voice every time he said them was the only reason I'd packed my bags and come on this trip.

I kicked my shoes off, laying my head against the back of my chair, a little sick of having this conversation again. "Bradley's the most liberal person in your family in generations. He's not going to be concerned about us splitting up at all." I said it confidently, although I couldn't fight the itch of doubt creeping in.

Zane switched into an impressive newscaster impression, picking up his glass and holding it like a microphone. "Bradley Xu, arguably the most popular candidate in California's senate race, has been covering up for his brother after he destroyed his long-term marriage with his doting wife by cheating on her with another man. If he's hiding this, what else is he not telling us? More on this story at six."

I cringed, grabbing my glass and taking a sip. "Okay, when you put it that way, it does seem pretty bad." We had gone through all that trouble of petitioning the judge to keep the records of our divorce sealed. Sure, if someone really wanted to find out that we weren't together, they could, but both of us had agreed to keep things quiet about the matter because of our own financial situations. He was a trust fund baby set to inherit billions, and I was the heiress to an international real estate conglomerate. We'd been perfect on paper, but not anywhere else.

But he had never done me dirty, so to speak. "You didn't cheat on me. For the record."

"Emotional cheating is real cheating, Iz." His eyes were sad as he took another drink from his glass without breaking eye contact.

I let out a sigh. I had forgiven him so many months ago, sitting in our therapist's office. It was going to take some time for him to forgive himself, however. "We both made mistakes. I wasn't an attentive wife," I said, remembering the day he told me about Caleb. How it hadn't hurt as bad as it should have. Sure, it was a shock, but my world wasn't shattered or anything. I didn't think I was going to die from it.

He held his free hand out, his palm open. "For old times' sake?"

I took it in mine and squeezed. "We can get through this reunion. And hopefully the rest of this election season." I tried to keep my voice light, but the doom of Bradley's PR team breathing down our necks was a little much.

I couldn't help but worry about the other member of our triangle. "How does Caleb feel about this?"

"Lizette. He knows I want to tell them. That I'm ready to tell them. But I'm afraid that meeting him will be too much for them. At least for right now. I want to show my parents that we're not any different just because we're not married anymore."

Maybe he wasn't any different, but I felt like a stranger in my own skin. And I wasn't sure if I knew what kind of woman I was becoming. Maybe this trip would help me figure out what I wanted next.

My purse vibrated on the chair across the table. I let go of his hand and scooped it up.

"What's in your Birkin bag, hon?" Zane asked, knowing that I never traveled light when it came to electronics.

"Just my laptop and phone." I set my drink down, unclasped the bag, and dug inside.

"How many phones?" he huffed a laugh, like he had a pretty good guess.

I bit my bottom lip, hating how well he knew me. "Only three."

He leaned over, looking into my purse. "You sure there isn't another one in there?"

"Obviously," I grumbled. His grin meant he didn't believe me at all. "Okay, I guess it's not obvious." I only needed three phones when I was away from the office for extended periods. My personal line, US business line, and my international one.

Just in case.

I pointed to his attaché case in the seat across from him. "Are you going to keep teasing me, or are we going to play what's in your bag, too?"

He laughed out loud. "Okay, true. But I was hoping to take a nap for the next five hours. What was your plan?" He also already knew the answer to this question.

I stared him straight in the eye, not willing to feel guilty for what I was about to say. "Work."

He smiled, leaning back against his headrest. "You love what you do, and you're damn good at it." Then he shrugged and pulled his sleeping mask over his eyes. "But don't you want more? A life outside of the office?" he lifted the mask off one eye, peering at me. "That was a rhetorical question, by the way. It's time for my beauty sleep." He covered his face again and reclined his seat.

I did want more. But there was too much on my plate to get there. At least right now.

I sat, facing forward for a few minutes, trying to just experience the present moment, something our therapist had asked me to try during the divorce. I counted the seconds . . . only making it to seventy before I pulled my computer out of my bag.

If Zane was going to sleep, I might as well check emails. Besides, the more I got done on the plane, the less I had to do when we got there.

I could be present when we landed.

I situated my computer on the table and took a final sip of wine before opening the company email going through anything I'd missed since leaving the office late last night.

A few hours passed. It was amazing how much I could get done in a quiet airplane with only the sound of Zane's soft snores keeping me company. A notification for an incoming email popped up, and I clicked it. It was from Aniyah, my right-hand woman at The Howell Group, with just the words "Urgent: The Azure Inn LISTED!" as the subject line.

A scream left my lips as I read the first lines. Zane pulled off his mask, throwing his hands up in the air, absolutely terrified. "What is it? Are we crashing?"

I stood up, clapping my hands together. "No. Oh my God. The Azure is for sale."

"Lizette!" he admonished me with the voice he always used when he thought I had lost touch with reality. He wiped at the drool that had spilled out over his chin.

More to myself than to him, I said, "This hotel has been my white whale since I joined the board. Do you know what it would mean for our company if I bought it?"

"You need to find a boyfriend," he mumbled under his breath before putting his mask back on and lying down again. I paced the aisle for a few moments, wondering what this property could mean for me. A minute later, he sat his seat up and pulled the mask off. "Wait. Isn't The Azure next to The Pacifica? Why do you need two properties next to each other?"

I felt the gleam in my eye when I looked up at Zane, and I'm sure I looked like some sort of zealot, but I didn't care. "When I buy The Azure, I can merge it with The Pacifica. It could be Santa Barbara's most popular mega-resort."

"I thought the whole point of The Pacifica was to take a step back from your father's corporate takeovers and leave the soul of the property intact?"

"I know, and it is. But don't you see how this could be something really special?" I continued walking up and down the aisle, thinking of the right words. "This has been the one property my father had his eye on but wasn't able to acquire. All over the world, that man walked into boardrooms and steamrolled people into letting him buy their properties for hundreds of thousands of dollars less than what they were worth. He slaps a little lipstick on them, and bam, they're hot spots for socialites and influencers."

"So you want to do the same thing to The Azure?" His eyebrows bunched together skeptically.

"No. What Blake and I did for The Pacifica renovations is what we're doing with The Howell Group from now on. The building has its own energy, its own life. But I do want to spend time in the property and get a feel for its bones. Maybe it would like being merged with The Pacifica." My fingers itched to send emails to our interior designers. "My dad would flip!" I clapped my hands together, looking Zane in the eye. "Imagine how he would react if this resort became the diamond in the collection because of all the work I'm going to put into it."

"There it is," he said, laughing.

"What?"

"Your umbilical cord is showing." He patted the seat next to him, urging me to sit down. "You know you don't need that asshole's approval to be happy."

"First of all, you do know we get our umbilical cords from our mothers, right?" I waved him off, refusing to take a seat. This was about me, not my father. Sure, The Azure Inn in Santa Barbara was my father's goal for so many years, but it was my goal, too. It's why we focused our acquisitions on Santa Barbara when he started preparing me to take over for him. Zane and I had moved there from Malibu three years ago just so I could be closer to the resorts in the area, which I might need to remind him was a big plus for how his life has changed so far. "And secondly, I said nothing about needing his approval." I hated how I felt so defensive over this.

The Azure had become the North Star of The Howell Group. And it was within reach.

Zane's face turned soft, understanding where I was coming from. "I know you didn't say it, but it's written all over you."

I looked down at myself like I could see what he was saying. "I want this for me. This is what will make me happy."

He cringed. "Are you sure about that?"

I went back to the table, leaning over my laptop, scanning the rest of the email. Aniyah had confirmed that they were taking offers, so we'd have to come up with something worthwhile if we really wanted it.

I thought about my dad and how he would feel if I could make this deal happen. Sure, he wasn't my favorite person, especially after things went down the way they did with my brother. Plus, he was retired, living his best life in Singapore with my mom. But Zane was right. I whispered, "I don't think I'll ever shake the need to live up to his expectations." Maybe I should go back to therapy to talk this out. I'd make an appointment when we got home from this trip. There would be a lot to discuss after this adventure was over, anyway.

"Well, knowing is half the battle," he replied groggily, knowing I was already lost to my work. He laid his chair back again, ready to continue his nap.

I reread Aniyah's email a few more times. There was no hotel on the West Coast I wanted more than this one. Obsessed was an understatement. I wouldn't let anyone know this, but I'd gladly sell all of our California properties for this one. Well, maybe not The Pacifica. But anywhere else was collateral.

There weren't many things I had an emotional attachment to, and it was probably my dad's fault, but I'd always dreamed of walking through the lobby of The Azure, knowing I'd made it my own.

I sat in my seat and typed my reply to Aniyah: *I don't care what we have to do to afford this. Let's make it happen.*

Her reply came within a minute, like she had been sitting at her computer waiting for me to respond: *I'm already on it. Let's schedule a conference call to discuss our strategy.*

I looked at my husband. Ex-husband. Pretend husband. I'd just have to slip away for a little while tomorrow. He'd understand.

So I replied: *How early will you be at the office in the morning?*

Chapter Two

We rolled our suitcases to the passenger pickup area to wait for David. Zane was on the phone with his mom, trying to calm her down—her own flight was delayed until tomorrow, and she would miss out on a whole day of fun. He tried to explain that we weren't there yet either, but she was beyond listening to logic.

If a damn flight delay was so upsetting, how would she react when we told her we weren't married anymore?

I fiddled with the zipper of my jacket, regretting putting it on, even though it was nearly ten p.m. I'd hoped being up north would be cooler this late into May, but I was wrong. I unzipped the jacket, not wanting to carry it around, or worse, tie it around my waist.

I noticed a chip on my fingernail and recoiled. I kept them long and red, never any other color. They looked pretty and powerful, but secretly the paint kept me from nervously chewing on them.

I'd spent my entire adult life projecting my boss bitch persona and, at this point in my life, I really felt like her most of the time. Hell, it had been a decade since I wore a single color. Just black and dark gray for me. It made me look unapproachable, which I loved.

But at times like this, standing in an airport with a speck on my armor, I wasn't sure if I even knew who I was anymore.

Sometimes all I wanted to do was give it all up. Sell all my properties, curl up on a couch, and spend the rest of my life reading romance novels with plenty of smut.

But I had thousands of people relying on me. I couldn't stop working. Who would replace me? I couldn't trust anyone else to put their soul into The Howell Group the way I had.

So that dream had to get quietly tucked into the back of my head once again.

I poked at the missing speck of nail polish with my thumb. This was going to be such a long vacation.

My business phone rang just as a fifteen-passenger van parked in front of us, blocking my view of the road. A big family piled out around me, which wasn't the best situation for whatever this call was about, so I stepped away for a moment. "I'll be right back," I said to Zane before finding a nearby planter.

I leaned against the concrete edge as Aniyah's voice came by on the other end without even saying hello. "Well, I have some okay news and some shitty news."

"Can you resolve the shitty part without ever telling me?" One thing I adored about Aniyah was her ability to handle everyone's problems, no matter what. Sometimes I wondered what she took care of without me, but I was too afraid of the truth. After all, she only brought the biggest problems to me.

She hesitated before answering. "I probably could, but you're going to want to hear this."

"Fine. Give me the okay stuff first, though." I promised myself I'd take this time off as a vacation, but the Azure deal might mean I would be working more than I'd wanted to after all. Lord knew it had been years since my last non-business related trip. I didn't want to figure out how long it had actually been.

"The holding company that owns The Azure would love to hear from us." She barely contained the excitement in her voice, which made me excited, too.

"Did they say anything else?"

"No. The email wasn't exactly personalized, so I didn't get a tone. Which is why I'm not sure if it's good or bad."

"Damn. Okay, what's the bad news?"

She let out a heavy breath as she hesitated, like she was dwelling on how to tell me whatever this was. "The Carlisles already submitted a bid. I think they knew about it before it went on the market. I don't doubt that we will come up with great numbers, but there's a slight chance that they'll buy the property out from under us."

"Which would make them neighbors with The Pacifica."

"Exactly. And I know you have some bad blood with—"

I cut her off. "It's not bad blood. They're vile people."

"Are they, though?" She said, skepticism filling her voice.

I felt myself growl. "James Carlisle is a wretched old man who screwed my father out of multiple million-dollar deals and spent decades trying to trash him in corporate real estate networks. They're not good people."

I could almost hear the grimace on her face. "But your father . . ." her voice trailed off.

"I know. My father is who he is. But as far as I'm concerned, our two families are like the Hatfields and the McCoys. We've hated each other forever and we aren't stopping anytime soon."

"I might be overstepping, but why?"

I let out a breath. "I don't know the whole story, but my father had worked for the Carlisles before he left California for Singapore. Before he met my mom. And then as soon as my mother and he began their business, the one company that stepped in and blocked them from almost every deal they tried to make was The Carlisle Corporation. They knew my dad had the potential to compete with them at a level they'd never seen, so they tried to crush him. It's the only possibility I can think of."

"But is this your fight? Is it worth it to get into the mix? We already own The Pacifica."

"Look, I want to do what we did for The Pacifica to this property. Which can't happen if the Carlisles get their way. They'll turn it into a cookie cutter just like the big corporations always do—like we used to do. We have to do whatever we can to stop them. They're terrible." I'm sure it would seem irrational to an outsider, but I'd been raised to think of the Carlisle family as the enemy. Getting something that they had their eye on made this deal even more important than before.

"Do you really think they'll ruin The Azure?" I wondered if she was thinking the same as me. What it would look like to get turned into a generic motel.

"It's personal now, with them bidding on the property next door. Who knows what they would do to drive customers away from us? We'll start with this, and then maybe we'll start buying shit next door to theirs." I paused for a few seconds, knowing I sounded like a maniac. "We can't let them win."

I had poured my entire life into this company. I'd given up sleep, a social life, and my marriage for the success that my family business had. If The Howell Group lost this deal to our top competitors, I wouldn't know what to do with myself. I'd be a disgrace to both of my parents. A disgrace to our board of directors.

"I have every bit of faith in you, and I'll do whatever needs to be done," she said before Zane's voice bellowed across the passenger pickup area.

"He's here!" He pointed to a large black SUV pulling up to the sidewalk.

I hung up my phone and went to grab my suitcase from where I'd left it near Zane, but it wasn't there. I thought he'd had an eye on it, but maybe I didn't communicate clearly enough when I'd walked away.

Panic rushed through me. I looked up and down the sidewalk, but my Louis Vuitton rolling trunk was nowhere to be seen. "Where's my luggage?"

I barely noticed David get out of the Escalade to help Zane with his bags as I called out to the guys, "Did either of you see where it went?"

They looked confused, so I gave up on them and rushed back inside the tiny airport.

It was gone. Gone. All my clothes. All my shoes. Sunblock. Cosmetics. My identity.

"Help!" I yelled, but the airport was nearly empty. I found a security guard locking up a gate around the concourse. "I need help. My luggage was stolen."

He looked me up and down, and I became very aware that I did not belong in this very small town so far from home. "Ma'am. That sort of thing doesn't happen here. Are you sure you didn't misplace it?"

My blood boiled. "Do you think I'm dumb enough to misplace a ten thousand dollar suitcase?" My voice screeched across the airport.

His eyes doubled in size. I really was out of place here. "No, ma'am, that's not what I meant. I can take a look around, but we've never had a theft in the twenty years I've worked here. You probably just forgot it somewhere."

"That is absolutely incorrect. It's been stolen," I practically yelled in his face, offended that he would accuse me of losing it.

He glanced up and down the tiny concourse. "Everyone knows each other here. It's not that kind of place."

I unlocked my phone, still in my hand. "What's the sheriff's number?"

He stepped from one foot to the other and rattled off the number. "Judging by how late it is, ma'am, he's probably asleep."

The phone rang and rang, finally going to voicemail. "Hello. This is Lizette Howell-Xu. I'm calling to report a theft." I left my numbers: the one for this phone, the one for my personal line, and the one that would reach my assistant back in California. "Please call me back as soon as possible."

Zane appeared at my side, his hand on my lower back. It was a gesture I had taken for granted for so long. Before our flight, it had been forever since someone had touched me. Something else to talk to the therapist about later.

I turned to him, explaining what had happened, and the security guard assured us he would figure out where my suitcase had gone. The fact that he waited until my husband came to save me was not lost on me at all.

I told him everything I'd remembered, which in the blink of an eye was not much. But as I tried to tell the story from an outside perspective, I remembered one annoying thing. "The van! I bet someone grabbed it when they pulled up." I wanted to throw up. To get back on the plane and go home. This was a complete disaster.

His eyebrows scrunched together. "The van that just dropped off the Heikkinens for their annual trip to Finland?" His next look told me exactly how crazy he thought I was being. "That's extremely unlikely."

I wasn't sure how the rest of the conversation went, as it became a blur when I blacked out from rage, but Zane got the man's contact information and made him promise to check the cameras as soon as he could.

My former husband escorted me out the door and

toward the waiting car. He murmured something I didn't quite pick up, but then he said, "I know that if I tell you they're just things, you'll rip my balls off and throw them in the lake, but I promise this isn't the end of the world. We can replace everything that was stolen."

It was difficult to breathe. My lungs felt like they were slowly being crushed.

"You're the one who was harping on me for bringing my work with me, but guess what I have left? My work bag. It's the only thing I have." Not just physically, but metaphorically, too.

This felt worse than when Zane sat me down and told me he was moving out. That was something I could move on from, or at least bury my head in the sand over. Having my belongings gone in the blink of an eye was a crisis I wasn't prepared for.

He gripped my shoulders, not hard enough to hurt, but enough to get my attention. "Your work is not all you have left. You have me. You have our family we are about to spend time with. You have the girls back home. You even have your brother, even if he is busy finding himself in Europe right now. We all love you, but I can bet that every single one of us would tell you to focus on the things you can control in this moment." When I started to protest, he said, "This is a small town and your luggage will be found in the morning. If not, we'll order you some more. Lord knows we both have enough to buy you a whole new wardrobe."

I closed my eyes. "You don't understand."

He inched closer to me, rubbing up and down my

arms. "You think I don't see you hiding behind your armor? Your black power suits are like chain mail." He let go of me, walking toward the car. "Use this as a moment to learn, Iz. A moment to discover who you really are."

I shook my head, but followed him anyway. I don't know what hurt more, losing two weeks' worth of clothes and toiletries, or his sharp words that rang true.

It was nearly midnight when we made it to the Lac Brumeux Resort. The hour-long drive had been mental agony, so I sat in the back seat, pretending to listen to David and Zane catching up.

The entire property was bathed in darkness, so I wasn't sure what kind of vacation we were embarking upon, but based on Zane's mother Alice's previous picks for family reunions, I would bet that this place was quaint, cozy, and had enough events to keep all of us busy while we caught up. There had to be an itinerary somewhere that had each of the next ten days planned down to the minute.

I strived to be as organized as Alice. Which was saying something, based on how many times in my life my own family harped on me for being an overbearing micromanager.

We pulled up to a large building, a log cabin surrounded by trees. It was two stories, but from the look of it on the outside, it was mostly taken up by a giant glass chandelier just inside the tall double doors.

Zane and I followed David into the building, which

had a small countertop on the other side of the chandelier, a restaurant to the left, and what looked like a gift shop to the right. When we got closer to the counter, I noticed a few desks in the back, framed by large windows. David pointed to one of the windows. "The lake is just on the other side of this building, down at the bottom of the hill."

There must have been a hallway behind the gift shop that lead to the little office area, because the sound of a door opening echoed through the whole place, and then a woman in her midtwenties came down the corridor. "Hi there. How can I help you?" she asked the man I was pretending to still be married to.

"Zane Xu, checking in." He had a bright smile on his face, despite the anxiety that I'd felt the entire drive here.

She checked her computer briefly. "Great. You're the last of your party staying in the small cabins to check in."

She went through the process of taking his ID and credit card for incidentals, but when she was done, she waved me over and laid a paper map on the counter. It was beautifully illustrated and showed just how sprawling the property was.

"You're here." She pointed to a drawing of the cabin we were standing in. It was to the far left, with the outline of the lake across the top of the page. Then she ran her finger along a trail to the right. "You can take the walking path this way to the cabins, or you can go back down the road you came to get there." While she double-checked her binder, for which tiny house was ours, I looked at the rest of the property. There was a small cabin about every hundred or so feet. If I guessed, I would say there were about fifteen of them. Six lined the lake, the rest of them were speckled through the trees on the bottom half of the page.

A large family-sized cabin sat on the bottom middle of the paper, and there was a swimming pool smack dab in the center of the resort that looked pretty impressive if the illustration was to be believed. Like a bookend on the other side of the property, there was a barn which looked about the same size as the building we were currently in. "Ahh yes, here you are." She took her pen and circled the cabin that was in the bottom right corner of the map. It looked deeper in the trees than the others. "This one's pretty far from here, but the privacy is amazing."

David pointed to a cabin close to the water near the building we were in. "This one is mine." Then he pointed to the one closest to ours. "Our sisters are sharing this one." Hannah and Ruby were even closer than Zane and David, so it made sense that they'd be staying together on this trip.

"All activities are scheduled from the barn. Horseback riding, kayaks, paddleboats, even guided hikes can be scheduled from there . . ." She continued with the check-in process, but I zoned out, fixated on the way the light shone through the crystals in the chandelier as she told the boys about breakfast and how to get to our cabin. I'd spent my entire life in hotels. I didn't need a lengthy explanation.

Zane's fingers brushed against my hand, and I jumped. "You ready?"

It took everything in me to smile and thank the woman behind the counter for her time, even though all I wanted to do was crawl under a rock and pretend this entire trip wasn't happening. A few hours ago, I had almost thought about relaxing. But now that all my things were gone, and I knew I was only here to break hearts, I didn't want to do it anymore.

I followed the boys out, robotically getting back into the rental car and riding to our cabin.

We pulled up to a building that was marginally smaller than it had looked on the map. There was no way it was over four hundred square feet on the inside. It did have a small screened-in porch in the front, which probably had a view of the resort and the lake behind it, but the small yellowing light at the front door left much to the imagination.

Zane held up the map the woman had given us, and David typed in the code to the door. As soon as he swung it open, my shoulders slumped even further than before.

There was a sitting room on the right of the entranceway that held a pull-out loveseat and an ottoman. To the left was a kitchenette, if it could be called that, with a small fridge, sink, and table for two. There was an open pocket door to a bathroom on the right side of the little corridor after the living space, and a door at the end. I took the three steps necessary to reach the door and opened it, revealing a full-size bed that took up most of the space and a dresser on the opposite wall. Not even room for a queen. My closet at home was larger than this space.

I could do this. I was a strong woman. I'd had to deal with corporate bullshit for decades. With a family that checked out when I needed help, encouraging me to handle things on my own.

But I was tired. So damn tired.

"I'm taking the bedroom." Was all I said to them as I closed the door behind me.

I started to undress until I realized I had nothing to change into. "Zanc!" I cracked open the door, peeking out to the living room where the two of them talked in hushed whispers.

He looked over at me, reading my mind. "Would you like to borrow one of my shirts?"

I nodded slowly. "Just to sleep in. Please."

His eyes looked sad, like he knew it killed me to be this unprepared. Because it did fucking kill me. There was no other emotion I hated more than vulnerability. "Only because you said please."

He turned his attention back to David, talking about his mother's itinerary for the next few days, but dug through his bag until he pulled out a soft white t-shirt with a tequila brand logo on it. I knew he was trying to play it cool, but I softened when I saw that this was the shirt I had always stolen from him when I came in late and needed a little comfort after a long day. We had gotten it at some bar in our early twenties, and it had been our shared sleeping shirt for longer than our marriage.

I'd really fucking missed it after he moved out.

He tossed me the shirt, and I gripped it in my hands. What a weird place we were in. Like the purgatory of relationships. Not together by any means, but not quite fully apart, either.

Thoughts like this were a sure sign I needed some sleep.

I closed the door behind me, hoping that Zane found some comfort on the pull-out loveseat. After changing, I slipped between the sheets and fell asleep before I could feel any guilt about leaving him out there on his own.

Chapter Three

I woke up the next morning, grabbing my computer so I could check my email as the sun crept through the curtains. It was a surprise that I'd been able to sleep at all last night, with The Azure on my mind and all of my belongings missing, but that mattress was quite possibly the best one I'd ever slept on. I snuggled back under the comforter and tried the Wi-Fi password three times before getting frustrated with the lack of internet in this little cabin.

"Connect, dammit," I whispered, like that would help.

When it didn't, I pulled out my company phone and tried to turn on the hotspot, but there were no bars in the upper right corner. I went as far as to stand on the bed, reaching toward the ceiling, hoping it would connect to some far-off satellite.

Nothing.

Instead of screaming, I took a long, calming breath. The kind the therapist had told me to try.

In for seven seconds. Hold for four. Eight long seconds to exhale.

Again.

One more time.

I still wanted to scream, but my heart wasn't flying out of my chest anymore.

Out of options, I swung open the bedroom door, about to ask Zane what kind of Podunk town he had dragged me off to, but I stopped in my tracks.

I barely registered my ex-husband standing off to the side of the room, clad in pajamas with a cup of coffee in his hands. Instead, my eyes scanned the blond Adonis perched at the top of a ladder in the middle of the room.

My mouth went dry at the sight of him. His arms reached up to the Wi-Fi box mounted above the kitchen cabinets as my eyes scanned the skin between his dark blue Henley sweater and his worn-leather tool belt. He looked firm, showing off that strong vee that drove me crazy on fashion models. As he adjusted his footing on the ladder, I couldn't help but focus on his legs. His thighs were so thick in his jeans, I thought the buttery soft fabric might split open.

I realized I'd been staring longer than was socially acceptable when he mumbled something about disconnecting a wire. "Oh, umm, sorry," I said without thinking.

Then he turned toward me, his eyes crashing into mine. Like waves of the ocean on a clear day, as blue as the sea.

There was an energy between us, something compelling me to take a step closer to him. His chin was covered in dark blond stubble, making me want to run my fingernails through it.

He licked his bottom lip, and I'm pretty sure I gasped. Something visceral that I'd never felt before ran through every cell of my body.

"Sorry if I woke you." He glanced at Zane, who I had completely forgotten about, before looking back at me. "Your husband called the front desk saying that the internet was out in the cabin and you have to work remotely."

I must have nodded, because he went on. His voice was deep, with a hint of a British accent. "I'll get it fixed as soon as possible, but you're more than welcome to work in the lobby if I can't get the issue resolved."

"Thank you." My voice came out weak, like I had slept with my mouth open. I certainly wasn't breathless because he was still up on that ladder, looking like a Michelangelo statue. I cleared my throat, repeating my thanks just as the front door of our little cabin swung open.

Zane's younger sister Ruby practically skipped in, dressed in leggings and a tank top, like she was about to go out for her morning run. "Izzy!" she yelled out, rushing to me and wrapping me in her arms before I knew it. She was practically my little sister, but I wasn't sure how to handle this. Now that she . . . wasn't.

My arms flopped at my sides like a fish out of water before I remembered I wasn't supposed to be heartbroken over potentially losing her in my life forever. Worried that this girl I had grown into womanhood with in the last decade and a half was going to hate me when she found out that I was no longer married to her brother. And that both of us had neglected each other for so many years, dooming ourselves, maybe even from the start.

I needed to be happily married to her brother until he found the courage to tell them the truth.

As if he had the same idea, Zane slipped next to me and wrapped one arm around my waist. It might have been because the charade felt forced, but it was an awkward gesture.

The man who had been at the top of the ladder moments ago made his way down and his eyes caught my own again. My chest did a little flutter thing I didn't recognize. Was that butterflies? I wasn't sure. He gave me a lopsided smile before saying, "I think it's a hardware issue. I'm going to bring the router back to the office and see if I can find a replacement. In the meantime, if you need a connection, I can set you up behind the check-in counter."

I think I imagined it, but Zane's grip on me tightened. Or maybe it was my skin tightening at this stranger's gaze. "That would be great. Thank you," I mumbled, shocked that my usual assertive disposition was nowhere to be found. "Um, if you'll please excuse me," I said to the room before slipping away from everyone and closing myself back into the bedroom.

I caught my reflection in the mirror and blanched at what I must have looked like to this man. My hair was a mess, my cowlick in the front was out of control, and my legs were completely bare. All I had on were a pair of black panties and Zane's tequila shirt that just barely covered my ass. Great.

I bet Sexy Tool Belt Guy thought I had slept with Zane last night, too. After all, he's my husband and I have no pants.

This was just my luck. The first man I'd felt any sort of attraction to in years, and I'm wearing my ex's clothes with bed-head.

Not that I could do anything about it on this trip, anyway. At least my tits were perky, even without a bra.

I ran my fingers through my otherwise straight black hair, trying to get it to flatten down. Having my straightener would have been really fucking helpful right about now. I sat on the foot of the bed, smothering my face with my hands.

All of my belongings were gone. I had no missed calls, nothing from the sheriff or the security guard from the airport. My suitcase, along with everything else, was probably in some dumpster by now.

There was a faint knock at the door. "Come in," I called out, thinking it was Zane, but in crept Ruby. She and Zane were only three years apart, but the way he babied her made it seem like she was barely an adult. Ruby had been an accident if you listened to Zane's mom when she had too much wine—not in front of her daughter, though. To her mother, she was the perfect addition to their family, even if she was wild and rebellious.

"Wanna talk about it?" She asked, a sweet smile on her face.

"Talk about what?"

She sat next to me on the bed and met my eyes in the mirror. "I dunno. There's a lot we could talk about." She nudged me with her shoulder. "Work . . . Your suitcase getting stolen . . . The fact that you and my brother are definitely not together anymore."

"What?" I jumped up, spinning around to look at her. "That's not true."

She laughed, having seen right through me. "I thought the era of being Zane's beard was finally over?"

I started picking at the chip on my fingernail, thinking of ways to handle this hiccup. Never in a million years would I have guessed that she'd figured it out. I wondered if I could play dumb somehow. "I honestly have no idea what you're talking about."

She stared at me incredulously; the look leaving no doubt that she was related to Zane. "I ran into them together, you know. About six months ago." I stepped back until I bumped into the tiny dresser as she went on. "I was in Cali on a shopping trip with some friends and I came out of the Boba shop to see him and some other guy holding hands."

"You must have been mistaken," I lied.

Her head shook. "No, Izzy. The other guy looked at my brother like he hung the moon. Like he was the only person who existed. It was only for a split second, but I had seen enough to know what it really was." She patted the spot next to her, urging me to sit back down before going on. "When Zane threw this dude's hand away like he had been burned, he was so hurt. There was something real there. Way more real than the two of you ever had." I must have made a face, because she added, "No offense."

"Caleb is . . ." I inhaled deeply before sitting next to

my now-former sister on the bed. "He's really an amazing guy. Sometimes I hate that they found each other, because it put all our flaws under a microscope, but he makes your brother so fucking happy." Rubbing my face with my hands, I felt a bit of relief knowing I'd have an ally here. "We just need to get through this trip."

She patted my leg with her hand, reminding me of my very obvious lack of pants. "I promise to make sure you have fun while we're here."

I uncovered my face and raised an eyebrow at her. "That's doubtful. I don't even have clothes to wear." Ruby jumped up, tugging her leggings down to her ankles. "What the hell are you doing?"

"Handling something I can control," she said, handing the pants to me. They were warm in my hands as I tried to track where she was going with this. "Put them on."

The look she gave me warned me not to argue, so I did as she said, wiggling into her baby-soft yoga leggings. Thank goodness they were the super stretchy-kind, or I wouldn't have been able to get them over my hips. "Okay, what now?"

"Take your ass to the gift shop and find something."

I cringed. "I'm not wearing gift shop clothes."

She pointed at me, just like my mother used to when I didn't want to go to dance practice as a little girl. "Your options are to get your butt to the gift shop and get a few days' worth of clothes or to hole up in this cabin during the entire vacation. One of those is not actually an option."

I let out a deep sigh, giving in to her demands, and

scooped up my phone, which still showed no service. "Fine. I'm going, but only because that maintenance guy said there was Wi-Fi there."

I was in over my head the moment I stepped into the gift shop. The room itself wasn't overwhelming. In fact, it was well organized and decorated much like the gift shops at many of my hotels.

The problem was the lack of clothing choices. Everything was pastel. Not a single dark article of clothing on any rack. I hadn't purchased clothing in any color other than black in ten years, and I really didn't want to do so now.

Black was my signature color. Like how Geri Halliwell made only wearing white iconic and glamorous.

I hadn't worn another color, let alone a pastel, in a decade. Dark clothing made me look formidable, polished, powerful. And I liked that.

A woman with long gray hair and a face that just screamed *get over here and hug me* smiled from across the room. "Hello, sugar. How can I help you today?"

The way her eyes crinkled above her genuine smile made me wonder if she could actually help me find something that fit my personality. "Hi. I've had an issue with my luggage and neither the airport nor the sheriff have called me back, so I need to buy some clothes in the meantime." I looked around the large room for a Wi-Fi code and didn't find one. "Also, I need to connect to the internet, but the maintenance——"

She snapped her fingers and her eyes went wide. "Oh! I have a message for you! The woman who came in last night on a private plane?"

I felt my eyebrows crinkle together. "Umm, yes, Lizette Howell-Xu"

"Follow me." I did as she told me and went through the lobby, behind the reception desk, and to a small desk covered in paper ledgers and folders. She flipped through a pile of sticky notes at her desk. She grabbed a blue one and let out a celebratory, "Ah ha!"

"Sheriff Mackey called early this morning. He found your suitcase and wants you to call him." She pointed at my phone in my hand. "He said he tried to call you, but our service here is always pretty spotty, so he called the front desk, too."

I had so many questions. "How did he know where I was staying?"

She smiled at me again, and something about her demeanor warmed me up, regardless of how frustrating this suitcase debacle had been. "Oh, in a town this small, it's hard to miss anything."

"Except for a suitcase," I said flatly.

That earned me a laugh from the woman. She turned, flipping her hair over her shoulder before reaching her hand out to me. "Hi, I'm Cathy, but everyone around here calls me Cate." She vaguely reminded me of Kathy at The Pacifica, and I wondered if she was a meticulously organized planner as well—but based on all the papers spread across her desktop, she might be the opposite.

Her hand was warm and firm around mine, and I had

a feeling that if this hadn't been the first time we'd met, she would actually pull me into a hug. "I'm Lizette, but you can call me Izzy."

I blanched a little at the admission. No one but my very close personal friends and family called me that. In fact, I didn't recall telling anyone to call me by anything other than Lizette. Someone had to know my brother first since the nickname came from when he was too little to pronounce my full name.

"It's nice to meet you, Izzy. Now why don't you take this and go down the hall to my office and call the sheriff back?"

I followed her direction, clutching the sticky note in my hand. As I entered the office at the end of the hall, I realized this Cathy—Cate—was nothing like our Kathy back home. There were stacks of binders with papers sticking out of them on every flat surface. It took me a few seconds to find the phone on the desk, and after I did, I had to find somewhere to place the files sitting on the office chair so I could sit down.

Once I was situated, I dialed the number, hoping it meant I would get my clothes back by this afternoon.

It rang twice before a man's voice answered, "Mack here, how can I help you?"

"Hi, this is Lizette Howell," I dropped the Xu, as I'd started doing a few months ago, but I wasn't sure why it felt weird this time. "My luggage was stolen last night. Cate told me you called."

"Oh yes, Mrs. Howell." I almost told him that Mrs. Howell was my mother, but I stopped myself. "I was able to check the camera footage and locate your luggage late last night."

"Perfect. Where can I pick it up? Do you need me to come file paperwork to press charges?"

"Here's the thing." He sounded defensive, which made my blood boil. "We know where it is, but it's going to be a while before you can have it back."

"Is it being held as evidence?"

"Evidence?" He sounded confused before cutting himself off. "Oh, no, this wasn't a crime, ma'am."

I blinked a few times, trying to hold my temper back. "So someone stole my suitcase and you're protecting them?"

He laughed in an easy way that proved he wasn't taking this seriously. "I'm not protecting them. I'm just trying to explain what happened."

"Which was?" I asked sharply.

"Well, ol' Essi Heikkinen was flying out to visit her family in Helsinki, and she got confused after her son dropped her off to go park the car. Before anyone realized it, she grabbed your luggage and checked it in as her own."

I barked out a laugh. "Are you fucking with me?" This story felt completely made up.

"Why would I do something like that, ma'am?" He sounded serious, like he'd never been accused of having a sense of humor.

"How does someone check in a suitcase that isn't their own?" It had a tag with my name on it, for God's sake.

He released a slow breath on the other side of the line, like I was overreacting and he needed me to calm down. "I checked the camera footage, and she went through security just like everyone else. Unfortunately, it's going to be another five hours before she lands, and then probably twenty hours or so for it to make it back here once the airline ships it back."

"So the fastest I'll be able to get it back is tomorrow evening?"

"Hopefully. I called the airline, and I'm waiting on a call back."

I rubbed my face with my free hand, not even caring what it did to my makeup, or lack thereof. I couldn't argue my way out of this. "Will you call me the moment you hear anything?"

"Sure thing. I'll give your phone a ring, and I'll call Cate if you don't answer."

Knowing that I probably wouldn't have service on any of my phones, I agreed. "Thank you for your help." I kept it cordial even though I wanted to scream, which was something I was well-versed in. I was known for not taking any shit, but I also wasn't rude when I could help myself.

He promised me one more time that he would contact me as soon as he heard from the airline, and I hung up the phone.

Laying my head against the chair, I wished I had another pair of shoes. Sitting here wearing Zane's shirt, Ruby's pants, and my heels was definitely the weirdest outfit I'd ever worn.

I spun slowly in the ancient green office chair, listening to it creak under me while I looked at the pictures on the wall. Cate was in almost all of them, smiles on the faces of all of her family members. A cute middle-aged husband and three children accompanied her in every picture. One girl looked familiar, and when I got closer, I realized she'd been the woman who checked us in last night when we got here. This place really was a family company.

I sat wondering what it was like to have it all—a loving husband, kids, maybe even a dog. I'd frozen eggs several years ago, but Zane never wanted to make an actual embryo. He assured me that when our careers were in the right place, we could move further in the process, but that had never happened. Hopefully it wasn't too late for me now.

Maybe I could do it on my own . . . make a baby. I could look into donors and find an IVF clinic. After I handled all the things I needed to take care of at the office.

I looked around the room again, finding a wall calendar with a picture of a sandy beach. Instead of thinking about any of my properties in California, my first thought was The Azure.

I should have brought my laptop, so I could check my emails. It would piss me off to no end if I lost the property to the damn Carlisles because I had no access to the internet.

I stood, straightening out my shirt, and remembered what I had come here for in the first place. Two days' worth of clothes. I was able to handle being the only woman near the top of my class in business school. I could handle two days of pastel-colored clothing.

Making it back to the gift shop, I scanned the racks.

There were a few sweaters, but I had a feeling it would be too warm for them. After a few minutes I'd decided on two tops and two pairs of sweatpants that didn't make me want to throw up on myself, and headed to where Cate was manning the cash register. At the last minute, I remembered I'd need a toothbrush, so I grabbed one from a spinning display next to the counter.

Cate was checking out a couple that were very obviously on their honeymoon, judging by the white sweatpants with a bedazzled 'Bride' across the woman's behind. I hated thinking that she probably had her damn suitcase and a cute husband that wanted her more than anyone else. Jealousy was not something I was accustomed to.

When it was my turn, Cate smiled sweetly. "Is this everything you'll need?" She took the pile from my hands and asked, "How did things with your luggage go?"

"Hopefully I'll have my stuff back the day after tomorrow." I plucked at the peach-colored pants. "This should be all I need."

Then I realized there was something more important I would need. I wasn't a prude, but I liked my privacy, so I leaned in closer. "You don't happen to sell . . ." the pause gave her time to pick up on what I was trying to tell her.

"Unmentionables?" she asked with a smile.

"Yes. The only underwear I have are the ones I'm wearing."

She drummed her fingers on the tall countertop between us. "Hmm." The gears in her head turned before her eyes went wide. "I have a few bikinis left over from last season! Let me see if they're your size." She jumped up and disappeared into a storage closet down the hall before I could stop her.

After a couple of minutes and some grunting noises, she came back out with two sets of identical bathing suits on plastic hangers. The tops were more revealing than I was comfortable with, even for bras, but the bottoms looked like they would get the job done. "Perfect!" I told her, thankful for her quick thinking.

She rang me up, telling me she was putting it all on my room. I should have stopped her, but Zane told me he would cover all of my incidentals for coming on this trip. He owed me.

I grabbed my new clothes and thanked her, stopping her from putting my purchases in plastic bags—you can take the girl out of California, but you can't take California out of the girl—and turned toward the door.

As I left the gift shop, I wondered what Zane would say when he saw me wearing the colorful tank top later. I didn't look ahead and bumped right into someone coming inside.

A bumbling "Sorry" slipped out of me as I looked into those piercing blue eyes from earlier. The maintenance guy.

He looked down at my purchases, and I couldn't help but notice a blush creep up his cheeks as he saw the bikini draped over the rest of my clothes. A thought of him helping me remove it flashed through my mind, and I knew if I spent any more time with him, I might ruin more than my pretend marriage.

He reached his hand out. "Hi, I'm Ben."

I shifted my new clothes into one arm and clasped his

offered hand in mine. My handshake was something I took pride in. I'd learned it from my dad, after all. *A firm handshake is the best first impression our company can make*, he would say. But Ben's grip was impressive. It felt like he'd also been well-practiced, but where my hand was soft from office work and manicures, his was rough and callused, like he'd grown up on a farm.

His eyes lingered on mine for longer than they should have, causing a shiver to run up my spine. I wondered if he saw the real me. Not the thick shell I'd built around myself; but Lizette, the lonely woman who'd filled her schedule with work so she didn't have to think about her empty life.

"Nice to meet you, Ben. Have a good day," I blurted out before letting go of his hand and rushing out the door.

The absence of his warmth traveled up my arm as soon as I stepped away. I tried to ignore the pull I'd felt toward him as I walked up the dirt path to my cabin in the trees, but it was difficult. I wasn't sure I'd be able to go back to ignoring my body's needs after meeting him.

Chapter Four

I made it back to my cabin, thankfully finding it empty. After a quick shower without washing my hair, I slipped into a brand new bikini and the peach-colored sweatpants.

I wasn't planning on wearing one of the tops, but the bra I had been wearing was well past its maximum sweat life and needed to be hand-washed before it could be worn again.

My breasts were average, but with these tiny triangles, I felt like I was going to spill out everywhere. I adjusted the top as best as I could and brushed my teeth using Zane's toothpaste. I even used a couple swipes of his deodorant. We had been married once, so it wasn't weird or anything to share toiletries.

It took a few minutes to decide between the cornflower blue tank top or the heather green tee-shirt. Since I didn't want to look like an actual peach, I went with the blue.

My main priority should have been meeting up with

the family, especially since Zane's parents had most likely arrived by now, but I couldn't stop worrying that we'd lose The Azure if I didn't at least check in with my office.

Pulling my laptop out of my bag, I opened it, hoping that maybe the Wi-Fi had been magically fixed. It took twenty seconds to determine that it hadn't, so I packed my stuff into my purse and double-checked the resort map.

A private trail I'd seen yesterday would help me reach the main building without running into anyone, so I slipped on my pumps, making my way to high-speed internet. The sooner I could get there and get my work done for the day, the better.

Cate wore a bright smile and waved at me when I came in the door. "Hi sweetie. Is there something else I can find for you?"

I gestured to my bag, with my laptop secure inside. "I still can't connect to the internet in our cabin."

She jumped up, motioning for me to come behind the counter. "Ben told me to tell you he had to order a part, but it won't be here for a few days. You're welcome to work here with me if you need to." She pointed to a rickety old desk that looked like it came out of a ranger station in the 1940s.

Knowing it was either this or nothing, I accepted her offer and walked around the counter to the desk.

Upon further inspection, it was in great condition, like it had been recently refurbished. The wood on the top had a smooth finish that was impossible not to run my fingers across.

I pulled out my computer and signed into my account. "What's the Wi-Fi login?"

"Ben wrote it down inside the center drawer because we always forget." I slid open the drawer and found an organizer with everything perfectly in its place.

"Is this his desk?" I asked, poking around.

"Yep. He likes to work here when he's at the main building." She paused, a proud smile across her lips as she watched me look over the museum-level organization going on in here. "He rebuilt it himself. Found it abandoned next to a dumpster and brought it back to life. His main office is in the barn building, since its quieter and has fewer distractions. But when it's his turn up here, that's his home away from home."

I skimmed my fingers across the drawer handles. "It's beautiful." Then I looked at her. "So he's a handyman and runs the front desk sometimes. Is there anything he doesn't do around here?"

She laughed. "I guess you could say he's got his hand in a bit of everything."

A couple came in the front door, and Cate got up to help them. I kept looking through the drawer and found a stack of white business cards. I pulled one out to take a closer look. Ben Montgomery, huh? The rest of the card was plain, with just an address for this resort and what I was pretty sure was the phone number to the front desk. Not even a job description for Mr. Montgomery. Interesting.

I tucked the card back into its spot and found the Wi-Fi password written on the side of the drawer in sharpie marker. Not very secure, but useful.

After setting up my computer and closing the drawer, I was ready to get some work done. A hundred and fifty unread emails stared back at me. I should have come here sooner.

Closing my eyes, I wondered how I'd even thought it was possible to take a real vacation. I imagined what it would be like to spend a whole day at the beach. All of my days were within a thousand feet of the ocean—or the lake if I were thinking about where I was right this minute—and I never put my feet in the sand. Why would it be any different here?

When I opened my eyes, Ben had appeared over by the reception counter and was talking to Cate. He'd lost the tool belt, but still looked ruggedly handsome. His jeans were smooth, but the muscles underneath were solid as they perfectly filled out every inch of the denim. He laughed at something she said, his eyes crinkling at the corners. I let out a sigh that must have been audible, swooning for him.

I tried to ignore him and the fluttering sensation in my belly by looking down at my emails, but the majority of them were unnecessary. My thoughts drifted off to my dating history. Not that I had one, really. Just Zane in college and no one since we'd split. Maybe this inability to stop thinking about someone I'd just met was normal?

I clicked through a few messages—I'd been cc'd on all of them—but my eyes kept drifting up to the imposing man who'd moved behind the counter and was standing three feet away from me. His hair was a little unruly, like it had been a few weeks since his last haircut, but it fit him. It was thick, with highlights bleached by the sun.

They were talking about plumbing in one of the cabins, and I couldn't help listening, pretending to care about the issues at my own hotels.

His accent was subdued. British, for sure, but only when he said certain words, like he'd lived in America most of his life. Usually, I could drown out the world when I sat at my computer, but I found myself more interested in the pipes in cabin three than in the payroll issue that had been found and fixed before I even saw the email thread.

He turned his attention toward me, propping his hip on the edge of the desk. He was so close I could touch him, but I didn't.

I thought about sitting on my hands so I wouldn't, but I rested them against my keyboard instead.

He leaned forward, his voice sultry. Or maybe that's just how it was in my head. "I'm sorry I couldn't fix the connectivity issue. I hope it's not too much of a pain to come up here for work."

Glancing at my screen quickly, I hoped he hadn't seen the heat creep up my neck, knowing I'd probably been caught staring. "It's no problem. I'm able to connect here just fine."

I looked around for Cate, but she was gone. Being alone with him was thrilling and a little scary. I'd been alone with plenty of attractive men, but this was the first time I'd wanted to do something about it. Maybe I wasn't as out of touch with my sexuality as I'd thought.

He settled on the edge of the desk, crossing his long legs at his ankles. My eyes trailed from his belt to his chest, then to the stubbly beard that made him look absolutely delicious. Like he knew I was imagining what he looked like under his shirt, he pushed his sleeves up to his elbows and folded his arms. The little hairs sprinkling them were mesmerizing. They looked soft in comparison to the strong muscles beneath.

I realized it was my turn to say something, and felt myself blush. "Working here is fine, really. I just have a deal I'm working on. I shouldn't be here much longer."

He smiled, genuinely interested. "What kind of deal?"

I waved my hand, trying to pretend that I wasn't about to invest millions of dollars on a property I'd been hoping to acquire for years. "I'm in real estate. Something came on the market that I'd been watching for a while. I'd hate to lose it because I was here." He shifted, causing his arms to flex, and I had to force my eyes back to my screen. The heat building under my skin blossomed into a fire. It was almost too much.

He must have felt it too, because his next words were, "How does your husband feel about you working so much on your family vacation?"

I clicked open another email. "He's not my husband." Then I looked back up at him, panic flooding through me. "Shit, please don't say anything." I was not one to just blab family secrets to strangers, so I was just as shocked at my words as he looked.

But then his shock turned into a smile, a mischievous one at that. "Who am I going to tell?"

"Our entire family is here, and they don't know about the divorce." His head tilted to the side and his eyebrow popped up like he didn't believe me, so I added, "We came here together to tell them, but we've been separated for quite some time." It had been over a year since he moved out, but I'd stopped counting months ago.

He nodded, unfolding his arms. "That's a lot to unpack." His smile had turned into a full-blown grin. "Can't say I'm not happy to hear it, though."

I bit my lips, looking back at my computer. I didn't have the skill to flirt back with him. If he was flirting with me, anyway.

He finally said, "Is this going to be one of those vacations where he gets you back?" His tone was flat, like he had lots of practice keeping his emotions and opinions in check.

"Oh, no. That ship has sailed," I blurted. "I am definitely on a vacation with a man who is not attracted to me at all. And to make matters worse, my luggage was stolen at the airport."

He pointed to my shirt. "That explains the outfit. I had a feeling you weren't excited enough about your trip to change into resort merchandise."

"You don't have women running around wearing Lac Brumeux clothes head to toe all the time?" I said mockingly.

"Not usually, no." He leaned forward and plucked the strap of my bikini top, which peeked out from under my tank top. "Cate was excited to get rid of last year's bathing suits, though. I'm glad they went to a good cause."

I felt a blush erupt across my cheeks. The bikini strap he'd touched practically hummed with electricity. "I'm glad you had this, at least. I don't even have a car to drive to town so I can find something more my style." Why the hell was I telling him this? There was no way he cared about my clothing situation.

He started to say something, but Cate emerged from the gift shop. "Thanks for covering for me," she called across the lobby, like it wasn't something he did every day.

He stood to his full height, which had to be over six feet. "Well, anytime you need to get some work done, you're welcome to my desk."

"Thank you. I appreciate it." I looked back down at my computer as he left, hoping the grin I felt in my cheeks wasn't as large as I thought it was.

I clicked through the rest of my emails, finding one from Blake. It was just a report regarding the kitchen project at The Pacifica. Even the changes we'd agreed upon after the incident that almost ruined my brother's wedding were taken care of and cleared by the inspector.

She ended the message letting me know that she and her boyfriend were moving out of his grandparents' house and into a place of their own. I'd offered to help her open a Bed and Breakfast if she let me invest, and we were one step closer to making that dream a reality.

I replied, telling her I was thrilled for her, both because of her adorable relationship, but also because The Pacifica could go back to making money again. Then I ended the email promising to go out for drinks with her and Camilla as soon as this reunion was over with. Hopefully we would also celebrate the purchase of this new property.

Finally, I started a message to Aniyah, since there was

still no update regarding The Azure, and asked her to send me anything she's found about the deal The Carlisle Corporation had been building. She had insiders all over the industry, so I had a feeling she knew someone that would be able to share some secrets.

I hated that I wasn't in California right now, getting this deal ready with the rest of my team. My brother's voice rang in my ear, nagging at me for micromanaging, but I've learned so many times during my career that things don't get done unless I do them myself. Well, the way I want them done, anyway.

As soon as I thought about Reece, I knew I owed him a phone call. I'd make one as soon as this fake-marriage stuff was over. I'd tell him the whole truth. And also apologize for what a horrible bitch I'd been the last year of my marriage when I was grasping for control in other areas of my life.

An email from Aniyah finally came through. She'd gotten an appointment with a board member of The Azure to discuss possible negotiations. We were on the right track.

"I thought I'd find you here." I must have been in the zone for quite some time, because Zane's voice made me jump in my seat.

I closed my tab and looked at the clock on the top of my screen. "Holy shit, I've been here for two hours," I said, more to myself than to him.

He was wearing a button-down shirt with an obnoxious Hawaiian print and a pair of board shorts. The man knew how to dress for an event, I had to give him that. "Mom and Dad just got here. Should we make our grand entrance?" He spun around in a circle, and I realized his outfit looked just as ridiculous as mine.

Feeling a little guilty, I shut my laptop. "I'm sorry if you were waiting. I didn't mean to be here this long." After packing up my things, I stood, wondering how the hell time had moved so quickly.

Once I came around the counter, he slung his arm around my shoulder, walking us to the door. "It's not like I expected you to ignore your responsibilities just because we're on vacation. You've got a lot on your plate." He squeezed me closer to him. To an outsider, we probably looked happily married. I kept my eyes forward, hoping the outsider I'd just imagined naked wasn't seeing us like this.

"True," I mumbled, but felt like maybe it was time to relax. Based on all the correspondence with the office today, the team was working well without me. I could trust Aniyah implicitly.

"Where's your head today, Iz?" Zane popped me out of my bubble.

"Oh, just thinking about The Azure and if they're going to let us buy it." Definitely not also wondering when I could catch a glimpse of the handyman again.

"I know you want to make your dad proud, but seriously, fuck that guy. Your worth is not tied up in some business acquisition."

I nodded as we headed toward our cabin so I could freshen up before the party. "I know. It's just hard to let some things go." I looked him in the eye. "No more work today. I promise."

His head tilted back as he laughed. "Maybe let's start with baby steps. How's a few hours sound to you?"

I rolled my eyes. "Give me five minutes, and I'll be ready for the party."

Chapter Five

Zane's parents were staying in the largest cabin at the resort, but the map didn't do it justice. The place was enormous. It had two stories, a walkout basement, and tons of windows. The best part, though, was the wraparound porch with a panoramic view of the lake just in front of it.

The two of us walked up the stairs of the deck and found a few people milling around. I recognized one of Zane's cousins I hadn't seen since the last reunion and waved excitedly. Hannah rushed to me, a red cup in her hand. "Izzy! It's been too long!" She practically yelled in my ear as she hugged me. She had always been wild, so I wondered how much she'd already had to drink today.

At thirty, Hannah was just a few years younger than Ruby, but she'd been the instigator in many of their poor decisions over the years. They lived in different cities, but when they got together, all hell usually broke loose.

One look gave her away as David's little sister. The only difference between them was that he was a foot taller. Her hair was cut into a short bob, with an edgy undercut, while he had one of those haircuts with short sides and curls on top. I'd wondered if he permed it, but had never wanted to ask. Otherwise, they could have been twins if they weren't five years apart.

I could smell the alcohol coming off her and started to inquire where I could find some of my own, but she asked me how I'd been.

Back at home, in my real life, I was always cool and collected. I knew what I was doing. But here, when I was Izzy instead of Lizette, when I was just another adult kid in the Xu family, it took me a few hours to get used to the chaos. I loved it, but it was jarring at times.

We were a small group that always stuck together at these annual events. We'd spent every reunion for the past fifteen years connected at the hips, except for last year, which Zane and I had managed to skip by pretending we had the flu.

But I was nervous about this year. With both David and Ruby knowing our secret, it was only a matter of time before Hannah knew, if she didn't already, and I had a feeling she'd be the weakest link. We had to tell his parents soon.

I answered with a generic, "I'm good. How about you?"

She didn't even respond before letting go of me, tugging at my shirt, and dragging me into the house. "I like the new look on you."

I laughed, knowing I looked ridiculous in sweatpants, a blue top, and a pair of black Louboutin pumps.

"Thanks. It's a long story, but I'm too sober to tell it without crying."

Before we could catch up, Zane's mother crashed into me, pulling me in for a bone-crushing hug. "Izzy, everyone's almost here!"

"Hi Mom," I muttered with the air that remained in my lungs. She let go of me, but only pulled back slightly. She looked every bit of the wife of a billionaire—tall, bleach blonde hair, in her 60s but still hot as hell—but she was kind and loving and honestly the best mother-in-law I could have ever wished for. Better than my own mother by a landslide.

"Let me look at you." She gently took my chin in her hand, analyzing my face. "When's the last time you ate anything?"

"I had a protein bar I found in my purse this morning," I admitted a bit shamefully, knowing I should have eaten a real breakfast.

"Oh, that simply won't do." She spun around, grabbing my hand and dragging me the rest of the way to the kitchen.

I blinked rapidly as I followed her. The impact of how our life had changed hit me like a ton of bricks. This woman, who had been in my life since I was nineteen, who had loved me and cherished me like her own, was about to have her heart broken when Zane and I told her the truth. We were going to tell her that we had failed her. We'd given her hopes and dreams that weren't going to come true.

Would she think about those frozen eggs that would

never become zygotes? Would she mourn the loss of grandchildren we hadn't even decided we were ready for?

I wiped at my eyes as we made it to the heart of the house. The kitchen was right in the middle of the open-concept layout. The island had seating for six and was flanked by a dining room big enough for a dozen people on the right and a huge wraparound couch on the left. A quick headcount assured me that there were at least ten people in the house. Most of them sat on the couch, eating and drinking, laughing like crazy.

Zane's dad, Andrew, and his two uncles sat at the table playing a card game, speaking to each other in Mandarin. I knew the language too, since I had been born in Singapore, but I'd never been as fluent as my father-in-law and his brothers. I struggled to even pronounce their Chinese names, and they insisted on using the names they picked when they moved to America as small children, so I never got the chance to practice.

My mother had stopped speaking Mandarin in our house when we moved to America, and she only used it on the phone with her sisters or friends. I don't think Reece even knew anything past a basic greeting. I guess that's what happens when you move to The States as a kid and there's no one in your pretentious private school that looks like you.

Zane's dad barked out a laugh, highlighting the contrast between our families. Zane's owned one of the largest international banks in the world, but unlike my family, they were loving and had actual hearts and souls. His dad and uncles were still heavily involved in the company, with Zane, Ruby, and their cousins all ready to take over when they retired.

But in this case, it was more of a passing of the torch and less "off with their heads" like my corporate training had been.

"So, how have you two been?" Alice asked, bringing me back to the present. She leaned her elbows on the quartz countertop of the island, making the question feel intimate despite being in a large room full of people.

I shrugged a little, reminding myself to stop picking at the paint chip on my fingernail. "You know us. Just focused on work."

"I've been keeping up with your company in the news. You're making quite a name for yourself now that your horrible father is out of the picture." My heart pinched at that, but she was right. She'd been the one person I'd always talked to when things were weird with my parents.

Having the secret of the divorce between us felt like a bigger betrayal now that I was in front of her. I had to shake off being Izzy for a few minutes and jump into being Lizette. Feelings couldn't come out right now. "Thanks, Mom. I'm hoping to get my hands on The Azure in Santa Barbara soon."

She squeezed my upper arm like she wanted to pull me into a hug but knew that I wasn't a huge fan of too much physical interaction. "Isn't that next door to the resort you bought a couple of years ago?"

"Yes, but I have a really great plan for it." I imagined all the things I could do to make it my own. Some cute Spanish-style tiles would look great on the walkway between the two resorts, maybe even some cantina lights cascading across the breezeway.

"Well, don't work too hard, okay? I'd like it if you remembered to take care of yourself sometimes, you know?" Her hand slid down my arm to my fingers, and I wrapped them around hers.

I'd heard that from practically everyone I knew lately. That I was working too much. "I will," I told her, not fully committed.

The next several hours were spent catching up with everyone, as much as we could with this giant secret lingering over my head, at least. I talked to every aunt, uncle, and cousin, and even chatted with a few of the little kids that belonged to more distant relatives.

Sandwiches for lunch turned into a dinner that Zane's dad and uncles grilled out on the wraparound porch. The food was delicious, but the company was even better.

Zane had pulled up a couple of chairs for us to watch the sunset, which left me a little breathless. We'd sat there since then, just enjoying everyone around us as the hours ticked by.

The big cabin was so close to the lake. If we jumped off the deck, we'd probably land in the water, but I didn't want to say that out loud because the cocktails had been flowing for most of the day and I didn't want to start anything. At these reunions, I usually had to pour water into my cup before someone refilled it. Except for today. Today I was letting alcohol fix all my problems.

The Xu's were also wildly competitive. There wasn't a challenge one of them wouldn't take. If I mentioned jumping off a deck into a pitch black lake, it would surely end in someone's legs getting broken. It wasn't worth it.

Zane reached over and took my hand in his. Quietly, he said, "My brother and Tippy are coming over. Look happy."

"I'm never happy," I said to him, jokingly.

His face shifted to concern for just a second before the fake smile took its place again. I gave him my corporate smile in response. "Yes, just like that," he said, squeezing my hand. His brother and sister-in-law's flight had also been delayed, and they'd only made it to the resort half an hour ago. Luckily, they were staying in the big cabin with Andrew and Alice, so they didn't have to worry about checking in.

A minute later, Bradley and his stereotypical trophy wife came over to us, Bud Lites in their hands. "Hey, you two. How've you been?" she asked before he could say anything.

I looked at Zane, silently asking if we should just rip the Band-Aid off. He shook his head slightly. "Just peachy. How about you?" I wondered if it was a dig at my pants, but I'd have to let it slide if we were pretending to still be married.

"Oh, you know how campaign life is," Tippy said, with a bright smile on her face. She looked like she could pass for a younger version of Zane's mom, save for the fake boobs and lip injections. I'm sure a therapist could spend weeks deconstructing her family history. She was a quintessential mean-girl, hiding behind her bright personality. Always handing out backhanded compliments. I got used to being her target years ago, so now I just laughed when she tried to get under my skin.

Glued to his phone screen, Bradley looked up only for a moment to say hello. I hadn't even thought of bringing my laptop or phone here, but it was good to know that the internet probably worked at the big cabin. Tippy nudged him with her shoulder. "He's been like this for weeks. I'm hoping bringing him here will give him a chance to relax before we hit the campaign trail."

Zane grinned and pulled my hand into his lap. "I totally get it. My wife's the same way. Married to her work first, and me second." If looks could kill, my darling husband would have turned to dust. He grimaced before whispering, "Sorry."

I stuffed the burn from his insult deep down, smiling brightly. Now wasn't the time to start anything. I had to play the role of the loving wife. "What do you have planned while you're here?" I asked, changing the subject.

"Whatever Mom has on her itinerary, I guess," Bradley said, finally looking up from his phone.

"I think we're all going horseback riding tomorrow. Isn't that exciting?" Tippy added.

Quite the opposite, I wanted to say. "I've never ridden a horse before, actually," I admitted.

"What! With your family's money, they never bought you a pony for your birthday?" She asked completely seriously, and I couldn't help but laugh.

"I'm sure if I'd asked, my parents would have given me one. But the thought of climbing on something I have no control over gives me the creeps."

Zane squeezed my hand. "Well, it's supposed to be a

short ride. And if you don't like it, we can find something else to do." I wasn't sure, but I think he was trying to make it sound like we'd go back to our cabin and fuck, but it missed its mark. We really were rusty. Maybe we'd never been good at that kind of thing.

We talked a little longer with the politicians before getting up and going inside, where we found our usual group that we hung out with during these visits.

"How is it already midnight?" Zane asked, yawning.

I looked down at my bare feet, having kicked off my shoes hours ago. "You're going to have to carry me. I can't make it on my own." Then I leaned against him, more drunk than I'd thought. "It will make them think you're still in love with me."

He pulled me close, pretending to gaze into my eyes. "Be careful, wife. There are ears all over the place." Then he hefted me up, throwing me over his shoulder. "But we did agree to keep it up until we told Mom and Dad." He called out to his sister and cousins, "We're going home. You're welcome to join us."

Chapter Six

The five of us clambered up the steps to our cabin, trying to stay quiet since it was late and they had warned us about a strict noise ordinance earlier in the day.

The funny thing about trying to stay quiet when you're drunk, however, is that it's impossible.

David helped Zane with the door, which was a struggle because of the ungodly amount of alcohol we'd all consumed, and the fact that Zane had me over his shoulder in one hand and my shoes in the other. Luckily, we all found our way into the tiny living room where we could relax without the pressure of a house milling with people we only saw once a year.

Zane and I sat next to each other on the couch. Ruby lay across the ottoman like a starfish, and Hannah sat cross-legged on the floor. Zane pulled my feet into his lap, and it felt like we had time-traveled to ten years ago. When we were lovers and best friends.

"I don't want to go to bed yet," Zane whined, even

though we definitely should have gone to sleep an hour ago if we were going to be bright and chipper for riding horses in the morning. It had been several years since I'd had this much to drink.

"Does your closet have board games? Ours had a few," David said, peeking around our tiny cabin. He somehow still looked put together in his button-down t-shirt and black shorts. Where Zane looked like he was dressed for a Hawaiian Luau, David looked like he was about to go tell the chef on his yacht that he was ready for a midnight snack.

Hannah, in her infinite wisdom, laid her empty beer bottle on the floor and spun it in a circle. "Let's play spin the bottle!"

Her excitement wasn't dampened by the rest of us staring at her like she had lost her mind. David sat next to her and put his hand on her shoulder. "No offense, but all of us are related. That's disgusting."

She spun it around again. "No, not like the kissing game. The one where you make people do stuff."

Ruby said, "You mean truth or dare?" Her voice was muffled in the ottoman, but we understood what she meant.

Hannah clapped her hands in excitement. "Yes! Let's play truth or dare." At that, Ruby and Zane both sat up, ready to take on a challenge. Hannah went on, "We'll spin the bottle to keep it fair. The last person who gets challenged has to spin. Whoever it lands on has to pick truth or dare."

I swallowed my groan. This had bad news written all

over it, but every other Xu had wild excitement blooming on their faces.

"I'll spin first." David said, rubbing his hands together, looking at each of us slowly, like he was coming up with personal challenges.

He spun, and it landed on Ruby. She lifted an eyebrow and said, "Truth," determinedly. Her shoulders went back, and she flipped her long black hair over her shoulder. Ruby's confidence was unwavering.

"What really happened to Mrs. Chesterfield's cat when it showed up on my mom's front porch with a singed tail?" David's grin meant he probably knew the answer, anyway.

She cringed before saying, "Can I switch to dare?"

I'd only vaguely remembered the story, but I had a feeling even if he said no, we wouldn't get the real answer out of her. "Fine. Do that impression of your mother."

Ruby fell into a fit of giggles before shaking her head, then her face turned serious. "Darling, have you seen my glasses?" She got up and walked around the cramped living area. "I can't find them anywhere. Zane, will you help me?" She patted her hands around the countertop before putting both hands on the top of her head. "Oh dear, they were here on my head the whole time."

We couldn't stop from giggling. Her voice was spot on. Even the way she swung her hips was exactly like Alice's. I had a feeling she'd practiced this one for a while.

She sat on the floor next to Hannah and spun the bottle. It pointed at her brother, and the look on her face caused both of us to squirm. I knew she knew our secret, but I hadn't told him yet. Zane looked her dead in the eye. "Truth."

"Tell us about your first kiss." She said it like she already had a plan with this very specific question. Frankly, it was terrifying.

He looked over at me and squeezed my feet in his lap. "Izzy and I were what? Nineteen?" His eyes were wistful. "We had only known each other for a couple of weeks. I remember standing in the grassy field right outside the student union, knowing that just one kiss from this bossy, tenacious woman would change my life forever."

Ruby groaned and lay down on her back. "Not your first kiss as a couple, dumbass, your first kiss. Before Izzy." She seemed to be digging for something, but either it had never happened, or he wasn't telling.

His gaze lowered to my feet in his lap. "She was my first kiss. We were both each other's first kiss." It was the truth. I'd known him well enough to be certain.

The pain of a 20-year-old lie pierced my chest briefly. But it was a secret I'd thought would be a nice kind. It wasn't as big as the secret we'd both been keeping from our families, but I'd never admitted this to Zane. To anyone. He'd made it such a big deal that our first kiss was, well, *our* first kiss, that I never had the heart to tell him. "Actually . . ." I started.

All eyes shifted to me. David was grinning like a maniac. "Go on . . ."

"Zane was my first real kiss. But I had one before him. It just didn't count."

Hannah leaned in, her eyes glassy from the alcohol.

She wore a shimmery sundress, so the wobble in her body seemed a little off-brand. "You have to give us details, Iz."

I rolled my eyes, regretting saying anything. "It's not my turn."

Zane almost looked hurt as he said, "Uhh, now it is."

I let out a deep breath. "When I was in sixth grade, I went to this horrendous gala with my parents. It was some real estate circle jerk event where we had to wear uncomfortable dresses and eat pretentious foods."

"Oh, come on, you love pretentious foods . . . and uncomfortable clothes." Zane cut in, giggling.

I bumped his thigh with my foot playfully. "Okay, fine, I do now, but when I was twelve, not so much."

"Tell us about this kiss. I'm dying." Ruby groaned.

"Well, I got bored and decided to sneak away for a little while. Back before I did anything with the business, it was easy to become invisible and disappear for a few hours." I hadn't thought about it for years, but that night came rushing back to me like a movie. "I slipped into the coat closet while the attendant was on the phone and found the book I had tucked into my coat for that very reason."

"What book was it?" Hannah asked. I'd only ever spent time with her at these reunions, but she always had her nose in a book. Usually something super smutty. I should have known she would ask.

"Umm, I think it was The Lion, the Witch, and the Wardrobe."

"Ooh, that's a good one."

Ruby kicked her cousin in the foot. "Shut up and let her finish, Han."

I laughed and thought about what had happened next. "After about ten minutes of peaceful reading, I heard a *thunk* in the aisle next to me. I could see the attendant's shoes from where I was sitting, so I knew it wasn't him. But I heard rustling and couldn't concentrate on my book anymore." Sitting up, I thought about the details of what happened next. "I got up and started looking, hoping it wasn't a mouse or something else disgusting. I had to cover my mouth when I found him, though. A cute blond boy with big eyes looked up at me from between two coats. He was also reading a book." I looked at Hannah before she asked. "And no, I don't remember which one it was."

I leaned back against the couch, letting that tingling feeling from that night fill my body. "Anyway, I sat knee to knee with him and we talked. He was the son of a real estate family, so we shared how our lives sucked in ways no one else understood." I paused, remembering the kindred stories from that night. "An hour or so passed with us hiding between the coats, but then I heard my dad's voice requesting our belongings and telling my mom to go see if I was hiding in the bathroom again.

"I hadn't even asked his name, but before I could, he leaned in and kissed me." I had a feeling that a dopey smile was painted across my face, but I didn't care. "He moved deeper into the coats, but right before he disappeared, I slipped my charm bracelet off and pressed it into his hand.

"When the attendant came around the corner, he saw me crouched between the aisles and screamed. It gave me a chance to come up with some stupid story about seeing my parents trying to leave and coming to get my coat before they asked me to." I looked over at Zane. "You know how my parents are."

He squeezed my foot. "Sorry they're the worst." Then, after a beat, he asked, "Did you ever find out who he was?"

I shook my head. "Nope. Sometimes I wonder if I had fallen asleep and dreamt up the whole thing. But it didn't explain where my bracelet had gone."

"Wow, wife. I can't believe you kept this from me," he joked, but I couldn't help but feel guilty. It had been so long since it happened that I rarely thought about it.

Hannah leaned forward, a sardonic grin on her face. "Looks like both of you have been keeping secrets." She was right. When I thought about everything Zane had kept from me in the past few years, the guilt quickly dissipated.

In a split second, I realized that Hannah shouldn't know that, though. Zane and I both leaned forward a bit. "What are you trying to say?" he asked.

She shrugged. "Ruby told me."

Zane glared at his sister, and my heart stopped. Both of us practically yelled, "Ruby told you what?"

"That you're cheating on your wife," Hannah said. I started to panic. Is that how it looked?

Zane shot to his feet, and I covered my face with my hands. "It's not what you think it is," I said before he could speak. I worried that our overprotectiveness of the situation had made it seem worse than it really was. Not that it had been a walk in the park, but it wasn't devastating.

Ruby stood, wobbling on her feet. "Okay, so I might have made a mistake."

David chimed in with, "Everyone, calm down. It's not that big of a deal."

"They're breaking up, and you don't think it's that big of a deal?" Hannah screeched.

Zane looked at me, pain in his eyes. He started to speak, but stopped. His fists clenched at his sides. I knew he wanted to tell them, but he was showing signs of spiraling into a panic attack.

"Listen." I stood up, resting my hand on Zane's shoulder. I kept my voice calm to try to reassure all of them. "Things didn't work the way we had planned, but we're still a united front." While I appreciated Hannah's anger at the loss of our marriage, I desperately needed everyone to calm the fuck down.

Hannah looked at us like we were both full of shit. Which we kind of were, I was starting to realize. We shouldn't have been surprised that people would be upset when they learned our secret. "He cheated on you with some dude, and you're a united front?"

I pinched my brow. "He didn't cheat on me."

Zane glanced at me sidelong. "Iz." I hated that he was still blaming himself. Yes, what happened was terrible, but so was living in a dead marriage for years. Both of us were at fault.

I put my hands on my hips, turning into boardroom Lizette in a heartbeat. "Zane."

I looked at the rest of them, who seemed mostly sobered by the shock of the topic, and told them to sit down and listen. And they did.

We told them the truth. The whole truth. How things had been before Zane found Caleb. How we went to therapy and worked through a lot of our issues after he told me how he was feeling. How we're happily not together anymore, but still talk all the time. "I love him the same way you do. It's a different love than a wife loves her husband. But it's still love."

By the time we were done, all of us had gone back to our spots around the living room. My shoulders felt more relaxed than they had been in months. It felt reassuring knowing that our secret was at least a little out, and everyone in the room understood and cared for us still. I nudged Zane with my elbow. "See, now we just have to do this one more time with your mom and dad."

Before he could respond, Ruby cut him off. "Bradley's gonna flip when he finds out."

"He's not going to find out. Unless you already told him, Ruby?" Zane looked scared for the first time this evening.

She shook her head frantically. "Do you think I'm insane?"

"Well, you told our cousins my business without talking to me first, so yes, I do." He sounded exhausted.

She let out a deep sigh. "I only told Hannah." Then she looked skeptically at David, "Why aren't you surprised?"

"I plead the fifth," he said before getting up and opening the fridge. Both Ruby and Hannah watched him with their mouths agape, but I didn't think it was worth it to explain further, and Zane didn't say anything either. David grabbed a couple of beers, passing them out before sitting back down. "Are we going to play this game or not?"

It was three in the morning before we'd run out of energy—and alcohol. There had been terrible karaoke performances, interpretive dancing, attempted self-elbow licking, and some juicy secrets about college roommates and ex-boyfriends spilled. David won the night, though, with the face he had drawn around his belly button with a permanent marker we found in a drawer. It was going to be a fun story to share when we were all at the pool later this week.

After sending the three of them packing, I turned to Zane. "You can sleep in the bed tonight, and I'll take the couch. But I'm keeping your shirt."

He shrugged. "I don't mind the couch at all." As if he was trying to prove his point, he reached down and pulled open the bottom of the pull-out.

His head tilted slightly to the side and, because I had known him so well, I knew he was about to say something that might upset me. He sat on the edge of the couch-bed and patted the spot next to him. "Talk with me."

I rubbed my face but did what he asked. He wrapped his arm around my shoulder, something he'd done thousands of times, but this time felt more important than any of those other times. Our secret was out, just a little. We could finally start being this new version of ourselves. "I'm glad we told them," I whispered to the floor.

He squeezed me tighter. "It feels like a relief to have people in our corner, for sure, but I'm concerned about you."

I pulled back slightly. "Why me?"

"It breaks my heart to see you the way you are." As he spoke, I schooled the emotion out of my face, trying not to react. This wasn't about me. "Yes. Just like that."

"Like what? I didn't say anything."

"I literally watched Izzy leave your body and Corporate Lizette take her place. In the space of half a second."

I rolled my eyes, pulling out of his arm. "That's not a thing."

"It is. You have built these walls, and I don't even think you know you do it. I'm afraid that you're isolating yourself." His voice was heartbreakingly soft.

"As a woman in my industry, I have to have boundaries." I knew he wasn't attacking me, but I couldn't help but feel like I was under a microscope. I'd had to learn early on how to school my emotions. If I ever felt anything, I'd come off as weak.

He waved his hands in front of him. "No, I get that. I'm not talking about work. I'm talking about your heart."

"I don't need a heart to do my job." I could hear the emotion in my voice, and I hated it.

He buried his face in his hands for a few moments. "I don't give a shit about your career, Iz."

I must have pulled back like he'd struck me. It certainly felt that way. Before I could respond, he spoke softly, "That's not what I meant. I'm proud of how hard you work and all of your accomplishments. But I care more about you finding someone who will stay up late with you. Who will take care of you when you're old."

I put my hand on his thigh. "I don't need anyone. I like being on my own."

"That's bull. Everyone needs someone."

"No, that's bull. There are millions of people who are perfectly happy on their own for the rest of their lives." I tried my best to keep my voice from wobbling. He was right, but I wasn't ready to admit it.

"Okay, fine, I'll let you have that one. But you are not one of those people." He waited a beat before adding, "It breaks my heart to see the person I've loved so hard for so long not find her happy ending. I want you to find your soulmate."

"My career is my soulmate." I raised an eyebrow, daring him to argue about this. "You've said it yourself."

He ran his fingers through his wavy hair. "Yes, but I was joking. You're not happy like this. You haven't been for a really long time."

I threw my hands out to the side, annoyed that he'd set his sights on my personal life. "Okay, genius. Where am I supposed to find someone at a family reunion where everyone thinks I'm married to you?"

"You've got to let your hair down and relax a little." The smile on his face reminded me of how conniving he could be in his own boardroom. "David told me there's a bar about half an hour from here where the locals hang out. You could find someone there."

"I'm not going to find my next husband in some bar, Zane."

"I didn't mean you need to marry the next guy you meet. But maybe you should get laid."

I let out a sharp laugh that echoed in my ears. "I could sleep with anyone I wanted to."

"That's the problem, though. There isn't anyone you

want to sleep with, is there?" Then he paused, looking at me accusingly. "Have you even slept with anyone since we split up?"

I don't know why, but I turned away. "That's none of your business."

"You haven't slept with anyone?" He stood, exasperated.

"I didn't say that!" I looked up at him, knowing I was full of shit, anyway.

"It's written all over your face." He looked up, tapping his chin with his finger for a moment. "What you need is a fuck buddy. Some guy from this small town who can jump start . . ." he gestured to my lower half, ". . . whatever your needs are."

I stood then, ready to walk out the door. "Absolutely not. Especially not with your mother sleeping just a few yards away from here."

"Well, I don't think you should fuck him here in our cabin. There are a lot of private places in these woods." He looked out the window. "Lord knows Hannah and Ruby are running around like they usually do. We could figure something out."

I felt my skin blanch. "There is no *we*, and if there was, we wouldn't be figuring out my sex life together. I'm perfectly fine with the way things are."

"No, you aren't. You're miserable."

I put my hands on my hips, hating that he was right. "I'm going to bed."

He stepped in front of me, blocking the tiny hallway to the bedroom. "No. I let you run off without finishing discussions for too many years. You're going to fucking stand here and talk about this with me." His voice was loud. He was actually upset over this.

"My sex life is not your business. And it hasn't been since you started fucking someone who wasn't me." When he flinched, I forced my shoulders to relax. This was not the time to have an argument. "That's not what I meant. I'm sorry." My hands started to shake, which made me hate myself more in this moment. "I just don't think finding a partner is the solution. I had you for years, and all I did was focus on work." I had to take a deep inhale. "I ruined us, Zane. I ruined what we had. Well before you left. And I know that whoever I find will suffer the same fate."

His arms were around me then. Strong and secure and comforting. He shushed me and brushed his fingers through my hair. "My sweet Lizette. You didn't ruin us. We were young and dumb and not ready for marriage."

I slowly wrapped my arms around him, holding on more than I thought I'd needed to. "Like you said before, my career is my husband. Success through The Howell Group is what I need to be happy. Adding someone to the mix would just end the same way we did."

"Izzy, I've known you for almost twenty years. You're not happy, and you haven't been in a long time. Maybe having a partner would help."

"We were together for so long, Zane. And I never loved you the way you deserved it. I don't know if I can love anyone the way they deserve it."

"Neither of us knew what love was back then." He pulled back, really seeing me in my weakest moment.

"But I know what it feels like now. It's beautiful and warm and messy . . . and I want you to have it, too."

I shrugged, a powerless motion I only did in his presence. "But I don't like messy."

"Promise me you'll let your guard down while we're here. Just a little?"

"But your family needs to think we're married. Your brother's campaign is riding on our perfect family persona." I stepped out of his hug, needing to bring myself back to reality.

"And we'll pull it off. We did it for years before this. What's another eight days?" He smiled, like he had already planned something. "But we should get you out there while we're here."

I felt a little nervous at the prospect of going out looking for a hookup while on this vacation. "Why can't it wait until we're back home?"

"Because here isn't real. Think of it like a practice run. A safe place to experiment with people you'll never see again. You can get your feet wet in the dating pool with the nearby support of people who know you best." His eyes lit up with excitement, a contrast to the discussion we'd been having. "We'll go to a bar in town, one that's away from prying eyes. Maybe find a guy who has a place you can visit while everyone else is busy."

"I just don't think it's my destiny to be in a relationship." This idea of his felt more complicated than what I was ready for.

"We're going to find someone you can fool around with. You don't need to fall in love with the guy." He stepped out of the way, opening the door to the bedroom and gesturing for me to head inside. "Now go to bed. The sun will be up in just a few hours, and in case you forgot, we've got to ride horses with everyone after breakfast."

I smiled at him, but it was fake. I wasn't sure what I was more afraid of, riding a horse tomorrow, or going to a bar to find a man. "Goodnight, husband."

"Goodnight, wife," he said before heading back to the couch.

Chapter Seven

I am not what you would call a *horse girl.* Unlike a lot of my contemporaries, I didn't grow up begging my parents for a pony. I never wanted one for my birthday, for Christmas, or any other time in my life.

The year Santa bought me a Palm Pilot was the greatest Christmas ever, which is basically the furthest thing from a horse I can think of. I've managed to live thirty-six years without having clambered on top of one of these terrifying animals either, and I had hoped that I could continue that well into my old age.

Of course this existential crisis was happening in front of ten of my closest family members and a very sweet looking, actual horse girl, who was helping them choose their horses and get situated before our ride today.

The knowledge that I was about to get on this living being that I could not control, combined with the brightly colored outfit and bikini I was wearing as underwear, was a perfect recipe for the worst day of my life.

Bright and early this morning, after only a few hours

of sleep, I'd gone to the main office to get some work done before breakfast. While I was there, I'd gotten a call from the sheriff. My suitcase had not only made it to Helsinki, but had also journeyed into a fifteen-passenger van and was taking a lovely vacation in some remote village in the middle of nowhere.

He assured me it would get back to us as soon as possible, but he had no actual timeline, so I called my main office and tasked a few people with trying to get it home faster.

But as much power as I have as the owner of an international real estate company, I hate using company resources for personal endeavors, so I had a feeling my things would be in Finland for quite some time.

I could only get an hour of work done before Zane dragged me out of there, not quite kicking and screaming, since he'd promised I could take the car to town to get clothes. I'd kept hoping Ben would come in while I was there, but I'd been unlucky in that department as well.

"Here. Rub her side a little like this, so she gets to know you." The horse girl smiled at me brightly. "I'm Michelle, by the way. Your husband just mentioned that you've never ridden a horse before, so I thought I'd come over and give you some extra help." Zane waved at me from where he stood with Ruby, about ten feet away. She gave me a double thumbs-up, like I was five years old and thrived on encouragement.

Great. Now I was the helpless wife who couldn't figure out how to tame a wild horse.

At that moment, the horse let out a huff, making me

jump back. "I don't know if I can do this," I said, more to the horse than to Michelle.

She rubbed the side of the horse, slowly and gently. "I'm not going to make you do anything you don't want to, but Checkers is the sweetest girl we have on property. She'll go slow, and she's gentle." She nuzzled her face into the horse's neck. "Aren't you, girl?"

I spent a few minutes getting to know Checkers, and Michelle assured me I was going to have a great time. She got me up onto the horse, and I felt as ready as I'd ever be. She walked Checkers and me around in large circles, helping me get my bearings. It wasn't as scary as I had originally thought, but it was still something I wanted to get over with in the next hour, so I could check in with Aniyah.

Suddenly, Ben came from the stable on a large brown and white horse that must have had some impeccable breeding history because it was large and gorgeous. The way his thighs gripped the horse made my breath hitch. The air around me grew warmer, more humid. Seeing him so confident with his flannel shirt and unruly hair while riding that wild animal made me feel brave. I finally understood the "Save a horse, ride a cowboy" song.

He let out a whistle, and the rest of our group looked his way. "Hello everyone, thanks for taking this ride with us today." His voice boomed over the crowd. All ten of us focused on him like he was the chairman of the board. "I'm Ben, and I'm going to be your tour guide. We're going to ride on the trail for about an hour, and then we'll hike up to the waterfall for another hour or so. Then we'll stop for a picnic lunch in the meadow before heading back here to the resort."

I looked down at the sneakers I'd borrowed from Ruby. Four hours on the back of this horse was not what I had agreed to, but when I looked back up, everyone else was positively delighted.

"Hey, if you don't want to go, you can stay back." Zane's voice called out to me as he brought his horse closer to mine. But that damn inability to show weakness crept through my bones. It filled my entire body, and there was no way I could get off this horse in front of this many people and live with myself afterward.

"No. I can do this," I said, even as my knuckles turned white around the reins.

"The rest of the family is riding tomorrow. You can try again then if you'd be more comfortable." I cringed at the softness in his voice. He'd always offered me an out, even when he knew I couldn't take it. For years I'd thought he was patronizing me when he spoke like this, but after a huge argument about ten years ago, I learned he was just trying to be kind.

I still hated it. But it was a *me* problem.

"I refuse to get off this horse until I've accomplished this. I said I would do it, so here I am," I said through my teeth. He rolled his eyes and looked at Ben and Michelle for more guidance.

Michelle lined up all the horses two-by-two, with Zane's mom and dad in the front, then Ruby and David, Zane and me, Hannah and her mom, and Bradley and Tippy. Michelle was at the back like a caboose.

Ben called out again, "Your horses have done this trip

hundreds of times, so trust them. There will be parts of the trail where the horses can only go one by one. Trust them. They know exactly what to do. Feel free to look around and enjoy the scenery, but please keep both hands on the reins at all times and avoid taking pictures until we are standing still in a safe location." He continued going over safety rules and describing how he wanted us to navigate the trails.

I couldn't keep my eyes off him. The way his muscles shifted as he moved his horse around was mesmerizing, sure, but the most attractive thing was how he spoke to the group. That quiet authority and self-efficacy was something I had rarely seen in men in my social circle. The ones I worked with were loud, boisterous, and used to getting their way.

I thought about the conversation I'd had with Zane last night, about finding someone to hook up with while we were here. The ache in my lower belly and the way my heart raced a little just by the sound of Ben's voice made me want him for my own. I'm sure it was the pressure of the saddle on my pelvis and not the sound of his voice making me horny as hell.

Maybe Zane was right. Maybe I should open my heart a little.

We began our ride up the trail, and I felt my muscles loosen up. This wasn't nearly as terrifying as I had imagined. After about half an hour, I felt more comfortable. There wasn't anything I'd ever failed at once I put my mind to it, so I just told myself this was a task I had to do to get to the next step. And Michelle had been right. Checkers was actually very sweet.

"He's not too bad looking." Zane had inched his horse closer to mine as we meandered down the trail.

"Who, Ben?" I asked, not sure I wanted to discuss who I wanted to sleep with on top of this horse.

"Yeah. He looks like he could be fun." Zane pointed ahead with a smile on his face that meant he was up to no good. "The way his shoulders move under that shirt is honestly distracting."

I shook my head. "I'm going to pretend I have no idea what you're talking about."

"He could be really fun to roll around with." He winked obnoxiously.

"Then go right ahead. I won't stop you."

He tilted his head to the side slightly, giving Ben another once-over. "No, he's not my type."

I stared at Ben a little longer, finding him absolutely perfect. "Shut up. He looks exactly like your type." I'd spent a little time with Caleb over the past year, and he had a much darker complexion than Ben, but they seemed to be shaped similarly. Ben might be a little taller.

Zane hummed, like he had seriously thought about it. "Besides, I have a boyfriend. We're looking for you."

I glanced around at the rest of his family. "Be careful what you say around here. They'll hear you."

Before he could respond, the trail shifted to something precariously narrow. Our horses took the lead and filed into a single line, going down the side of the valley. As the sun beat down on us, I started to look toward the lake, but quickly closed my eyes, worrying that vertigo was about to knock me off this giant creature. Riding a horse was not something I ever wanted to do again.

The trail stabilized a little, and I opened my eyes, finding us still traveling narrowly in a single-file line. As soon as I felt it wasn't so bad after all, something slithered across the trail. Checkers must have seen it at the same time I did, because the moment I yelped, she took off, up the side of the hill, away from the trail.

I heard Zane yell, "Snake!" as the horse galloped away from the group. My hair whipped around me as sweat coated my skin.

This horse was supposed to be sweet, not a fucking lightning bolt. I screamed, gripping the saddle horn for dear life. As we barreled into the trees, I leaned my body against the horse and closed my eyes, preparing for my fate.

The temperature dropped, like we had gone even deeper into the forest, but I was terrified to open my eyes. It was probably less than a minute, but it felt like a lifetime. I had to do something, so I released one hand from the saddle and dug my fingers into the reins, trying to pull back, to do anything to stop this bullet train from killing me.

But then a loud whistle came from behind. It reverberated through me, and Checkers slowed down. Lifting my head slightly, I opened one eye and found Ben astride his horse, looking like one of those oil paintings of men going into battle. I tugged a little more on the reins, and Checkers tossed her head, trying to pull away from me. Ben pulled up next to us, reaching for the reins, and I let go, going back to white-knuckling the saddle horn.

He slowed his horse somehow, without speaking, and

pulled on Checkers's reins. As soon as Checkers met the pace of his giant beast, I sat up fully, watching him.

"Come here sweet girl, it's okay," he said, his voice calm and collected. It made me feel safer, so hopefully it was working on the horse, too.

Checkers lifted her giant head toward him, and he went on, "It's okay, it's just me and you." I wondered if he was talking to me or the horse, but I felt a fraction of my body's tension leave, anyway.

Sitting up a little straighter, I still wasn't sure of the animal under me. My skin was slick, covered in a thick sheen of sweat. "What happened?" I asked, more waver in my voice than I liked.

Ben ran his hand down Checkers's neck, making a soothing sound, but she yanked away, taking me a few feet deeper into the woods. I bit back a scream, my heart pumping into overdrive. He followed us, still holding on to her reins, trying to calm her down.

"Ben, I'm scared." It squeaked out of me on its own volition.

"There's no need to be afraid. You're safe with me," he said. His voice was low, meditative almost. He moved along next to us, shushing quietly, and after several feet, Checkers finally conceded, nuzzling her neck against his horse.

"That's it, sweet girl. You're okay." He reached over, rubbing her neck, and she relaxed under me. I leaned forward instinctively, running my hand against her coat, despite my inner terror. It helped calm my heart a bit, but adrenaline was still blasting through me.

I repeated my question to Ben, my voice a little stronger. "What happened?"

"The snake must have spooked her. She's usually not like this." He slid off his horse, coming up to my side. He kept rubbing her, and she pressed further into Ben's horse for comfort.

"I want to get off," I stammered. I didn't care if I had to walk all the way back to the cabin. I was over this.

"No. You're staying on the damn horse," he said. It came out commanding, but soft. His hand moved from Checkers's coat to my thigh, slowly rubbing in circles. When my eyes met his, a blaze flared inside of me. It was almost erotic, being told what to do in an uncontrollable situation. No one gave me demands. But I liked it.

I licked my lips, thinking of what it would feel like if his hand came up further. It had to be the emotions pumping through me, going from scared to whatever this was, but my body was so sensitive, so ready for him. "Okay, I'm staying on." It came out breathless, and I watched his gaze linger on my lips.

It would be so easy, so simple, to weave my fingers through his hair, to press against him for a kiss. But when I thought about logistics, I knew I'd have to lean down to pull him against me, and I wasn't brave enough to move like that on top of this animal that I was still very unsure of. Against all the alarms going off in my head, though, I reached for his shoulder. "Thank you for saving me."

He started to speak, but something crashed behind us, and Zane called out, "Izzy, are you okay?"

Ben took a step back, and I found my husband on the back of his horse ten feet away. "I'm fine, Zane. Thanks for all the help." I was trying to lighten the mood, but I cringed a little when it came out more judgmental than I'd planned.

Ben turned away and mounted his horse in one muscular shift. My eyes scanned his body, thankful that he was here when I needed him. "She's fine and so is the horse, but I'm going to keep a close eye on both of them. No need to worry." His tone didn't leave any room for argument.

Zane simply nodded his head. "Thank you."

Ben reached for Checkers's reins, making a clicking noise and pulling us beside him. "Keep a hold on her reins. I want her to know that you're still in charge," he said to me, and I followed his direction without a thought.

We continued like this for the rest of the way down the trail. Michelle had taken the lead for the rest of the group, and Ben, Zane and I took up the rear, moving at a pace that Checkers found comfortable.

We made it to a clearing with a paddock for the horses. Michelle appeared practically out of thin air and started helping everyone dismount. Ben, however, was still riding next to me. "Here, let me help you."

He was off his horse in a second and reached his hands up toward my hips, but didn't make contact yet. Instead, his eyes scanned slowly up my thighs. All I could think of was how he had touched me earlier. How my body had responded. I opened my mouth to stop him, but realized he would see the effect he had on me if I protested too much.

"Sure. Thank you," I mumbled, and his hands gripped my waist. The second he touched me, I knew it had been a bad idea. I let out a gasp as the heat from his hands seeped into me. He lifted me up and out of the saddle and gently lowered me to my feet without effort. I had to stop myself from leaning into him, from burying my nose into his neck to take in the pine scent of him.

Ben's tongue dipped out briefly, wetting his lips, and I was entranced. His eyes met mine, and for a second we were the only people on earth. His eyebrow perked up slowly. "How are you feeling now, Izzy?" His words were quiet. Intimate.

I reached up to brush a piece of hair out of my face, and his eyes snagged on my wedding rings. The energy between us shifted as his brain obviously registered what they represented. I shouldn't have felt remiss, especially since to everyone else, I was supposed to be married to Zane right now, but the emotion left me a little breathless.

I started to speak, but Hannah rushed over to us, smacking her hand on my shoulder. "You didn't die! I'm so proud of you." Then she noticed Ben was standing with me and turned to him. She looked him up and down like he was a big chunk of meat and said, "Hi. I don't think we've officially met. I'm Hannah."

I used this as an excuse to disappear before I did or said anything I'd regret in front of Ben. I've always excelled at taking my emotions and burying them so I can get my job done. If anything, I'm more productive when I avoid my feelings. I'm sure it's why my brother and I have such a strained relationship. He says I turn into an asshole when there's something going on in my personal life.

And I think he's been right about me this whole time.

Shaking my head, I glanced back at Ben and Hannah as they walked together, leading Checkers into the pen. He had a smile as bright as the sun, and she said something that had both of them laughing. She touched his arm as they walked, and unexpected jealousy arose in my chest. Of course the cute guy who spent his days socializing with tourists would have his pick of women to sleep with. I just didn't want him to choose Hannah this week.

I wanted him to pick me.

I took a few more steps away from the family, trying to catch my bearings. My backside was sore from that treacherous ride, and once I was away from the group, I took a few lunges to stretch the muscles in my legs. "Hey babe, where you going?" Zane called out to me.

"You don't have to call me babe. They can't hear you," I said, folding forward over my legs, giving my hamstrings some tension. I'd been doing pilates and yoga for well over a decade, but there were muscles in my body that I didn't think I'd ever used before today.

He laughed quietly. "I hadn't said it on purpose. Old habits die hard, I guess."

I stood up, smiling at him before stretching my leg in front of me again, trying to relieve some tension. I was worried about how my body was going to feel later, especially since I was finally feeling calm and collected again.

He held his hands out. "Let me help."

I stepped closer to him and he took my thigh in one hand, rubbing the side of my bottom with the other, stretching my glutes and rubbing a knot that had begun to form. "Caleb taught me this one. It really helps after long rides on my Peloton."

I started to explain how his bike was different from what I'd just been through, but he hit just the right spot and I closed my eyes, gripping his shoulder. "Right there. Yes. That's amazing." He went a little deeper and I let out a moan that ventured on indecent.

"Oh, pardon me." Ben sounded startled and when I opened my eyes, I realized Zane and I had been standing in a semi-private copse of trees, far away from the rest of the family. My thigh was in his hand, his front pressed tightly against mine as I dug my fingers into his shoulder.

Ben's hands flew up. Embarrassment from finding the two of us so close together was all over his face. "No worries. I was married once before. I know what it's like."

The sounds I had been making must have given the impression that we were doing something much different from an ex-husband using a trick he learned from his personal trainer boyfriend to release muscle strain. I thought about our conversation the other day, when he'd asked if this was a trip for Zane to win me back. I had to set him straight, especially since I'd rather be in his arms right now than Zane's.

"It's not what it looks like," I admitted as I pulled away from my ex-husband.

Zane pushed my shoulder playfully. "Yeah, I don't even like her like that," he said, humor in his eyes.

Ben shook his head, probably thinking that we were the weirdest couple he'd ever found practically fucking in the woods. "We're about to head up to the waterfall. You're welcome to join us or . . ." he looked over the two of us again, "keep doing whatever you've got going on here." He walked away before I could defend myself further. His movements were stiff, like he was just as mortified as we were. I almost yelled out to stop him, to explain, but I didn't want to call attention from anyone else.

I shoved Zane's shoulder the way he had done mine. "Some wingman you are."

He laughed and motioned for me to give him my other leg. Since the damage had already been done and my ass was sore from the horse, I did.

Zane's voice was close to my ear as he stretched my muscles. "Okay, so maybe we ruined your chances with that guy, but we're going to the bar tonight. I'm sure we'll find another one."

Chapter Eight

Once we got back to the resort, the pull to touch base with my office became too strong to deny. I took a quick shower and changed into a clean set of resort clothes, thankful that the girls and I were going into town in a few hours, even if I was on the verge of complete exhaustion.

I sat at Ben's desk, ready to knock out some work. The first email I saw when I booted up was from my father. Great.

"I heard from a contact in Santa Barbara that The Azure is up for sale. Have you put in a bid yet? You're going to have to develop an aggressive plan so it doesn't turn into a bidding war.

I have faith in you, but I also need you to step up to make this happen. That hotel was meant to be ours."

He didn't even sign it at the end. Or give an update about his trip. Not a word about my mother. Just business.

I shouldn't be surprised.

I sat, thinking of what to write in my reply. There were no words that I could use to assure him I had it under control. I knew I did. But he wouldn't believe me.

My biggest fear was saying the wrong thing and making him think he should come out of retirement and do the work himself. I'd have to double down if I wanted to show him I could make this happen.

I took a deep breath, planning my reply, but Ben cut off my concentration. "Looks like the ship made it back into the harbor."

I glanced up at him, confused. "I'm sorry, what?"

He propped himself on the edge of the desk like he had last time we were alone in here. I looked around, noticing that Cate had yet again chosen the right time to disappear. "You said the ship between you and your husband had sailed. But the two of you were awfully close earlier."

I laughed, but it didn't have much humor in it. "I assure you, there was nothing going on."

He folded his arms, which seemed to be his favorite resting position. "I noticed some pretty intimate touching afterward, too."

I closed my laptop and leaned my elbows on the desk, close enough to smell the sunlight and pine of him. "There is no way in hell Zane and I are getting back together."

"So you're just friends with benefits?" He was genuinely concerned, his brows bunched together. "One last hookup while you're away from your real lives?"

"Not that it's anyone's business, but he's got a boyfriend back home that he absolutely adores. The two of them are probably soulmates, actually. We're just pretending until we find the right time to tell his parents." I sat back in my chair, knowing I'd set him straight, just like I'd done a thousand times to men who didn't believe me in the boardroom.

That answer had the shock I was going for. He stepped back, clapping his hands together quietly. "Oh shit. I am so sorry I pressed. You were right, that absolutely was not my business."

He was cute when he squirmed.

I thought for a second about what it felt like to tell someone the truth. To admit to the entire world that my husband really did love someone else.

And it was nice. Refreshing, even.

It made me want to throw caution to the wind—to just get our truth out there. If it weren't for the stupid campaign, I think I'd walk right up to the big house right now and scream it from the porch. Instead, I softened my tone just a bit, giving Ben more of the story. "It's not a big deal, I promise. He's my best friend, and I had a tight muscle from my horse running away into the woods, in case you've forgotten. That's what you walked in on."

He had a private smile peeking through his beard. "So you're really single, then?"

"As single as they come." I thought about mentioning that I'd been accused multiple times of being married to my work, but he could probably tell that about me already.

"Well, then." He stepped away from the desk, but leaned in, putting a hand next to my laptop as he came in closer. The smell of his minty breath had my mouth watering. It took all of my will to not close my eyes and inhale deeply. "I have an extremely important question for you," he said seriously, his voice low.

I leaned in, mirroring his movements. Licking my lips, I watched his eyes dart down briefly before meeting mine again. A fleeting thought that this was turning into something I'd want to call Blake and Camilla about later popped into my mind. "Ask away."

He was so close I could feel the heat—could smell the sunshine coming off him. "When you eat breakfast, do you put the cereal in the bowl first or the milk?"

It took a second to register, but when I did, I barked out a laugh. "That was not where I thought you were going."

He smiled coyly, standing up to prop his hip back on the corner of the desk. "What did you want me to ask?" His voice was even deeper than usual.

Oh, he wanted me bad, too.

"I'm not telling," I said, feeling a tingle from my core travel up my body.

He messed with the pens sitting in the glass jar on the desk, like it was my workstation, not his. "Well, what is it? Cereal or milk?"

I had to think about it, even though I knew the answer. The question felt like it had come completely out of left field, but I thought he had asked it to disarm me. To get me to stop worrying about my relationship situation, maybe. So I answered honestly. "What kind of psychopath puts the milk in first?"

The smile my answer earned actually took my breath away. "I had to make sure you weren't crazy before I asked you out."

"Good call." I narrowed my eyes at him. "You're not a milk first guy, are you?"

"Oh, God, no. There is something wrong with those kinds of people." He looked mischievous. I wanted to lean in and kiss him.

As he spoke, I realized what he'd just said. I felt more adventurous in this moment than the entire time spent on the back of that horse, especially when I'd thought I was about to die. "A few of us are going to a bar tonight. I don't know what it's called, but it's half an hour away."

"I know the one. Maybe I'll see you there." He flashed another smile, but this one was darker, like he wanted nothing more than to spend time with me somewhere else. Somewhere dimly lit and private.

I tried to think of something flirty to say. Something to relate to his ridiculous question, but before I came up with anything, he looked down at his watch. "I've got to lead a hiking tour in a few minutes." His eyes trailed down to my hands before placing his palm next to my forearm. Heat radiated off him. "Enjoy my desk." Then he stood, a crooked smile gracing his lips.

As he walked away, I thought about how he'd saved me today. Like it was nothing. And yet here he was, ready to go take another family on another tour, like rushing into the woods after runaway horses was part of his daily routine. My eyes scanned over his back, down to his ass that had no right to look as firm as it was.

I'd somehow missed her come in, but Cate cleared her throat. I looked over at her, finding her wiping down the counter. I wondered if she'd been eavesdropping on our conversation. Instead of being irritated, it made me want to laugh. I really, really liked her. She sent me a wink and whispered, "I didn't mean to listen, but your secret's safe with me."

I cackled, winking back at her, while also wondering just how much she'd actually heard. "Thanks, Cate." I didn't think anyone in the family was spending any time with her, so I was sure she'd be true to her word.

I tapped my fingers on my laptop. As much as I wanted to email my father back to let him know I had everything under control, I also didn't feel like logging in again. I wanted to go back to my cabin and take a nap while I waited for the girls to head to town. Maybe spend some time replaying Ben's fingers moving up my thighs while I had the cabin to myself.

So I got up, said goodbye to Cate, and did just that.

Chapter Nine

We pulled up to the Walmart, which was a 45-minute drive from the resort, and I wasn't sure how to feel about it.

We'd passed by a few boutique stores, but they all had shit like pink feathers sewn to the collars of the shirts in the display windows, and I just couldn't bring myself to get out of the car.

So here we stood next to the Escalade—Hannah, Ruby and me.

I stared at the large logo on the front of the building, wondering how I'd even gotten here.

"Have you ever been in a Walmart?" Hannah asked, looking at me with dripping skepticism.

I mulled over it for a second before glaring at her from the corner of my eye. "Don't act like your daddy isn't a billionaire."

She burst into laughter. "Yes, but unlike you, I know how to find a deal once in a while."

Ruby cut her off before she could finish explaining.

"She likes to come here to pick up dudes." Hannah gasped, her cheeks turning pink. Ruby's hands flew to her hips, like she was ready to argue if her cousin wanted to. "She says it's a fun way to find someone who isn't into you for your money, huh, Han?"

I rolled my eyes. "The two of you are going to give me a heart attack, I swear."

Ruby weaved her arm through mine. "Come on, let's go in."

Hannah took the lead, but looked at me inquisitively. "So if you've never been to a Walmart, how do you get your groceries?"

"Online. I put in what I want and the store delivers it in a cooler the next day." Not that I really did much with the groceries. Cooking was not my thing at all. It wasn't Zane's thing either, so when we'd lived together, we usually got takeout delivered. We'd never really been home at the same time, anyway, so it wasn't like it mattered.

"What if you need emergency tampons? Or like, cough syrup in the middle of the night?" Ruby asked.

"I call my assistant?" I tried to ignore how out of touch my answer made me sound, but it felt like a lump in my chest.

Ruby squeezed my arm a little tighter. "Well, are you in for a treat today!"

The girls dragged me through the front door, and I was overwhelmed. The smells coming from the bakery on my right were delicious, but having it right across from the swimwear department was jarring. This place was huge. Enormous. And I think they sold literally everything.

"Okay, here's the list," Ruby said as she pulled a piece of notebook paper from her back pocket. I glanced at it over her shoulder. Drinks, snacks, breakfast items, and even pool noodles were there. I had no idea where to start. "Mom said we needed enough for thirty people or we'd be at risk of snack starvation by this time tomorrow. So dramatic."

Hannah grabbed a shopping cart and rolled it toward me before grabbing another one for herself. "Okay, I think we're going to have to divide and conquer in order to find everything before we meet the boys at the bar on time. Iz, do you want one of us to come with you and the other one can get started on Aunt Alice's list?"

I scanned the front half of the store. This place was intimidating. The fluorescent lights were bright as hell and the number of people milling around like zombies was more than I would have preferred. But I was a grown ass woman. I could handle a shopping trip on my own. Plus, I hadn't been alone in a few days and needed a little bit of a recharge. "You two go, and I'll holler if I need help."

The girls took a sharp left, and I went right, headed for the women's department. I tried to remember the last time I'd been in a store, but faltered. Every so often, I enjoyed going out to buy new shoes or a handbag, but as far as everything else, a courier at the company was either paid overtime to pick it up or it was brought right to my front door.

If I couldn't get it delivered, I didn't need it.

But now, when I was wearing my last clean bikini under lilac sweatpants and a green t-shirt, I knew it was time to handle this myself. I'd refused to even look in the mirror when I'd left the cabin. There was no way I would like what I saw.

I pushed my cart around, trying not to be overwhelmed by the sheer amount of merchandise stuffed into this corner of the warehouse. The underwear department was my first stop, as I thought it would be the easiest. Boy, was I wrong. I scanned row after row of brightly colored packages. Bikini-cut, hip-huggers, boy shorts, and so many other styles were sending me into overload.

Each plastic-wrapped package had a smiling, nearly naked woman on the front, clearly living her best life, with about a hundred measurements on the back. I didn't know I would need a measuring tape to find out which panties were best for me.

I took a deep breath and did the first thing that came to mind, but after dialing her number and putting the phone to my ear, I secretly hoped she wouldn't pick up.

"Hey Lizette, what's going on?" Blake sounded like she was in the middle of something. I was already ready to hang up.

"What kind of underwear do you wear?" Her laugh burst through the phone, and I realized I was a prime candidate for an HR investigation. "That came out so wrong. I'm sorry."

"Please, this might be one of the best moments of my life." I could hear the grin on her face. "This totally makes up for you walking in on Sal and me at the wedding."

I cringed, thinking about finding them hiding in an office at Reece's wedding, completely naked. This absolutely made up for that mortifying moment, making me want to fall into a pit and never come back again. "I shouldn't have called. I just don't know what I'm doing." Fuck. What a thing to admit. My entire life was spiraling out of control, and I was ready to get off the ride. I reached for the first pair of underwear I saw. The woman on the cover looked a bit like me. This would be fine.

"No, it's okay. Just give me some context."

I let out a sigh. "My luggage was lost, and we thought it would come back soon, but now it's in Finland and I'm at Walmart and I don't know what kind of underwear to buy." It spilled out of me like a waterfall of word vomit.

"Wow. That is a lot, okay." I imagined her pushing her keyboard away from her, like she sometimes did when she was problem-solving. "Do you usually buy your own underwear?"

I rubbed the bridge of my nose. "Does it make me sound pretentious if I say no?"

"Not at all. If anything, I'm envious." Thank goodness she sounded like she was smiling and not judging me.

"Usually I hire a shopper when I need new ones and she gets them." I paused. "And yes, I am realizing how that sounds now that I've said it out loud."

Blake walked me through the vocabulary of underwear styles. She stayed on the phone with me until I'd found a few different packs to try and tossed them into my cart. I thought about asking her to stay on the line while I looked for the rest of my clothes, but I knew she was busy. She was running one of my most lucrative hotels, for heaven's sake.

"Thank you for being my friend. I wouldn't have been able to do this without you." It came out before I could think. I wasn't used to any sort of vulnerability, and this felt a little raw.

She might have paused a second before saying, "No worries. We're friends first. Coworkers second."

I had an out-of-body experience for a second, thinking about that part of *How The Grinch Stole Christmas*, when his heart gets bigger. I'd spent my whole life working hard to be a success in my parents' eyes, not really cultivating relationships, and look at where it brought me. In the underwear aisle at a Walmart, wondering if I liked hipsters or bikini briefs more.

I thanked her for her help and hung up, promising to send her pictures from the trip later, and made my way through the clothing aisles. I walked up and down until I found a few dresses that would have to work.

Black wasn't in season, apparently, and most of what they had in my signature color looked like it was made for extras on *Little House on the Prairie*. But I found a few charcoal gray sundresses and even a dark blue pencil skirt that felt soft and stretchy.

I had hoped my bra could handle a few more days, but even after handwashing it in the sink again, it had developed a smell I didn't exactly love. I'd been wearing the bikini tops since then, and really wanted something that would actually support the girls, so I went to the bra department. It was just as daunting as the panties, and I thought about calling Blake again.

Not wanting to come off as taking advantage of a friend, I flipped through a bunch of different bras, looking for my size. I found a couple that looked comfortable, even one without an underwire to try, but then I came upon a black lace bra that looked more like racy lingerie than everyday support.

I ran my finger across the soft scalloped edge and wondered what Ben's face would look like if he saw me in it. Sure, it didn't have to be Ben, but so far I hadn't found anyone else I wanted to throw myself at.

Thinking about anyone other than Ben made me want him that much more. Maybe he would come to the bar tonight.

I took the bra off the rack, tossing it into my cart, and was taken aback by how badly I wanted to move on from Zane. Just a week ago, I'd thought I would be content to never sleep with another man. Like that part of me was dead.

But coming here, with the fresh air and the gorgeous man I kept running into, had changed something in me. Suddenly I went from being afraid of moving on and finding someone new to this woman who was ready to climb a man like a tree. I looked down at the bra, lying on my slightly colorful new clothes and quietly thanked it for giving me this kind of courage.

I meandered through the rest of the store, picking up all the other things I would need. I even grabbed a cheap carry-on suitcase to take everything home with me, too.

After tossing some sunblock in the cart and browsing

the magazine aisle for some things to read, I sent a text to Ruby: *I think I've got everything. Where are you?*

While waiting for her to reply, I pulled out my work phone and checked for messages from the office. Aniyah had sent a short email:

Lizette-

I think I'm getting closer to finding what The Carlisle Corporation is bidding for The Azure so we can make sure our offer is better. I dug through some tax records of the trust that holds their properties and surprisingly found that they've purchased something in the same county you're staying in, but my person on the inside said they had no record of the sale, so it was probably a family home. I'll keep looking and let you know when I find something useful. In the meantime, start being cordial to any old dudes you come into contact with, just in case one of the Carlisle brothers is living in the Upper Peninsula of Michigan. Maybe we can get some internal info that way.

Almost done compiling numbers, but I think it's going to be a great bid. I'll let you know when I'm ready to share with the board.

Ruby's incoming text on my personal phone told me to meet them at the checkout, so I went back to my business phone and typed a quick reply:

Thanks for the info, Aniyah. I know she's a pain in the ass, but maybe reach out to Aimee to see if she can dig up some information. She's got the internet stalker thing down, and her mother knows everyone.

Aimee was a subcontractor we used for our social media management. She worked at her mother's agency, which was the best in the business. There had been some bad blood between her and my little brother when he was deep in his addiction, but I'd never learned details, and frankly, didn't want to. I'd heard through the grapevine that she'd tried to sleep with him and he shut her down, but I did my best to avoid hearing anything about Reece's sex life.

I hated working with Aimee. She was a spoiled brat, but dammit was she good. Plus, I owed her mother a lot of favors over the years, so throwing her a bone by giving her a job every so often was easy.

Just as I tucked my phone back into my purse, I saw Ruby and Hannah passing by with their shopping cart loaded to the brim and rushed to catch up with them. They'd obviously taken their task seriously. We'd never go hungry, or sober, again.

Chapter Ten

I snuck into the bathroom at the bar and locked the door. Anyone that had to pee would have to wait—this was the kind of thing that couldn't be handled in some piss-stained stall. I'd blindly grabbed an outfit from the car when we parked and stuffed it into my purse.

See Zane, I'd wanted to say. *I can put more than work stuff in my Birkin bag.*

Pulling tags off the clothes felt more secretive than it should have, but the first thing I started with was a pair of hipster underwear.

I pulled off the resort clothes, tossing them in the trash can. I never wanted to see them again. They'd been comfortable, but I was ready to wear real clothes again.

The new panties felt like a dream. Like the most comfortable thing I'd ever worn in my life. A warm hug from a lover you'd had for years. Or so I imagined.

I stuffed the rest of the pairs into my purse, since I didn't want to lose them. Then I got dressed, slipping on the charcoal dress I'd selected for tonight's festivities.

After popping off the tag and tossing it in the trash, I slipped it over my head. I finally smoothed it down and checked myself out.

The dress was actually really pretty, which was a surprise. The halter-straps were thin but didn't dig into my skin. I ran my fingers over the empire waistline, glad that it showed off my curves but not in an overly-sexual way. The fabric wasn't the softest thing I'd ever felt against my skin, but it was close.

The best part was the pockets. I never wanted a dress without built-in storage again.

Tonight I had opted for my black pumps, but the more I thought about the cute little flats I'd bought at the store, the more I wanted to go back out to the car and get them.

I finger-combed my straight black hair and reapplied my red lipstick—one thing I'd never leave home without.

I was as ready as I'd ever be.

The snick of the lock echoed across the tile room as I opened the door, and I was met by a few irritated faces waiting in line. "Sorry, it was an emergency," I said as I walked down the hallway to find my people.

David and Hannah were sitting at a tall table, and I spotted Ruby at the bar. Just as I was looking through the crowd for Zane, he appeared next to me, a drink in his hand. "Here's your vodka soda, my dear."

I took a sip, which was mostly vodka. Other than these family reunions, I wasn't a big drinker. Sure, I went to happy hour about once a week, between friends and clients and coworkers, but when I was out, I rarely had more than one alcoholic drink. It was different at family reunions, though, knowing I could let my hair down a little.

Looking around the bar, it felt more like a honkey tonk than any of us were used to, with the tongue-and-groove wood and the posters of old country musicians on the walls. I'd be lying if I said I wasn't hoping to find Ben, but I didn't see him anywhere.

"You might not find Prince Charming tonight, but there's at least some cute guys you could flirt with." Zane's voice pulled me back to reality. I wasn't sure if I wanted to find some random guy. After feeling Ben's fingers on my leg this afternoon, I knew just who I wanted.

Zane motioned for me to follow him to the table just as Ruby arrived with her drink. The five of us stood together, a stark city contrast to the reclaimed wood of this dimly lit bar. "How did you get here?" I asked Zane and David.

David answered, "Funny story. We took an Uber, but I think it's the only one in town. We watched the car on the map, and it came from here to pick us up. I bet the guy just goes back and forth all night long."

"Judging by the size of this crowd, I'd assume the whole town is here tonight." Hannah said. The building was larger than it'd looked from outside, so the mass of people had plenty of space. There were tables all around the dance floor, and even a small stage in the opposite corner for a live band. I didn't know if I'd ever pick a place like this to visit, but now that I was inside taking it all in, it seemed like a lot of fun.

Ruby drummed her hands on the worn wooden table.

"Enough talk about transportation. We're on a mission tonight." She glanced around conspiratorially. "We're looking for a horse for Izzy to ride home on."

"Maybe not a horse," I said, remembering how scared I had been earlier. The shock on my face must have been huge, since they all laughed at me. Absentmindedly, I rubbed my backside, which was still sore from the actual horseback ride this morning.

"First things first," Ruby said excitedly as she reached for my hands.

"What are you doing?" I asked, confusion running through me as she pried my wedding rings from my finger. I rubbed my thumb around the now-empty space and wondered how they had gone back to feeling comfortable in just a couple days of wearing them.

Almost a year of them tucked away in a box had been forgotten in less than forty-eight hours.

She planted a hand on her hip. "No one is going to want to take you home with a three-carat ring on your hand."

I reached for them, panic in my voice. "Please don't lose them." They weren't a symbol of undying love anymore, but they were still special.

She rolled her eyes, just like the little sister she was, and unclasped her necklace from her neck. "Stop worrying. I've got it all planned out."

Zane leaned in. "You really should worry if Ruby is the mastermind."

"You," she pointed at him, "need to make yourself scarce. No one is going to ask her to dance with you looming over her like that."

"I'm not looming. I'm wing-manning." He wrapped his arm around my shoulder, smiling proudly.

"This is exactly what I'm worried about." She pointed between the two of us.

"What?" He said, letting go of me. "I know her better than anyone else. I can find someone she's going to like."

"I've changed my mind. Ex-husbands are banned from being wingmen."

The two of them stared each other down until Zane picked up his drink, knocking it back. "Fine. David and I wanted to go back to the resort, anyway."

"We did?" David protested. Zane kicked him under the table, but David kicked him back. "Why the hell did we come all the way out here if we were just going to hang out for an hour?"

Hannah jumped in. "Ruby's right. I hadn't thought about how weird it would be until we were all here together." She looked at me and then at Zane. "It's weird, right?"

Ruby nodded, and I tried to keep a neutral face. It was a little odd, but I didn't want to chime in.

Zane folded his arms on the table, looking at David. "Fuck. She's right. Lizette needs to find a man without us."

Hannah held up the keys. "The car is filled with alcohol. You'll be fine. We'll catch the Uber driver on his way back."

The worry that always bubbled up as people left a bar must have shown on my face. Zane grabbed my hand. "David hasn't had anything other than soda. He's okay to drive." I nodded. "And you can have more than one drink, you know." I opened my mouth to argue, but he said, "You are not your brother. Three or four, hell, even six drinks aren't going to ruin your life. You can hire a ride back to the resort whenever you want." He pointed to Hannah and Ruby, who had their heads together, whispering something they didn't want us to hear. "I know I don't have to tell you this, but please don't let them pressure you into anything you're not comfortable doing. However," he squeezed my hand, "if you're comfortable staying out late and channeling your inner woo girl . . . I'd be very happy for you."

I smiled. "I promise to keep an open mind. But that's as far as I'm willing to go."

"Call me if you need me, okay?" He and David waved their goodbyes and went out the door. It wasn't until my first drink was empty and they were long gone that I remembered there was no service where they were going, so I wouldn't be able to call. Maybe Cate would pick up if I called the front desk.

"Ready to work the room?" Ruby asked, lifting her long hair into a high ponytail. The way she twisted the hairband around it told me she was taking this task very seriously.

"I'm going to need another one of these." I held up my empty glass.

"Think of it as an undercover assignment." Hannah said. "Pretend you're someone else. A secret agent. You don't even have to use your real name."

We went to the bar and ordered another round while I thought over the logistics of her plan. "Ooh, he's cute." Hannah pointed to a guy wearing sunglasses inside.

"Nope," Ruby and I chorused.

"Hmm, okay." Hannah scanned the crowd. There were small groups of people filling the whole place, even a few couples dancing on the parquet floor in the middle of the room. "What about him?" She pointed.

"The guy with an orange shirt and bleached tips in his hair?" Ruby asked, disgusted.

Hannah let out a sigh. "This is harder than I thought it would be."

"We need to walk around." Ruby grabbed me by the arm, pulling me along.

I felt like a debutante in a regency novel, taking a turn around the room, hoping to fill up my dance card. Except instead of a husband, I was hoping to find a random hookup. Maybe.

The girls led us through a few groups of guys, introducing us and chatting about work. Ruby told the first two guys we walked up to that my name was Izzy, and I was a real estate agent, which wasn't exactly a lie, since that's what the family called me, and I did have a real estate license. I just wasn't the queen of selling suburbia, as Ruby had claimed.

No one really gave me the butterflies, not that I had expected as much, but the guys we talked to sounded like normal humans. Even the guy with the sunglasses came over at one point, and I worried that Hannah was going to throw herself at him. "Standards, Hannah. You don't want to sleep with someone you wouldn't be willing to get accidentally impregnated by," I warned her.

We took another lap around the bar before coming up to a group of very tall, broad-shouldered guys clad in flannel shirts and cowboy boots. Ruby took my glass in her hand and held it in front of us as she addressed them. "I'm sorry, but my sister's glass seems to be empty. Do any of you want to buy her another one?"

Heat rose in my cheeks. I had never in my life asked someone to buy me a drink, and wasn't planning on starting now. "Sorry, guys, my sister is mistaken." I yanked the glass out of her hand. "I can buy myself a drink." I turned around to go back to the bar, maybe even to walk out the door.

"What are you drinking?" a familiar voice asked.

Chapter Eleven

I turned, meeting his eyes as if I'd done it a thousand times before. The same pull I felt when he was propped against Cate's desk yesterday brought me right back to him. "Ben. You came."

He reached for me, running his hand along my arm, and I had to hold in a gasp at his touch. "Sorry it took me so long. I got stuck taking care of a faulty propane tank." He pointed to his group of friends. "We come out here a lot, but this is the first time I've had someone waiting for me."

Hannah jumped in, not having heard him. "We're looking for some cute guys to make out with. Know anyone?" Her grin made me wonder how intoxicated she was. Or maybe how often she did this.

Ben stepped a little closer to me, speaking quietly. "And your husband is okay with that?" The charming cadence of his voice made my toes curl a little.

I bit my bottom lip. "Um. He's the one that talked me into coming out tonight." I pushed my hair behind my ear, a nervous tic I thought I had broken myself of years ago.

"Did you tell the family . . . ?" he motioned between us with his hands, not finishing his sentence.

I shook my head. "His sister knows the truth. And his cousin. No one else is here tonight."

His eyebrows scrunched together, but he looked conspiratorial, not concerned. "Tell me what you're drinking, and I'll get one for you," he said with a smile.

I asked for a vodka soda, and he took off toward the bar. Hannah and Ruby took up court with the rest of the group, giggling, flipping their hair, and putting their hands on flannel-covered shoulders at just the right time in their conversations.

While I was excited that Ben had shown up, I didn't know what to do with my hands—a rarity for me. Now that he was here, what was I supposed to do?

I used the girls' distraction to slip away, finding a high-top table several feet from the crowd. It only took Ben a few minutes to get drinks and meet me in my little corner, which provided a nice break from the noise of people chatting over the country music. He slid into the chair next to mine as I took a sip of my drink. We were close enough that I could bump into his shoulder with mine, although I didn't have the guts to do that. Not yet, at least.

He leaned in so I could hear him over the music. "So, how's the family vacation with your ex-husband going?"

I thought about it for a few seconds. "Honestly? Really nice. I was worried I wouldn't enjoy a single moment of it, but it's starting to grow on me."

He lifted his glass to his lips, taking a long sip of the amber liquid. "How much longer are you going to pretend you're still together until you tell them the truth about your . . ." he paused for a beat, "situation?"

"I've been a little busy with things at the office, so we haven't really scheduled anything. But hopefully soon." I took a sip of my drink. "Sorry, I'm sure the last thing a guy I'm interested in wants to hear is complaints about my job and ex-husband."

He flashed a boyish grin, making his ocean-blue eyes sparkle. "So, you are interested in me?"

I shrugged, thinking how easy it would be to scoot my chair closer and kiss him. Why had I been so worried that it would be hard to move on? He was easy to talk to, and the spark between us was palpable. "You do fill out those jeans nicely. And your eyes don't hurt, either."

He knocked back the rest of his whiskey. "Dance with me?"

"No. I don't dance." My tone was sharper than I'd anticipated.

His eyebrows bunched together. "Not ever? Why?"

Avoiding the risk of spilling family trauma that shouldn't be shared for at least five dates, I kept it short. "It's a long story, but when I was a kid, it was kind of forced upon me and I hated it." My mother's obsession with ballroom dancing was not something I wanted to discuss. My brother had enjoyed it. Me? Not even a little.

Instead, I'd wanted to spend my time curled up with a book or bothering my dad with questions about the family business. And it seemed to have worked out for me.

"Understandable. There are a lot of things I hate

doing just because someone used to make me." I wondered who the someone was who made him do things. Maybe it was the ex-wife he mentioned when he'd caught me and Zane *not* doing it in the woods earlier.

"It's not that I don't ever dance. My brother got married recently, and I didn't stand against the wall the whole time." I thought about what I hated about dancing. "Slow dancing is the absolute worst. Jumping around with my friends? Sure. But I'd rather sit at the bar and talk than sway back and forth in uncomfortable silence."

He scooted closer as the DJ's music got louder. Our thighs were almost touching at this point, a thrill ran through me. I could feel his warmth radiating over to me, intoxicating me more than the alcohol I'd consumed. "Maybe you need a better dance partner."

I laughed even though he was being serious. "I just realized that the only person I've ever slow danced with wasn't actually attracted to me. So you're probably right."

"Wow, that's . . ." he started to say, but I was already mortified about what I'd said.

"Sorry, that was terrible to just throw out there. I'm really bad at this." Right now would be a great time for the floor to open up and devour me.

"So, what do you do in the real world?" he said, changing the subject.

I took the last sip of my drink, feeling a little tipsy, but not enough to start spilling about my latest obsession. "Real estate," I said, choosing to go along with the story I'd told earlier. "It's pretty boring, really."

"I don't know, I bet you meet all kinds of people doing what you do." He'd turned toward me, completely ignoring the rest of the bar, and our knees touched. The fact that he was gorgeous and actually interested in what I had to say was a little disarming.

I tried to come up with some positives of running a corporation. "I spend most of my time analyzing numbers and profit margins. I really don't get to go out in the field anymore."

"My last job was a lot like that." He gestured around the room. "This is much less stressful."

"How do you even become a handyman at a resort in the woods, anyway? Judging by your accent, you're not from around here, but I can't quite put my finger on it."

"When I was thirteen, I was sent to boarding school in England. Then I went to Oxford for my undergrad. After that, I went to grad school and worked in a few different countries for several years, and now I'm here." So it was a British accent I'd heard in some of the words he said. But that didn't explain how he got here, in the Upper Peninsula of Michigan.

"How did an intensive education on the other side of the world bring you to the middle of nowhere to install Wi-Fi routers and take people on horseback riding adventures?"

He pulled back slightly, stretching his shoulders. "That's a story for another day." He made me want to ask more questions, but his tone meant he wouldn't budge. It might put other women off, but his assertiveness made me regret not dancing with him. He didn't press me about my issues, and I wouldn't press him about his.

A few moments went by without either of us saying a word. The gravity of his body pulled me closer. It felt comfortable, like coming back home after a long trip. It also gave me a chance to look at him without staring, which was a plus.

His blond hair had a slight wave, like he'd tried to style it, but it couldn't be tamed. His beard seemed thicker than when we'd met, like he only shaved once in a while. Only the top button of his flannel shirt was undone, and I wondered what it'd feel like to undo the rest of them. To run my fingernails against his bare chest.

"Did you like living in Europe?" I asked, breaking the silence.

"I did, really. But a couple of years ago, I had some loose ends I needed to tie up, and I was ready for a fresh start. So I packed up what was important to me and found my new home." I wondered if the need for a fresh start had been because of his divorce.

"I grew up living in hotels, but we never spent a lot of time in Europe," I told him, the words spilling out of me. Maybe it was him. Maybe it was the liquid courage in my blood. But I felt like sharing more than I ever had before. "When I was born, we lived in the penthouse of a hotel in Singapore," I told him.

His eyes lit with excitement as he slipped into perfect Mandarin. "I love Singapore. I lived there for two years after I finished my MBA." My heart fluttered at Ben's use of my first language.

"Your Chinese is much better than mine," I said, dusting off the language I hadn't spoken in so long. His intelligence was just as sexy as his well-toned body.

He switched back to English. "I don't get to use it

much in Michigan, but every so often I have to take a call or talk to a client, and it helps."

I shook my head slowly. "I can't believe you've been hiding in the U.P. this whole time. You'd be really successful back home in California." I wanted to kiss him, but we were in public. Fuck, I wanted to wrap my arms around him and claim him right here. But I was afraid. What if I'd been reading his signals all wrong? What if he was just being nice to me because I was staying at his work?

He nudged me with his shoulder. "This place might grow on you, too." Before I could say anything about the likelihood of giving up my California lifestyle, he held up his empty glass. "Want another one?"

"Yes," I paused, unable to keep my eyes from tracing his soft lower lip. Wondering what it would taste like. "Please," I added, when I realized he'd been staring at my mouth, too.

He was only gone for a few minutes, but watching him walk away made me wonder how smoothly his body would have moved with mine. He walked with such confidence and strength. I bet he would feel heavenly on top of me.

I was in trouble with this one. Even with the apprehension I felt about moving on.

Our eyes met on his way back, and my chest fluttered again. "Here you go." He sat next to me, handing me another vodka soda with a slice of lime. His fingers grazed mine as he handed me the glass, and the tingle ran all the way up my arm.

I loved that he remembered what I was drinking. That

he'd been paying attention. Maybe he'd remember other things that I liked later on, too.

He pulled his chair a little closer than before, pressing his knee against mine under the table. The spark in my chest was brewing into an inferno.

Fuck. I wanted him bad. More than I'd ever wanted anyone.

"I'd like to know about your guilty pleasures," I blurted out, wanting to get to know him more.

His eyebrow perked up. "Oh really? Like what?"

I bit my lip, thinking for a few seconds. There had to be a question that could match his cereal question from earlier. When I thought of it, I grinned from ear to ear. "What's the dumbest movie you've ever seen, but you secretly loved?"

He laughed, taking a sip of his drink like he was really mulling it over. "That Will Ferrel movie where he plays basketball. All of my friends hated it, but I thought it was so damn funny," he said, a smile brightly lit across his face. "What about you?"

I couldn't hide my grin. "The Will Ferrel one where he plays a professional ice skater." I covered my face with a hand. "It's so stupid, I know."

He replied without hesitation, "That's a really great one, too. Dumb movies are the best!"

"I know, right?" I felt both relieved and excited. Never in a million years had I thought he'd say something I'd seen, let alone liked.

The two of us continued talking long after our drinks were empty. Not only was he funny, sweet, and actually attracted to me, but the longer we talked, the sexier he became. He wasn't just a pretty face. He was smart as hell and genuinely listened when I spoke.

When we reached a lull in conversation, he ran his fingers down the side of my dress. "Looks like your luggage showed up. This is nice."

I laughed, thinking of how not-nice the entire suitcase situation had been. "Oh, these are not my clothes." He raised one eyebrow, wordlessly asking for more information, so I added, "Well, technically, they are. I went shopping earlier. But these aren't the clothes I packed for this trip."

I looked down at my outfit, wondering how different I'd feel if I were wearing the Prada dress I'd packed for a night out with the girls, but Ben didn't seem to care one bit.

"Damn. Any word on when you'll get it back?"

I let out a frustrated huff. "After its own family reunion in Finland, unfortunately. I'll probably be home before my suitcase makes it back to Michigan."

"Well, as frustrating as all that sounds, you look cute, so I'm not complaining." By the way his eyes scanned my body, I knew he was being completely honest.

"I think this is the first time anyone has used the word *cute* to describe me." I felt the urge to twirl my fingers through my hair. What did cute girls do with their hands?

He rested his hand on my thigh tentatively. I had to remind myself to breathe. It reminded me of when he'd helped me off the horse earlier, but in a safe way. I wasn't scared. "That's a damn shame." He licked his lips, his eyes intense. "What do most men call you?"

I thought for a second, and since we were basically

alone, I leaned in to his touch. "Intimidating. Outspoken. Bitchy."

"None of those words come to mind when I think about you." My core ignited at his admission. Shifting in my seat, I moved my legs, which were crossed at my ankles, to cross at my thighs, desperate to release some pressure from my apex.

Feeling brave, I grazed my fingertips across the pocket on his flannel shirt. "You've been thinking about me?" I hoped it came off as flirty as it meant.

His eyes dipped to my breasts and then rested on my lips for a moment before meeting mine again. "What things would you want me to fantasize about, Izzy?"

Chapter Twelve

I was not adventurous enough to answer him, so I said, "I'm surprised you haven't said something about finding a quieter place to be alone."

He leaned back slightly, checking out my body before coming close enough to smell the whiskey on his breath. "Thinking of you in those shoes makes me want you right here." Every inch of my skin burst into flame. Squeezing my thighs tighter together wasn't helping the heat between my legs. "We don't need a quiet room."

The deep tone of his British lilt was the final decision-maker. I was going to sleep with Ben before this trip was over. I'd never see him again, so there'd be no strings attached. It was the perfect plan.

Someone slammed an empty glass down on our table, shaking me from my vision of vacation hookup logistics. "There you are!" Ruby's voice was loud, and a little slurred. "You ready to head home?"

"Or are the two of you gonna rub some fuzzies

tonight?" Hannah cut in loudly, right as the DJ switched songs.

I stood, scraping my chair across the floor as I moved away from the man I probably would have gone home with if we were back in Santa Barbara. But I was tipsy and embarrassed by what Hannah had just yelled for everyone to hear.

I turned to Ben, hoping my drunk family wouldn't turn him off. "Sorry about them." I reached into my purse and pulled out my phone, checking the time. The rest of the family was probably expecting us to be back soon, since Alice was such a mother-hen. "We really should get going." I hated to break the spell he'd had me under, but I was already thinking about how we'd find time to be together soon.

"Can I have some chapstick?" Hannah blurted out as I tried to close the latch on my bag. She reached in, blocking me. Before I could swat her hand away, she yelled, "Oh my gosh, is this your underwear?"

I slapped her hand, knocking the dark panties back into my bag. "Yep, it's time to get you home," I muttered, wildly embarrassed that she had told the whole bar my underwear was stuffed in my bag. As I secured the latch, it hit me that everyone must think I wasn't wearing any. I looked up at Ben, and the grin on his face told me he was thinking exactly that. Then I looked down at my phone, opening the ride share app and avoiding his stare. "I'm going to see if I can pay the Uber driver extra for rushing."

Ben's eyes followed my hands, and he pointed to my

phone. "If you ladies are relying on a ride share, you're out of luck."

"No, Zane and David said there was one guy going back and forth all night," I replied, refreshing my screen.

Ben gestured to a man who looked like he'd guzzled an entire bottle of whiskey, dancing by himself in the middle of the bar with a bandanna tied around his head. "That's him. He finishes his last trip around ten every night, and his wife drives him home when she's done tending the bar."

I audibly groaned, but Ruby and Hannah took it as a challenge and went over to dance with him. "How the fuck am I going to get us back?" I said to myself. Then I looked up at Ben, an empty glass in his hand. "How are you getting home tonight?"

I might have caught a blush spread across his cheeks. "Niko's dad is driving us back. His name is Eino." He motioned to an old man who looked like he'd been fishing every single day of his life. "He always comes to get us when we go out. There's space in his minivan if you want to ride with us?"

Ten minutes later, I found myself stuffed into the middle row of Eino's van. The third row sandwiched Hannah and Ruby around Ben's friend, Niko, who seemed to be very much enjoying their attention. I sat behind the passenger seat, with Ben in the middle. His thigh was pressed against mine, and I tried to ignore every inch of my skin that begged for his touch. Another friend, Mattias, sat on the other side of Ben, and one more guy around our age sat up front, a plastic bag in his hands as if he was anticipating his drinks coming up on the ride. I thought his name was Oliver.

It wasn't exactly the sexy alone time I'd imagined this night turning into, but at least I could smell the whiskey and pine coming off Ben.

I hadn't experienced a night like this in my twenties, so it was fitting that I'd be living this life in the last half of my 30s. Just another way for me to be a late bloomer, once again.

As the drunks in the third row started singing off key to the songs on the radio, Ben took my hand in his. It was such a cliché, but a current of electricity flowed from his body to mine. Pursing my lips together, I tried to tamp down the excitement I felt.

Fueled by bravery and vodka, I moved our clasped hands to my lap, inviting Ben to come closer. He shifted sideways, running his nose against the sensitive skin in front of my ear. A shiver ran down my spine as he whispered, "I had a good time tonight."

Glad for the loud people behind us and the lack of any streetlights as we traveled down the mountain road, I reached up with my free hand and tucked my hair behind my ear, giving him better access. "Me too."

His lips grazed just under my earlobe and my breath hitched, stopping me from speaking any further. I sucked in a deep inhale, trying to keep the arousal from overtaking me. I think he felt the shift. He let go of my hand and instead ran his fingers up my thigh to my hip, pulling me against him.

I grabbed his bicep to steady myself, unable to suppress my grin. His muscle under my palm was rock solid. "Everyone can see us," I whispered back to him, my heart racing. I wanted him badly, but I never thought I'd actually make it here. It was one thing to fantasize about hooking up, and quite another thing to have his hands gripping my skin.

Now fully turned toward me, he looked at Hannah and Ruby out of the corner of his eye. My gaze followed his, watching the two ladies and their new friend sing their hearts out to an old Journey song. "I don't think they realize that we're still here," he said before brushing his nose against mine.

I shuddered at the touch of his skin. It would only take a centimeter to press my lips against his. He smelled delicious. Manly. And I knew at any other time, in any other place, I could have him. "We can't do this here."

His fingertips grazed the skin on my face as he cupped my cheek. "We'll be home in twenty minutes. Come with me." The hand he had on my hip ran down my thigh again. "Didn't I hear something about your panties being in a bag?"

I pressed my hand against his chest, not sure if I needed a breath or needed him closer. "That's a long story for another time." Wondering what it would be like to share a bed with him, I took one of his buttons between my fingers. Then, as if my brain was out to betray me, I thought about the drama of Zane's parents finding us together, catching us getting out of the van entwined in each other's arms. "I want to come with you, I do. But it might not be the best idea right now."

His thumb ran across my bottom lip. "True. But

sometimes I get so tired of doing the right thing all the time."

Then came the most horrible sound I'd ever heard in my life from the passenger seat of the van. I pulled back, unable to hide my disgust as Oliver emptied the entire contents of his stomach into his bag.

Ben rubbed his face briefly with both hands, disappointment painted all over him, before he leaned forward, checking on his friend. Judging by their rushed words, everything had made it into the bag, so we were going to keep driving.

Eino cracked the windows open and turned the music down a little, and that's when I knew the magic had fizzled out of the moment.

Ruby leaned toward me. "Is he okay?"

Twisting to face her, I answered, "Yeah, I think he just drank too much."

Ben laid back against the seat, blowing out a breath. I could barely make out the smile he gave me in the dark. He nudged his shoulder into mine. "Well, I hadn't expected that to interrupt us."

"What are you guys talking about?" Hannah asked.

I looked him up and down, not ready to tell the girls that I'd almost kissed him, right in this crowded van. "Ben was telling me about the broken components of the Wi-Fi system and how he's going to make sure they get fixed tomorrow."

His eyebrow shot up. "No, I was telling her how it won't get fixed, possibly during the entire duration of your stay, so she's going to have to make other plans."

I bit my bottom lip, wondering why his answer felt

more like a euphemism than it should have. Before I could think of a response, Hannah asked him about other activities they had at the resort, and I'd lost him. He'd twisted sideways to speak to her and Ruby, but after a moment, his hand slid forward, privately reaching for mine. I had to admit, even though the current situation was absolutely insane, I liked the feel of him next to me. The chaos of the situation would have driven me mad if we were back home, but here it was invigorating.

The rest of the drive went by quickly, especially with our hands secretly clasped, and I felt a little remiss when we parked outside of Hannah and Ruby's cabin, even if the van still had a weird smell to it.

The reality of our situation sank in my stomach like a stone. We were just a hundred yards from the cabin I was supposed to be in right this minute, with my loving husband.

"Can I walk you to your place?" Ben asked, and I wanted to say yes, with every cell in my entire body. But I had come here to be Zane's wife. Not to hook up with the handyman. Even if I felt a warmth I'd never felt before, sitting so close to him.

The porch light of my cabin flicked on. Not knowing who was in there, or who else could see us, I pulled my hand from his. "No. I can't risk it," I added more quietly, "Not yet, anyway."

The door next to me slid open, with Eino standing there, helping me out. I hadn't even noticed him leaving the driver's seat. It wasn't very cold out, but I shivered now that I was away from Ben's warmth.

Ben followed after me, and Hannah and Ruby began

climbing over the seat, loudly singing a song that no longer played on the radio.

I reached forward, shaking Eino's hand. "Thank you so much for the ride home. I appreciate you getting us here safely."

"No problem," he said, his Finnish accent thick. "You girls make sure you take some aspirin and drink a big glass of water before you go to bed, okay?"

I promised him we would before turning back to Ben. The girls were giving him hugs and waving at the other guys still in the van.

"I'll see you tomorrow?" I said quietly, hoping we could find our way back to what we'd started.

"I'm counting on it," he said, his tongue running over his lips.

"Oh, don't forget these." Ruby interrupted, before pulling her necklace off. She removed my wedding rings, handing them to me. I wrapped my hand around them tightly, trying not to think about how they tied me to a life that I didn't want anymore.

After thanking her for keeping them safe, I looked back up at Ben. "Sorry. That was . . . awkward."

He smiled, the darkness casting him in a deep shadow. "I know how hard it is to let something go. Don't worry about it."

As I walked to my cabin, back to my pretend life, I could practically feel Ben watching until I got in safely before going to wherever he lived nearby.

Chapter Thirteen

We'd shown up at breakfast tired and hungover, so Alice cleared the family itinerary so we could spend the day at the pool. While everyone was napping before meeting this afternoon, I'd planned to get some work done in the main building.

Cate wasn't there, but her daughter was sitting at her desk hunched over a handwritten spreadsheet.

"Hi, I'm here to use the Wi-Fi." I really didn't want to go into the whole story.

She smiled, brushing her long brown hair off her shoulder. "Sure, my mom told me you'd probably come in right about now. Ben's desk is all yours."

I settled down, starting with the most important emails first, and forwarded any that didn't matter to the team holding down the fort while I was gone. My bottom was sore from the runaway horse, or maybe from sleeping on the sofa last night after forcing Zane to take the bed, but I was thankful for this comfortable leather chair. After about an hour, I closed my laptop and looked up at Cate, who had just walked in from the lobby. "Thanks for letting me work here. I've got so much going on."

"I've got a question." Concern was painted across her brow as she met me at Ben's desk.

"Sure." I wondered if she'd noticed the energy between me and Ben yesterday. I hadn't seen him today, but I'd be lying if I said I didn't look for him every time someone had walked through the door.

"Why the hell did you come here, to literal paradise, to spend the whole time working?" That was not what I thought she was going to say. When I didn't answer, she went on. "We have a lake, a pool, hiking trails, everything! And here you are, young and full of life, and all you want to do is hang out with me."

I started to give her some bullshit answer, but I knew she would see right through it. "Well, to be honest, I didn't really choose to come here."

"So someone gifted you an amazing vacation and you're wasting it?"

I glared at her playfully, and she laughed. "When you put it that way, I do sound like an asshole, don't I?"

"You said it." She propped one hand on her hip.

"Okay, I promise I'll relax while I'm here." I stood, ready to leave. I had a feeling if I stayed longer, she'd see through even more of the walls I'd put up around myself and start asking more questions.

"What time will I see you at Ben's desk tomorrow?" She gave me no room for argument.

"I will only work for an hour tomorrow," I swore, tapping my fingernails on my laptop case. Her eyebrow went up. She knew I was full of shit. "Okay, half an hour."

"Deal." She held her hand out and made me shake on it.

I came through the front door of our cabin and found Zane standing in the kitchen, loading up a cooler bag with beers and waters from the fridge.

He had a white t-shirt and bright red swim trunks on, like a stereotypical tourist. "You're here just in time. Everyone else is headed to the pool." He was smiling brightly, and I wondered if I could feel as relaxed as he seemed if I let my work stuff go, too.

"Give me five minutes, tops," I said, before rushing into the bedroom. I thew on the black bathing suit I'd bought yesterday. It was a one piece, but now that I saw the amount of skin showing in the middle and the back, it was more like a bikini with the sides sewn together.

After freshening up my red lipstick and putting my hair in a ponytail, I picked up the bag I'd bought for the pool and filled it with sunblock, the magazine I'd gotten at the store, and a bag of chips. I slipped my dark sunglasses on my face and looked over myself in the mirror. It was the first time I'd felt like myself since we landed.

Zane looked me up and down. "You never cease to amaze me. How you can take a ridiculous situation and still look amazing is beyond." Holding out his hand, he asked, "Ready to go?"

I almost didn't take his hand, but I saw Tippy heading down the dirt path in front of our cabin. She was far enough away not to hear us, but I knew she'd spot us eventually with Zane's bright swim trunks.

Holding his hand made me wonder if one day I could find someone who wanted to do this with me as much as Zane liked to with Caleb. I'd never been one for public displays of affection, but I wondered if I would think differently if it was a different man with his hand entwined in mine.

It made me think of the callouses on Ben's hand. What they'd feel like if it was him walking with me instead.

It also made me wonder how Caleb felt about this whole thing. Was he at home worried about Zane? Was he jealous that I got to hold his boyfriend's hand?

I didn't think about it until now, but it must be hard for Zane to not get to call or text him while we were here, too. If we weren't about to be inundated by his family, I'd ask.

I leaned closer to him, just to be sure prying ears couldn't hear me. "Are we going to tell them sometime today?"

He pinched the bridge of his nose with his free hand. "I don't know. I almost did yesterday when we got back from the horseback ride, but my dad and his brother started in on a conversation about the lack of economic education amongst millennials, and I lost my chance."

"Maybe we should ask them to sit down with us at dinner tonight?" I really wanted this to be over with.

He shook his head. "Mom said we're all going to town. She heard about some steakhouse and wants to try it out. Maybe tomorrow morning?"

I nodded. "Okay, but today or tomorrow. I don't like lying to them." Plus, I needed this out so we could really, truly move on.

His eyes scrutinized me. "You seem different."

I waved my hand between us, like swatting at a bug. "Stop analyzing me."

"No, I mean it." He let go of my hand and reached up, squeezing my shoulder. "You're not walking around like you've got a stick up your butt."

I gasped. "I have been acting in no such way." He laughed and wrapped his arm around my shoulder so we could keep walking.

As we went through the gate surrounding the pool area, the tension I'd felt for months started to dissipate. Like all the anger and hurt that I hadn't realized was there when we first split was gone. "I don't know. Maybe I've finally forgiven the universe for what it did to us."

"Maybe we should have gotten you kidnapped by a horse months ago." He chuckled, guiding me down the walkway around the pool.

"I think I'm finally ready," I said as we approached the cabana that the family had reserved for the day.

"Ready for what?" Zane's mom asked from under a giant floppy hat.

"For me to shove her into the pool." Zane said without missing a beat, making his mother laugh.

We sat our stuff down, and he passed beers to his cousins and aunts and uncles. I grabbed my magazine before standing at the edge of the pool, checking the place out.

This resort was gorgeous even without the pool, but

this area really felt like the crown jewel. Marketing ideas spun through my head as I looked over the area. There were three pools. One in front of us. One to the left that was about six feet higher than this one, with a waterfall that poured into the middle one. Then, to the right, there was a wading pool that looked to be about a foot deep before dipping deeper with a rock-clad water slide on the other end. That pool was filled with children of all ages. Their screams and laughter were usually something I would avoid, but today it felt welcoming and joyful.

Damn, maybe Zane was right and I had changed. I still liked who I had been before, but this version of myself felt more open. Happier, even.

A hand waving to my left, followed by some obnoxious bird-calling brought me to Hannah and Ruby. They were lying on loungers outside of the cabana where many people from the rest of the family were hanging out. As I approached them, Zane joined us, but he was talking to David, who was in the pool closest to us, leaning against the edge.

We jumped right into conversation, but a few minutes in, Zane must not have been able to resist himself. He nudged me with his elbow. "Well, you ladies were certainly out late last night."

I tried not to look around. "I don't think this is the place for this conversation, babe. I assumed you weren't interested when you went straight to bed last night," I ground out between my teeth.

Ruby piped in, "Oh, come on, Izzy, tell us about that TV show you stayed up watching last night after the boys went to bed."

My forehead crinkled in confusion. Hannah added, "You know, the one about the hot maintenance guy?"

Fighting the embarrassment of not picking up the code fast enough, I mumbled, "It was fine."

"Are you going to watch another episode soon?" Ruby asked, a gleam in her eye.

I met her gaze. "I should probably finish the season finale of the one I started earlier. Don't you think?"

Ruby giggled. "You'll have plenty of time later to finish that one. For now, I want to hear about this new show."

Zane cracked open a beer. "Okay, someone is going to have to let me in on whatever is happening. I didn't hear the TV at all after I went to bed."

Before I could decide how much or how little to tell them, David let out a whistle. It was the same kind he always used when we were about to get caught doing something we weren't supposed to.

A hand gripped my shoulder, and I relaxed when it was just Zane's dad, Andrew. He was shorter than me, but had a bright smile and a beer belly. With his orange board shorts and a drink in his other hand, you would never guess that he was the heir to an international bank, with a trust fund worth billions of dollars. Zane and Ruby got their height from their mom, but their wavy hair and humor came from this man right here. "How are all my kids doing? You all don't look too hungover?"

"The boys chickened out last night and went home early." Ruby said, stifling a yawn. "But I wouldn't turn down a few more hours of sleep."

Zane's shoulders suddenly straightened, like he was

about to talk about interest rates or capital expenditures. I recognized the gesture as something I also did when my father was around. "Hey Dad, Lizette and I have something we'd like to run by you later." The fact that he used my full name felt like a red flag.

Andrew straightened, but his smile grew deeper. "Why? Are you pregnant?"

Sweat slicked my entire body. "No, nothing like that," I blurted out.

He wrapped his arm around me, squeezing me into a hug. "Well, whatever it is, I'm sure it's going to be a great idea." Then he turned his head over his shoulder, looking toward the cabana. "But your mom's itinerary is pretty full. We could go visit the hot tub and discuss whatever you've got on your minds."

I looked to the hot tub and found Bradley and Tippy sitting awfully close to each other. "I'm not sure if that's . . ." I started to say, but then Andrew saw them there, too.

He cleared his throat. "How about tomorrow morning, at breakfast? We can sit somewhere private."

Zane gave him a smile and bobbed his head. "Sounds perfect, Dad. Thanks."

We chatted for a few minutes about nothing in particular before Andrew made his way back toward the older folks in the cabana.

The next few hours went by smoothly. It was almost like old times, swimming around with aunts and uncles, catching up with their lives. I felt a little fraudulent every time I had to pretend that I was still head over heels for

Zane, but luckily I had realized that I never really was, so as long as I reminded myself that he was still one of my best friends, I stopped being afraid I'd say the wrong thing.

Most of the older family members had started packing up, getting ready for tonight's dinner festivities, when we found ourselves back where we had started. Ruby, Hannah, and I were on lounge chairs, Zane at my feet, and David in a chair facing us. The giant smiley face that had been drawn on David's belly two nights ago was still just as bright as it had been when he put it there, and none of us had been able to take anything he said seriously all day because of it.

After several minutes of discussing what they thought Bradley's plans for the next part of his campaign would be, Ruby looked at Zane and asked, "So, once the cat is out of the bag, who should we hook her up with back in California?"

Zane perked up on the end of my lounger. "Caleb's got a friend that I've been hoping to connect her with. He's really easy on the eyes."

Hannah sat up, crossing her legs under her. "I think she needs someone with a business degree. Someone on her level."

"I'm right here, guys. You don't need to talk about me like this." I closed my eyes, covering my face with my half-read magazine.

Hannah continued like I hadn't spoken. "There's a guy at my firm that's single. He makes great spreadsheets. They could talk about bottom lines and acquisitions over candlelit dinners."

"I think it's going to be best if I just stick to work." I really wanted to disappear.

"No, you just need to get laid," David said, pulling the magazine off my face and tossing it into my lap. Luckily, I didn't think anyone had overheard.

Ruby took what he said and ran with it. "He's right. Get one out of your system to kick start your libido again." I gave her a look to try to get her to stop talking, but she ignored it. "We're not saying you need to fall hopelessly in love. But you need to dust off the cobwebs."

I gasped, sitting up. "I do not have cobwebs."

Zane burst into laughter. "Okay, maybe not cobwebs, but dust bunnies?"

I glared at them. "I hate you all so much."

"Let's find someone dull and adorable to get it out of your system when we get home. You don't even have to like him," Zane said, reaching down into his bag and handing me a water bottle.

I opened it, wondering seriously for the first time what going on dates would be like.

But I didn't want dull and adorable. If I was being honest with myself, I wanted what my brother had. Someone who was not only my best friend, but a person I couldn't get enough of. A man I couldn't wait to get home to at the end of the day.

"Speaking of adorable." Ruby's voice pulled me out of my thoughts.

I scanned the area until I found where she was looking.

Ben emerged from the pool in front of us, slicking his hair back with a muscular arm. It was just like in those

80s movies, where he seemed to move in slow motion. The water dripped from his head, down his chest, and trickled over those abs that had no business looking so indecent. I had to force myself to inhale as I scanned his torso.

Zane let out a low whistle. "I still think he'd be fun for you."

"The two of them got pretty close last night at the bar. Huh, Iz?" Ruby said, too loudly for comfort.

"Shut the fuck up, both of you," I whisper-yelled.

"Oh, so Ben was the TV show from last night. Nice." Zane said, with a smile in his voice. I hadn't realized I was still staring at Ben until his eyes caught mine and he gave me a sweet little wave.

"Guys, guys, guys, look natural," David whispered loudly, in a way that drew more attention to us than if he had just kept quiet.

Ben climbed the rest of the way out of the pool, giving us an amazing view of the skin right above his light blue swim trunks, slung low across his hips. "Jesus, Izzy, you have twenty-four hours to lock him down or I'm going to sleep with him instead," Hannah said breathlessly.

He padded over to us without a clue that our group, and probably every other hot-blooded adult in the area, was eating him alive with their eyes. "Hey there," he said as he approached us, his accent thicker than usual. One corner of his smile was up higher than the other. He nodded a little toward me. "Izzy. How did you sleep last night?"

My heart fluttered like I was a teenage girl. "Hey,

Ben." His bare chest was wildly distracting. "Um, I slept great. How about you?" My voice didn't sound like my own, all high pitched.

"Would you like a water?" Zane asked him, reaching into the bag that was better stocked than I'd remembered.

"Sure, thanks," he replied to my ex-husband before turning to me again. "I could have slept better."

Beside him, Hannah made a "whoa" face and fanned herself, picking up on what I had hoped was him flirting with me. She turned to him, fiddling with the straps of her bathing suit top. "So, why's a hottie like you working a maintenance job in the middle of nowhere?"

David jumped from his chair, interrupting her. "I think it's time to place bets on if Zane's too chicken to go down the slide. What do you think?" Thank goodness for David.

"I'm not chicken. I just don't want to get my hair wet," Zane said with a hand on his hip.

David clucked like a chicken a few times, making Ruby burst into giggles.

I looked at Zane. "Guess you better go prove it then, huh?"

Zane stepped toward David, grabbing him by the shoulders before pushing him into the water. "It's on, asshole."

"To the slide!" Ruby yelled out, and the three of them rushed to the other side of the pool, standing in line behind several children who had no idea how messy it was about to become over there.

"Do you want to go somewhere else?" I asked Ben once we were alone. "I think it would be more fun to watch them kill each other from a distance." Really, I was more concerned with moving away from the cabana filled with ears than actually watching these adult cousins acting like ten-year-olds.

"Sure. There's a spot over there that's got good shade." I tossed my magazine onto the lounger and followed him to a couple of chairs under a thick tree. From this spot, you could see all three pools, but the tree mostly covered where Zane's family was packing up, oblivious to the two of us.

David, Zane, Hannah, and Ruby made it down the slide and started wrestling in the pool, splashing everywhere. It made me wonder if they had been like this when they were little, before I knew them. They certainly had always acted like this since I'd known them, which was almost half my life.

I turned to Ben. "What brings you to the pool today?"

"Since I live right there," he pointed to a cabin a little bigger than ours, a few hundred feet on the other side of the fence, "I usually spend some time at the pool every day. At least during the summer."

"Okay, Mr. Fancypants business degree. Why are you really out in the middle of nowhere in Michigan? Shouldn't you be running a Fortune 500 company or something?" I started to wonder if my question was too forward, but I'd never worried about that with anyone before. I brushed the thought away before I could worry about it any longer.

He laughed, and my eyes lingered on the muscles of his neck as he threw his head back. "Well, Ms. Lady Who Reads The Economist At The Pool." He pointed to the magazine I had left on the lounge chair several feet away. "I was burned out. There had been . . ." he paused, his eyebrows bunching together. "A situation that I needed space from. My grandmother had lived here in the U.P. and I wanted to get to know her better, even though she's not around anymore." His eyes scanned the trees in the distance. "I didn't think I'd like being so far away from civilization, but I love it here." He tapped my knee with his, making me fully aware of how close we were sitting. "How about you? Why did you leave Singapore?"

"We moved to California when I was five. My parents' business had taken off, and they wanted to take their chances on the West Coast real estate market."

"So that's why you're in real estate? Because of your parents?"

"That's why I started, I think. But when I got my MBA from Stanford, I realized I was doing it more for myself than for them. I like what I do."

"Nice humble brag, Stanford Alum." He laughed.

"Whatever, Oxford." I noticed the rest of my crew getting out of the pool, drying off. My time alone with Ben was becoming limited, which was frustrating. "How has your day been so far?"

"Busy, for a day off. I had to run into town to get a temporary fix for the Wi-Fi in one of our cabins. The guest staying there has been insufferable about the lack of connection," he said cheekily.

"Oh, I hope she's not a total pain in the ass."

"Her ass is something, that's for sure." Our eyes locked for a moment, the challenge in his making me want to be irresponsible. Crazy, even.

I leaned toward him, challenging. "Maybe you should do something about it." I had no idea where those words had come from, but I was glad I'd said them.

He gave me a lopsided grin before his eyes travelled over my shoulder. I followed his gaze and saw my ex-husband coming toward us, in conversation with Tippy and Bradley. "Have dinner with me tonight?" he asked quietly.

"We have a family thing," I said, disappointed. Fuck, he looked delicious. His thighs taking up the chair like it was made for him made me wonder if there was any way I could get out of dinner. "I'll try to move some things around. I'll come to your cabin if I can."

Wow, I was really thinking about doing this. My heart rate doubled in speed.

"You're not just interested in my internet connection, are you?" He popped an eyebrow up, and it looked much more seductive than it should have, especially with the skin on his chest glistening in the sun.

I shook my head at him, my decision set in stone. "I'm going to take vacation more seriously for the rest of the trip. I promise to trust my assistant with her job." Then I leaned in a little closer. "It will give me more time for . . . other things."

As Zane, his brother, and sister-in-law approached, Ben leaned back in his chair. "So you'll only need my desk for two hours tomorrow, then?"

Before I could reply, Tippy held her hand out at Ben, ever the politician's wife. "Hi. I'm Tippy Xu, and this is my husband Bradley. It's nice to officially meet you. We had a lot of fun on the horseback ride yesterday."

Ben shook her hand. "What an interesting name, Tippy." Tippy's deep Southern accent made Ben's British lilt come out a little more. It was adorable.

She smiled, just like she had practiced over and over during the years she was a Miss United States candidate. "Thanks. My real name is Tiffany, but my older brother couldn't pronounce Tiffy correctly, and, well, it just sort of stuck!" She giggled like she'd said that about a million times before and was well rehearsed.

Zane moved behind my chair and put his hands on my shoulders, which to anyone who didn't know our situation would think was awfully possessive. He leaned down, pretending to give me a kiss on my cheek, and whispered, "She seemed worried that you were getting close with 'the ranch hand.' Her words, not mine." He squeezed my shoulders, making it look like a loving gesture instead of a warning that our family was going to start asking questions we weren't ready to answer if I spent more time with half-dressed men I wasn't married to.

A lie left my lips without a second thought. "Ben was just telling me about a program he uses to make investments with the spare change from transactions from his debit card. I thought it might be worth looking into for the company." I'd actually been using the app myself for a couple of months, which was why I thought of it so quickly.

The corners of his eyes crinkled briefly, but he went along with it. "Yes, I just started using it a few months ago. Before, that money just sat in the bank, useless."

Tippy rolled her eyes and waved her hands like she

didn't really care. "Leave it to Izzy to find the one other person who wants to talk business at a family reunion." She looked up at Bradley, who didn't seem to buy my story completely. "We'd be surprised if she hadn't found someone to bore with her obsession with work, huh, sweetie?" Typical Tippy. I didn't even react to her words anymore. She would have no idea how to handle half the shit I took care of on a daily basis.

"Actually," Bradley said, his dimples and public speaking skills shining through. "We're taking the whole family out for dinner tonight. What do you think about the steakhouse on Main?"

Ben sat up straighter, and I wondered how many people he encountered that saw him as just a worker-bee, not an actual person. "It's amazing. Make sure you order the sweet potato casserole with the ribeye. It's not to be missed." He gave Bradley a few more recommendations, like he had the menu memorized.

Bradley looked down at his watch and then at Tippy. "I think it's about time to go clean up. What do you think?"

She pushed up on her toes, kissing him on the cheek. "I think that's a great idea, hon."

Zane patted my shoulder. "I'm going to go grab our stuff. I'll meet you back at the cabin?" he said, but gave Ben a little wink.

Once they were out of earshot, I turned back to Ben. "Sorry about that. We're going to tell them the truth tomorrow."

He paused, looking me over like he wasn't even fazed by the drama that was my life. Suddenly, I felt naked in my skimpy bathing suit. "Don't worry. I understand how family dynamics can be sometimes." He stood up, stretching his arms above his head before looking back down at me. It wouldn't take much for me to lean in and bite him on the hip if we were in another place.

I'd never thought that about anyone before. I felt brave, maybe even a little hopeful. Maybe after tomorrow, after the whole family knew our secrets, I could get what I really wanted.

"I'm going to eat dinner at my place around seven. If you decide to slip away and join me instead of going out with everyone else, that's where I'll be."

Heat surged through me the same way it had last night when we'd talked alone. I looked around the pool for the people I was supposed to be socializing with instead. Those that were still here were preoccupied, collecting their things to go back to their cabins, but I switched to Mandarin anyway. Only Zane's dad and his brothers were fluent, and they weren't anywhere nearby. "Who knows, maybe I'll end up with a killer headache later and have to stay in."

He smiled, his water bottle at his lips. "See you later, Izzy."

Chapter Fourteen

Fifteen minutes had passed after the last set of tail lights left the resort, and I was sure all the Xu's had left the property. I crept out of my cabin feeling like a fifteen-year-old girl.

I made it ten yards before I heard a twig snap and sucked in a breath. How did people do this all the time?

I really should go back inside and rest, like I told Zane I was going to. Even after he did that bouncy thing with his eyebrows and told me he was going to cover for me.

I'd yowled, "I really do have a headache. Go away."

Except he knew me better than anyone else in the world. "You've never had a headache a day in your life."

That's when I'd thrown a pillow at him and told him to leave me alone. Possibly forever.

The air was still warm from the day, even though the sun was getting closer to the horizon. It wasn't dark enough for me to be completely incognito, but my deep burgundy flowy tank top that was tucked into my navy pencil skirt kept me pretty well hidden. I was a little let down that I hadn't been able to find anything black at the store, but at least this outfit was dark enough to feel like my own.

When I was getting dressed, I'd started to put on my new flats because they were comfortable, but then I'd reminded myself that I wasn't doing this to be comfortable. I was being wild and impulsive, so I kicked them off and put on my pumps instead. But now that I was trying to sneak into a cabin across the resort, I wondered if that had been the smartest idea.

I snuck into a shadow under a tree, waiting for a couple on their way to the lake to pass. I didn't recognize them, but I didn't want to meet them accidentally tomorrow and have them mention that they saw me being weird in the woods.

Was I ready to do this? Hook up with a virtual stranger?

What would his hands feel like on my skin? Would they be soft, or coarse because of the hard work he'd put into this resort over the years?

No, I told myself, this was just dinner.

But hooking up would be okay, too.

I looked down at my hands and picked at my chipped fingernail. I should have gotten it fixed when we were in town yesterday.

Self-consciousness crept in a little. What if he didn't want to hook up with me?

I'd only imagined his bare ass a hundred times today. Whatever happened after that would be something for me to worry about later.

Ben's cabin was about a thousand feet away, and the porch light was on.

I was really doing this. I was going to someone's house with the intention of sleeping with them.

Well, after dinner.

Clicking my fingernails against my thumb, I forced myself to stand up straight. In the office, I was an ice queen. I was able to shut off all feelings and tell everyone what to do. So why was this terrifying? He was just a person. A person I'd never see again at the end of this vacation.

Shaking my hands, I let out my extra energy, pulled my shoulders back, and inhaled deeply. As I walked the rest of the way toward the forest green cabin, I gave myself a pep talk.

I was Lizette Howell-Xu. I could do anything.

The steps creaked under my feet as I went up the stairs of his house and knocked on the door. Just a few seconds passed before it swung open, and there he stood, a bright smile on his face and an apron tied around his waist, covering a blue button-up shirt that made his eyes look iridescent.

"You came," he said, like he hadn't believed I'd actually show up. It reminded me of how surprised I'd been to see him at the bar the previous night.

"I did" was all I could say.

He wrapped his fingers around the nape of my neck and gripped my waist with his free hand, pulling me through the doorway. My body stiffened briefly at his contact, but the smell of pine and something savory enveloped me as he kissed me quickly, turning me to putty almost instantly.

The kiss was intense. I opened my mouth slightly, and his tongue met mine. My fingers dug into his shoulders instinctively. He let out a groan I'd only ever imagined. Fire spread from my toes to my lower belly.

He released me, his eyes scanning mine. "Oh my God, I'm so sorry. I've been wanting to do that for days and I just . . ." He looked pained. "I'm sorry."

Glancing behind me briefly to make sure no one had seen us, I kicked the door closed. Then I gripped his shirt in my fists. "Don't apologize. Unless you're not planning on kissing me again."

A grin spread across his face, and he did just that. Slower this time, like he wanted to taste me fully. He pressed me against the door and dragged his lips down my neck. "I'm so fucking glad you're here," he mumbled into my skin.

Pushing up on my toes, which was a feat in these shoes, I cupped his face with one hand, pulling him back to my lips. I wanted to get to know him more, but in this moment, the last thing I wanted to do was talk.

We moved together, his hands gripping my hips, my waist, then the underside of my breasts. Mine explored every muscle of his back. After a few moments, he guided me backward to the couch.

He laid me down like I weighed nothing and pinned a knee on the cushion between my legs, hovering over me. His lips left mine, trailing down below my ear, and I let out a moan just as goosebumps prickled my skin.

He pulled back again. "Is this okay?" he asked, breathing heavily over me, a hand sliding up my thigh.

I caught my bottom lip between my teeth, taking in how dark his eyes had become. "Yes. More than okay."

"Good," he whispered, kissing me deeper than he had so far. His tongue met mine, and I gripped his upper arms, eager to get him closer.

I'd never been kissed like this before. I hadn't even understood the appeal until now. Sure, seeing people make out in movies always looked sexy, but it didn't make me want to rip buttons off clothes until this strong, capable man climbed on top of me.

In this moment, with Ben's hands all over my body, his teeth tugging on my lips . . . I could live like this forever.

The ding of a timer went off somewhere behind us, and Ben let out a growl. "Don't move. I'll be right back." He slid off me and I used the space to catch my breath.

Sitting up, I straightened my shirt and shifted my pencil skirt so it wasn't bunched up anymore. My palms were sweaty, so I rubbed them on the couch cushion and waited patiently, hoping my lipstick wasn't smeared across my face. From the kitchen, I heard pots and pans clanging, and even a quiet curse. After a minute, I got up to check on him. He had set the table for two, with candles and everything.

He stood at the counter on the other side of the room, putting the finishing touches on what smelled like a beef roast.

When he noticed me standing in the entryway, he tossed a hand towel over his shoulder, walking over to me.

"I thought I told you to stay on the couch." His hand slid around my waist. His tone was authoritative but sexy. I liked it.

"You took too long," I said, pressing my hands against his chest, leaning in for a kiss.

After his lips slowly met mine, he mumbled, "We've got about twenty minutes while the meat rests. What should we do until then?"

I'd had one lover my entire life. And the thought of me naked had made him feel gross—his words in therapy, not mine. He'd apologized for them immediately, but I'd never forgotten the way they'd made me feel.

The likelihood that I was going to be any good at this was probably zero. So, of course, that's when the dumbest question on planet Earth came out of my mouth. "Should we play a game? Do you have Yahtzee?"

He laughed quietly, and I wondered if he thought I'd been joking instead of panicking internally about my ability to please him. "I bet we could think of a few things to play."

"Oh yeah, like what?" The way he'd kissed me earlier flooded my brain. It made me think about the promise of his skin against mine.

His fingers dug into my hair as he pulled me in for a slow kiss before leaning back, his blue eyes intense. "Or we could do something else."

Leaning into him, I pulled his bottom lip between my teeth. I was ready to ignore any doubt creeping in.

I took a step back so I could watch him as I said, "Monopoly?" This time it was a joke, and he took it just the way I wanted him to.

"I had something more enjoyable in mind." Grabbing the sides of my tank top, he tugged it out from where it was neatly tucked into my skirt. His lips grazed my neck right before he pulled it over my head, tossing it on the floor behind him.

His eyes scanned my breasts, covered only by the lacy bra I'd bought just yesterday. "Fuck," he whispered. His hands covered them like wildfire and his lips met my neck again, sucking and biting my sensitive skin. "You are so fucking beautiful."

I let his words settle in, believing him. He guided me backward until I bumped into something solid. He'd pressed me against a full-length kitchen cabinet, his hands moving from my breasts, down to my hips and back again. Ben bent lower, his mouth grazing the cups of my bra.

His eyes sparkled as he glanced up at me, tugging on one lacy edge with his teeth. I was going to come just standing here. It was the sexiest moment of my life.

"I knew these would be gorgeous after seeing you in that bathing suit earlier." He licked at the lace before pulling the cup down, freeing my breast. "But I never could have imagined these perfect tits."

I dug my fingernails into his hair, not sure how to respond. No one had ever made me feel so sexy before, so seen. He took my taut nipple into his mouth, and I let out a moan. My leg inched up, wrapping around his hip. I knew he could have me anywhere he wanted me.

I reached for his shirt, frantically working the buttons, needing to feel all of him against me.

My bra dropped to the floor at the same time I shoved

his shirt off his shoulders. We were doing this. And I felt more confident than I ever had before.

The only sound was our heavy breathing as he looked me up and down. "I've wanted to do this since the moment I first saw you." He reached up and tucked a hair behind my ear. A surprisingly gentle gesture for how assertive he'd been so far. "You came out of that bedroom with these legs on full display." He gripped my thigh, raising my pencil skirt up around my waist, and brought my leg up even higher. He pinned me against the cabinet with his hips, making me feel his hardness trapped behind his jeans.

I reached down, gripping his waist before running my thumb across the tan skin right above his pants. "I'm not going to lie, you were on that ladder and your skin was showing." Running my thumb across him again, I outlined the crease that led to the top of his boxers. A wild thrill ran through my body, like I was waking up from a long hibernation. "I would have let you fuck me that day if you'd asked."

His eyes turned molten as he murmured my name. I arched my back, unable to contain my desire as he lowered down in front of me. He shifted my leg to his shoulder, pushing my skirt up even higher.

Had I known all I had to say was "fuck me" and a man would drop to his knees in front of me, I would have done it years ago.

His fingers slipped into the sides of my panties, and I held my breath, waiting for his next move. When I got dressed tonight, I'd wished I'd bought something black and lacy to match my new bra, but never in a thousand years would I have guessed I'd end up here, pressed up against a cabinet, with Ben's face between my thighs.

But when he leaned in and softly ran his teeth against the front of my new hipsters, my entire mind went blank. He looked at me, his blue eyes blazing, watching my reaction. "That's the single hottest thing I've ever experienced," I gasped.

His smile went crooked, like he took it as a personal challenge. He rubbed his nose against me, finding my clit through my panties, and then took it between his teeth, not quite gently, and hummed quietly. My thighs squeezed together on their own volition, the stubble on his face scratching against my skin. I slammed my hand against the door behind me. "Holy fuck."

"There's nothing holy in what I'm about to do to you." His voice was deep, full of lustful promise.

Without warning, he shoved my skirt the rest of the way up so it sat just below my breasts, then looped his fingers under the sides of my panties. He pulled them down slowly. In the next breath, he picked me up by my hips and sat me on the cold countertop.

As he crouched down, he pushed my knees apart, asking, "You good up there?"

I dug my nails into his shaggy hair. "More than good."

He licked me once, twice, and went in with a passion I'd never even read about in a romance novel. I was so close to losing myself. My toes curled in my shoes.

He slid a finger in, thrusting in a way that had me gripping the edge of the counter, calling out his name. I was right on the edge, ready to spill over, when he added a second finger.

Waves of pleasure rushed through my body as I found my release. I gasped for breath as he stood, licking his lips, his fingers still moving slowly inside of me. "Ready to move somewhere else?" He reached around, unzipping my skirt with his free hand. "I'd like to get you out of this." He kissed me, slipping his tongue in for just a moment. He tasted sweet, with a lingering hint of *me*. "I want to see all of you."

"Back to the couch?" I offered, telling myself that my choice was because I was impatient to get him on top of me and not because doing this in his bedroom might feel like more than just a hookup.

"Sure." He grinned, stepping back. He removed his long fingers, achingly slow, before licking the moisture off them. Cold air brushed my skin for a moment before he gripped my hips, setting me down on my feet. His hands pulled on the hem of my pencil skirt, sliding it down to the floor, helping me out of it. I was left in just my shoes.

As if he had the same thought, he pulled in a breath between his teeth. "Fuck, Izzy."

"That's exactly what I'd like you to do." I grabbed at the button of his jeans. Once I had them undone, we moved in a frenzy.

"The shoes stay on." His demanding tone almost had me coming again. I'd made the right choice in wearing them this evening. I needed to remember to trust myself with men more often.

He moved me to the couch, with my legs wrapped

around his waist. His boxers had disappeared somewhere between the kitchen and the living room, and his ass felt as perky as it had looked in his swim trunks earlier.

Once his forearms bracketed my head, his kisses turned sweet. We could take our time. He rustled in the drawer of the coffee table, pulling out a condom. As I watched him tear it open and roll it on, I felt a bit of apprehension—something I wasn't used to feeling in any other aspect of my life.

It had been so long since I'd been intimate with someone.

But he finished his task and leaned in, kissing me in a way that eased my mind completely. His hand cupped my cheek. "Hey," he whispered, and my eyes met his. "We don't have to do this if you don't want to." He looked over his shoulder. "I think I might actually have Yahtzee in a cabinet somewhere."

I shook my head, my hands drifting to his hips. "No, I want to. I just . . ." I trailed off.

"I know." He paused, settling over me. "Me, too." We just stared at each other for a few heartbeats. Connecting deeper than I'd thought possible.

I shifted one leg up higher and reached between us. He sucked in a breath as I took him in my hand, guiding him to me.

Just feeling him against my skin, against my sensitive nerves, I knew it was just me and him. My body was relaxed. Ready.

Lifting my hips slightly, I encouraged him to follow where I guided him. His lips caressed mine while he slid into me slowly. His fingers trailed through my hair. Ecstasy trickled through me like warm honey, all the way to my toes.

Once his hips were flush against mine, he paused, letting me move under him, adjusting to the fullness of us. "I've been thinking of this since the first moment I saw you," he whispered as he kissed down my neck, moving steadily inside of me. His hand slipped down my leg to my ankle. "Even more once I spotted you in these shoes."

I tried to think clearly to respond, but the sensations rolling through me were overwhelming. Rocking my hips into him, I couldn't stop. "What took you so long, then?"

He pulled almost all the way out, teasing me. "You know the answer to that. It's taken me everything to not touch you. To get you under me, just like this." He pushed back in torturously slowly, leaving me breathless.

I dragged my fingernails across his back, encouraging him to move faster. "I felt the same way when I saw you."

He pulled out almost fully again, looking at me intently. "I wouldn't have done this if you were actually married. I want you to know I'm not that kind of guy." And I knew in that moment somehow that he wasn't just a man who took advantage of bored married women on vacation. "I saw you and felt . . . this," he said, filling me to the hilt once more.

Something about the confession felt sacred, but I had a feeling it was because I never would have dreamed that a man like this would think I was irresistible.

Our speed increased as we moved together. He shifted us, sitting with his back against the couch as I straddled him. The toes of my shoes dug into the edge of the cushion. I moved like the inferno flowing through me, taking exactly what I wanted.

Something about grasping control of our speed sparked a deeper desire within me. Without thinking, I said, "God, I've never felt so powerful in my life."

His smile grew, and he leaned forward, twining his fingers into my hair. "You have so much fucking power over me." His kiss was deep. Carnal.

I rode him hard until my thighs were tight, and I was holding in a scream. When I came, it was harder than I'd ever come by myself by far. As I began trembling, he moved us again, laying me down, hooking my heels over his shoulders.

Pressing a kiss to the sensitive skin of my ankle, he groaned. "I could fuck you like this forever."

Part of me wanted him to. If only this could be real for both of us.

He found his release after I'd found mine a few more times. The feel of him pulsing inside of me satiated me to my bones.

When he caught his breath, he rolled to his back, taking me with him. We lay together, my head on his chest, quietly connecting. He ran his fingers through my hair gently, a stark contrast to the tugging he had been doing just a few moments ago.

I had the errant thought that work never made me feel like this. My career had never given me this much satisfaction.

Had my love for my job been robbing me of a connection like this for decades?

As his fingers trailed down my back, rubbing languid circles around my spine, he asked, "You hungry?"

That's when I noticed the smell of the roast wafting through the house. "Starving," I replied with a kiss.

Chapter Fifteen

His hand patted my bare bottom a few times. "I'll start the shower for you and meet you in the kitchen when you're ready."

That unnerving feeling crept in again, like this was more than just a one-night thing. Taking a shower in his house felt too intimate. But it also felt like just what I needed, which was scary. "No, I can shower at my place. I'll just clean up a little before we eat." He looked at me, the question in his eyes, so I answered, "I'm weird about the body wash I like to use."

"I get that." He didn't seem to notice that I'd started overthinking what we'd just done. What it meant to me. Which was kind of a relief. "Let me get your clothes." He shifted me to the side and stood, heading to the kitchen.

Seeing his perky ass with streaks from my fingernails made me wonder if I really was a one-night-stand kind of girl. The urge to get up and grab him was a sign that this could be deeper than I'd originally thought.

I stood up, looking around for the bathroom. This

cabin was cozy, but at least twice the size of the one I'd been staying in. Probably 1,100 square feet, if I were to estimate. Not too big, but not too small. I really hadn't had a chance to check it out when I first got here.

Not that I was complaining.

The entire house looked like a magazine spread of a hunting cabin in the woods, even with the fishing rods hanging on the shiplap walls and goulashes by the door. The appetizing smell of dinner really tied the whole place together.

Ben came back from the kitchen, his boxers back on, holding my neatly folded clothes in his hands. His eyes scanned my body, from the tips of my stilettos to my eyes. He sat my clothes on the coffee table and reached for my hips, pulling me toward him.

"I've never seen a woman make a set of heels look so fucking sexy before," he said before kissing me hard, wrapping one hand around the back of my neck with the other gripping my ass.

"I bet you say that to all the ladies," I said, trying to lighten the conversation.

"I wish you knew how untrue that statement was." The conviction in his words was a tangible thing between us.

"So, you like my shoes," I said, spinning the toe of one of them, showing it off.

His kisses trailed down my neck before he bit my shoulder gently. "If you give me a few minutes, I can prove to you how much I like them. Again." The hand he had on my ass pulled me tighter against him as he rubbed his still-hard cock against me.

My stomach chose the absolute worst moment to growl, causing him to chuckle a little. "Maybe after we eat?" I asked, feeling a little self-conscious.

"Good idea." He'd said it with a smile, but it felt more like a promise.

I glanced over my shoulder. "So, where's the bathroom?"

"Use the one in my room." He pointed to a door a few feet to the right. "It's through there."

"I'll be right back." I stepped out of his embrace to grab my clothes, pausing to give him one more kiss before leaving the room.

Ben's bedroom was what I'd expected it to be when I took in the rest of the house. A total bachelor pad, complete with a comforter that could have been on display at a Bass Pro Shops.

As I walked past his bed, I caught myself in the full-length mirror. I stopped in my own tracks, looking at myself the way Ben just had. My skin was flushed, my hair wild, and my lips swollen.

Was casual sex always this empowering?

I kind of wanted to ask Ruby and Hannah, but I was afraid of their answers.

I found the bathroom and cleaned myself up. Fully dressed, I met Ben back in the kitchen. He'd gotten dressed, too, but didn't finish buttoning the top three buttons of his shirt. He'd rolled the sleeves up, too, revealing his solid forearms.

He'd plated our dishes and lit the candles while I'd been gone. The roast looked delicious, like it had been served in a restaurant.

Motioning for me to sit in the chair he'd pulled out, he tilted his head slightly. "You're not a vegetarian, are you?"

I waved him off as I sat down. "No. I tried it once in college. It wasn't for me."

He laughed, sitting across from me. "I'd like to hear about other things you might have tried in college."

"Oh, I was boring and married pretty much the whole time," I said, before I realized it was the wrong thing to bring up on a first date . . . or whatever this was.

"Wow. That's a long time to fake a relationship," he said, amusement in his voice.

"It wasn't fake until about a year and a half ago." I paused, spearing some meat and a perfectly cooked carrot with my fork. "It was just bad before that."

"I'm sorry to hear that, but I've got to admit I was wildly jealous when I thought you were married." He said it so casually as he poured us each a glass of wine. "Especially to someone who didn't seem like he was in love with you."

I moved the fork to my lips, but stopped, wondering how he'd known. "What tipped you off?"

He took a sip, smiling over his glass. "I can't imagine being married to you and not wanting to kiss you or hold you every second of the day."

I tried to hide my smile as I took my first bite. My eyes closed on their own. "Sweet Baby Jesus. You made this?" I said after I could speak again.

He laughed. "It's my grandmother's recipe. I can show you how to make it."

"Oh no, I don't cook. But you can make it for me

anytime you'd like." I continued eating, enjoying the savory flavor of the meat with the sweetness of the vegetables.

"Good to know. Nana would be proud." He sat his glass down, watching me, and I realized I'd looked like a woman who'd been starved.

I looked him up and down, feeling butterflies all over again. "You're gorgeous, good with your hands, and you can cook. Your ex-wife must have been insane to let you go."

"Late wife." He coughed, using his fist to cover his mouth.

"Oh, shit. I am so sorry." I felt like a total asshole.

He shook his head. "No, there was no way you could have known."

"I just assumed when you said you'd been married . . ." I was digging a hole under my feet, which was rare. "I'm just—sorry."

He reached across the table, taking my hand in his. "Izzy. It's okay. She probably would have said the same thing." His smile was bright, but I noticed a hint of sadness in his eyes. "Losing Summer is what brought me here, to Michigan. After a year of wallowing in my own self-pity, I realized there wasn't anything left for me in London anymore."

He picked at the edge of his napkin with his fingertips and went on, "The only other person who'd ever cared for me was my grandmother. I'd spent a lot of time with her before I was sent away to school, but when she passed ten years ago, I thought my work was too important to come say goodbye."

He was quiet, but I knew he wasn't done. Sure, I'd lost my marriage, but I couldn't imagine how bad it must have been for Ben. He started speaking again a few seconds later. "Once I realized that I wanted to be a different man, one Summer would have been proud of instead of the man who couldn't get out of bed, I opened a map, looking for a place that reminded me of the cabin Nana had lived in. Luckily, I found this place." His wistful smile made me wonder if this place was going to be a catalyst for me the way it had been for him. Something that taught me to stop worrying about my job when I had so many people to care about. I could feel his hope seeping into my soul, too. "The next morning, I reached out to Cate. I've been here four years this December."

I squeezed his hand, still in mine. My heart ached for his loss. "That sounds like it was a lot to overcome. I'm glad you found something that makes your heart happy."

He chuffed out a laugh. "I didn't realize how miserable I'd been until I got here and breathed the fresh air for the first time since I was a kid." He took another bite, thinking while he chewed. "There are absolutely days that I miss it. The intensity and interactions with people from all over the world were like nothing else. But this life is slow and easier on my blood pressure."

"I get it. Like a balm for the soul." It'd been the only place other than Santa Barbara that felt like home in a long time. "I think you found the antidote for depression." It'd had an effect on my workaholic lifestyle, that's for sure.

He let go of my hand, thrumming his fingers on the table. "It really is. We book mostly families on vacation trying to get away from their real lives, but the occasional influencer gives me a call. They don't like that I don't believe in social media." He laughed, and I was quietly excited that he felt the same way I did about keeping a private online existence.

"How could you worry about social media in a place that has such terrible internet?" I motioned around us, trying to make him laugh. It worked, and I adored the sound.

"Especially with employees who don't fix anything on time," he said, and I tried to suppress a giggle. An actual giggle. What was he doing to me?

We ate quietly for a few minutes. I was glad that I'd already slept with him, but knowing he could cook like this made me want him all over again. "So, what did you do in England?" I wondered how someone so well-educated had given it all up for life in the woods.

He leaned his head back and forth, forming his answer. "Kind of the same thing I do here. A little bit of everything, really."

"Did you work in the hotel industry there, too?" I wondered if we'd crossed paths before. I'd done a lot of business with European companies, so it wouldn't be surprising. But then I remembered, while I was here, I was supposed to be Izzy Xu, real estate agent to soccer moms or whatever.

He chewed on another mouthful, the same pensive look on his face from my last question. I had a feeling he was thinking of a way to avoid answering it. "It's kind of a long story, and not one I'd like to get into right now," he finally said. After a beat, he looked me square in the eye with a crooked smile. "I've got a confession to make."

Unable to hide my smile, I sat my fork down. "Uh oh. What did you do?"

He tapped the table again. Maybe it was a nervous tic. "I had a conversation with your father-in-law today."

"Former father-in-law," I corrected him.

"He seems really cool. He mentioned he's in the banking industry?"

"You could say something like that." I laughed. "His family owns XIB—Xu International Bank."

His eyebrows perked up. "Holy shit, I knew they had money, but . . ." He whistled.

"They're just people at the end of the day." He looked like he wanted to say something, probably relating to the enormous family history of the Xu's financial empire, but he didn't speak. "Why, does it intimidate you?"

"No, if anything, it makes me proud of you. That you're the kind of woman who can hold her own against a bunch of narcissists."

"They're not like that."

"Sorry, I didn't mean to accuse them of anything. I'm sure they're great people." He paused, taking a sip of his wine. "I guess I'm projecting. I . . ." his eyes dropped to his plate as he pushed a potato around. "At my old job, I had to deal with a lot of red tape caused by rich pricks who only thought about their own investments. I realized that no one in the boardroom had a soul. I couldn't live like that anymore."

It was hard for me to disagree. Especially since I was one of those soulless board members. The knowledge that

I'd only cared about purchasing The Azure while I was on vacation with the only family that had ever loved me hit me like a punch in the chest.

He looked up from his plate, a small smile on his lips. His eyes had a spark to them, filled with amusement and maybe a little embarrassment. "Sorry, that was an awkward way for me to tell you that I think we have a lot in common."

Just looking at him soothed the ache inside of me. I could take this trip more seriously. I could be less of a corporate zombie and find where my soul was located. If it really existed.

The rest of the meal was a blur. We talked about our favorite foods and what they reminded us of. It was weird telling him about my grandma's Char Kay Teow that I'd never attempted to make but always wanted to try, but he was interested. Excited to find a recipe, even.

I had to tiptoe around a few things to avoid admitting that I came from the Howell family—America's second largest real estate magnate, only behind The Carlisle Empire. I wasn't sure exactly why my gut told me to keep it from him. Maybe it was because he hated corporations. I told myself it was because I wanted him to see me as a person instead of someone he had literally fled to the woods to avoid.

After he cleared the plates and refused to let me help clean them, I stood, stretching my arms behind my back, still sore from that horseback riding adventure that felt like it had happened a lot longer ago than yesterday. Ben really had saved my ass and then made it all better. "Thank you so much for dinner." I looked at the clock on the stove, nervous that Zane's family might be back from dinner already. "It's getting late, though. I should head out."

Ben turned to me, taking a step closer. "Or you could stay."

As much as I wanted to lean into this private time we had together, I knew Zane would start looking for me soon. "The last thing I need is to get caught in a stranger's cabin when I'm supposed to be in bed with a headache."

He shrugged a little, like he didn't think it was something to worry so much about. "Want leftovers? I can pack some up for you if you'd like."

I was tempted, but wasn't sure how to explain it if someone found them in my fridge. "I wish I could, but . . ." I bit my bottom lip.

"I get it. Evidence would be tricky." He walked me to the living room, his hand grazing my ass. "Thanks for coming."

I blushed, thinking of all the ways I'd come tonight. "Anytime," I said awkwardly. I was going to have to ask Hannah and Ruby how they ended these things, too.

We were almost to the door. I faced him, resting my hand on his chest, not quite ready to leave even though I knew I should. "I had a lot of fun tonight." He gripped my hips again, like he really couldn't keep his hands off me.

"Will I see you tomorrow?" He sounded hopeful, which made me glad that this might not be a one-and-done thing for him, either.

"I'm sure I can slip away to do a little work as long as the Wi-Fi's still broken."

His grin was conspiratorial. "I guess I'll have some free time, since I don't have to worry about fixing it, then."

I gave him a peck on his lips. "I've never been so excited for no internet."

He reached for my ass with both hands, pulling me fully against him once more. He was hard again, which caused heat to travel all through my body. "I'm sure it's the internet that's got you all hot and bothered in here, too." His tone was barely controlled.

I kissed him fully this time, slipping my tongue into his mouth and dragging my fingernails through his hair. He groaned before pulling back. "Izzy, if you don't leave, I'm going to bend you over the back of this couch and fuck you until the sun comes up."

I stepped back, giving each of us some space. "Tomorrow?"

He nodded. "Tomorrow."

As Ben opened the door for me, he stopped, pulling me in for one more kiss while I was still in the darkness of the foyer. When his lips pressed against mine, it felt more real than just some random hookup. Like he expected me to move to Michigan and stay in this tiny little cabin with him.

The thought should scare me. I was supposed to want to run out the door, hop on a plane and go back to my real life. But as I melted into him, as my arms reached around his ribs, bringing him closer, the thought was comforting.

I'd spent so many years afraid of connecting, but now that I'd done it in the safety of a vacation bubble, I knew it could happen back home, too. We stepped apart, and I blew out a slow breath. "Tomorrow," I repeated again as a goodbye.

As I walked back to my cabin, thankful that the sun had finally tipped over the mountain, I wondered what it would be like if Ben lived in Santa Barbara. If I could have him for real.

I slipped into my dark cabin, and as soon as I closed the door behind me, the living room light flicked on. My ex-husband sat on the couch, like the concerned father of a teenager past her curfew. I let out a scream, and the look on Zane's face went from distress to hysterics. He clapped his hands, laughing. "You did not do what I think you did?"

"I went out for a walk," I said, my voice wobbly.

"Your skirt is on backward," he said, and I twisted, looking for the zipper.

"It is not, you asshole." I grabbed a throw pillow from the couch, chucking it at him.

"Yeah, but you checked. Thus proving my point." His eyes widened slightly. "What happened to your lipstick?"

Rolling my eyes, I stepped toward the bathroom. "I'm taking a shower and going to bed."

He slapped the cushion next to him. "The hell you are. Now get over here and tell me everything."

Chapter Sixteen

I slid into the booth of the resort restaurant the following morning next to my ex-husband, across from his parents. It was the fourth day of this vacation, but the first one that felt like I was actually relaxing.

It could have been the prospect that I was about to be fully divorced from my husband, or, more likely, it was from the sore but welcome feeling between my legs.

I hadn't seen Ben anywhere on property yet, not that I was looking for him or anything. Zane patted my leg, pointing at the menu in front of me.

"What are you gonna order?" I asked, automatically.

"It's time to tell them the truth," he said a little louder than he probably should have. The people from the table next to us glanced over for a second.

Alice looked confused, but she didn't have a chance to speak. Bradley and Tippy walked up to the table, smiles on their faces. "Aww, we didn't know you were coming here for breakfast today!" My sister-in-law practically hollered. I wondered if she'd already dove into a bottomless mimosa, since the family had eaten in this exact spot every morning since our arrival.

Alice patted Andrew's leg, motioning for him to scoot over. "Sit down, you two. Have you eaten?" Zane shot a look at Andrew, but he only shrugged, like this was out of his control.

Bradley sat down next to his mom, bags under his eyes like he'd been out too late last night, and Tippy sat next to Zane, forcing me to scoot over to give them both some space.

I leaned against Zane, whispering, "Well, there goes our plan."

He nudged me with his elbow. "Actually, this might work out better."

The rest of our party was busy discussing their breakfast choices, so I doubted they heard Zane when he spoke, but my heart stopped when I heard him quietly admit, "Mom, Dad. I'm gay."

Instinctually, my hand went to his knee. But it seemed like no one had even noticed. He cleared his throat and his mother looked over her menu at him. "I'm sorry, sweetheart. What were you saying?"

He looked at me, our eyes locking in solidarity. I nodded, letting him know it was okay for him to go on if he wanted to. He looked across the table at his parents. "Lizette and I. We're divorced."

I didn't know what I'd expected. Maybe screaming. A little crying. Even a heavy dose of denial.

Shit, even anger.

But no one flinched, not even an inch, and Alice went back to her menu before saying, "We know, hon."

I wasn't sure how to react. Never in a million years would I have thought this was how the conversation would go. I felt Zane tense up next to me, something like shock simmering under his skin. "Um," I started, "how?"

It was Tippy, of all people, who responded, "Because of the background checks, you idiots."

Zane and I both turned to her. "What background checks?" he asked, the hurt in his eyes flowing through my veins.

She pointed to Bradley, who answered for her, "When we were thinking about running, we had our manager do background checks on all the family members. You know, mostly to find old social media posts that might be racist or to discover pictures of Halloween costumes that might not be culturally sensitive and whatnot." He flipped through pages in his menu like the conversation we were having wasn't the most important one of mine and Zane's life.

"Anyway," he continued, "we found a few things Ruby needed to have scrubbed off the internet." He glanced at Zane's dad like it was his fault before looking me dead in the eye. "But the weirdest thing came up when we got to you."

"Oh, really?" I wasn't sure where this was going. I'd worked my ass off my whole life to always follow the rules. To do what was asked of me. I wasn't a fuck-up, like my brother had been before he got clean.

"There was practically nothing. No Twitter posts, no

Instagram. Not even an archived Myspace account they could find on some abandoned server. There was your corporate email address on The Howell Group's website, and that's it."

"Well, I take my privacy very seriously."

Tippy jumped in, "No one is that private. We knew something was up." She locked eyes with Bradley before dropping the next bomb. "So we hired a private investigator."

"What the fuck?" Zane yelled at the same time I said, "Excuse me?"

The waitress picked the worst moment to show up, asking for our orders. The six of us ordered quickly, handing over our menus so she would go away. It was tense, like we'd been forced to pause in the middle of a heated property negotiation.

"Okay, so tell us more about the person you hired to delve into our business instead of, you know, asking us," Zane demanded.

Andrew spoke up first, surprising all of us. "We didn't think they'd uncover a secret like this."

I felt the rage bubbling over inside me. "You were in on this, too?"

He laid his hand on the table, making me aware of how loud I'd become. "Bradley hired them before telling us, but yes, we knew. He came to Mom and me for advice after the fact. We knew that your brother had a run-in with the law a few years ago, so that's what we thought the initial issue was. But the investigator found more information online about him than he did about either of you."

Bradley leaned in, taking over the conversation. "But it only took him a couple of days to find divorce documents. And then when we had him follow you——"

"You had him what?" Zane yelled, causing the couple next to us to turn our direction again.

"You're making a scene, love. This isn't the best place for this conversation," Alice said. She'd seemed apprehensive this whole time.

Tippy looked at Zane like they hadn't just shattered our trust. "It was for your own good. We wanted to make sure you weren't being taken advantage of."

"Just who would be taking advantage of him?" I asked, ice in my voice.

She tilted her head, smiling with too much teeth. "Honey, you have money, but you don't have Xu money. A divorce would be a perfect opportunity to funnel funds into your own account." Zane's parents both cringed at her accusations, but they didn't admonish her, either.

If I hadn't been stuffed into this booth, I would have stood and left, but I was trapped. I inhaled slowly, steeling myself. "I'm sorry. While my parents were busy building an international conglomerate worth over a billion dollars, what were your parents up to?"

She turned to Bradley, ignoring me. "See? I told you this would happen if we told them."

Zane shifted, facing her, his rage palpable. "You need to leave."

She had the audacity to roll her eyes, but Bradley read the room. "Come on babe, let's let them talk this out together." He reached for her hand, not even attempting an apology.

The two of them took off, talking to the waitress on their way out. Zane rested his hand on my thigh again, like he was looking for a lifeline. "So, how long have you known?" His voice was soft, like he was afraid of the answer.

Andrew replied, smiling at his son like the last five minutes hadn't happened. His voice was soft. "About the divorce or about your boyfriend?"

Zane's jaw dropped, as if he was the one who had just learned personal news about his parents, not the other way around.

His mom reached across the table, but he waved her hand away. "Sweetheart. We've always known you marched to the beat of your own drum."

"You never even asked me." His reply was high pitched and defensive.

Her fingers tapped against the table quietly. "We thought you'd figure it out it on your own and tell us when you were ready. And then you went to college and brought Izzy home that first Thanksgiving. You were both so young." Alice looked at me, sadness in her eyes. "You were quiet and shy and had your nose in a book, but you made him so happy. We figured that the two of you connected and that was that." Her eyes welled up, and she dabbed at her face with a napkin. "And then you both grew and became the powerful adults you are today. We just assumed that what you had was working."

His dad leaned in. "We love you both so much. We should have told you about the investigator as soon as Bradley told us, but we thought it would be better just to forget about it. I'm not going to lie and say that we weren't hurt when we found out the way we did, but not for the reasons you might think. We just wish you'd been comfortable enough to talk to us about this."

I blinked rapidly, the emotional whiplash in this moment overwhelming me. "I thought he told you." Then I paused, realizing it sounded like I had blamed him. "But we should have. We should have sat you down and told you the truth. Together."

The waitress brought our food, telling us that Tippy and Bradley had taken theirs to go, not that I cared. While we ate, Zane told them about Caleb. They seemed genuinely excited to hear about him. Like all the worrying Zane had done was for nothing.

It was cathartic and freeing. Like we were finally about to start being our most authentic selves.

Hell, if I wanted to, I could kiss a stranger in public.

Not that I would.

But I could kiss Ben without worrying about what people would say.

Near the end of our talk, when all the food had been eaten and cleared by the waitstaff, Zane's mom and dad made it perfectly clear that when we left the resort, we needed to pretend we were still together . . . for Bradley. At least until the end of the election.

Apparently some data cruncher at the campaign had already looked into the possibility of Bradley having a newly divorced brother and felt that it might lose too many votes in a few counties. They'd done what they could to stop his opponent from getting their hands on our news, but could only do so much to keep the secret close to the family.

I started to ask why one son's public life was more important than their other son's personal life, but I knew the part I'd been playing my whole life. The part that was the perfect daughter of the perfect parents who were planning on taking over the real estate world.

It wasn't real, but it was only for a little while longer.

"Would it be better if I just went home?" I asked. Maybe if we went back to our normal lives, this guilt and shame creeping into my chest would go away.

"No. We love you as our daughter, regardless of paperwork. You're ours. Always," Alice said, and I knew it was true.

I tried to put myself in her shoes. In Bradley's shoes. Sometimes family meant sacrificing your needs for other people. I really fucking hated this, but I could do it. For them. "Okay, I'll stay."

"But no funny business." Andrew added. We must have looked surprised, so he added, "I mean it. No running off into town for hookups. No nightclubs."

Zane threw his hands in the air. "Where are we even going to find a nightclub?"

"You think Ruby didn't tell us that you all went drinking at a bar the other night?"

I shook my head, trying to stop this conversation. This was absolute bullshit. "Look, I'm okay with pretending when we're out, but I'm not faking this when no one else is around."

This was awful. I'd really wanted to hold Ben's hand around here instead of Zane's. I was ready to move on.

Clenching my teeth, I couldn't let this anger go. If we were covert enough, we could make it through. They couldn't stop what we did privately.

The looks they gave each other said they'd had this conversation many, many times before. Just based on body language alone, it looked like Andrew was more willing to give in than Alice, which made sense; Bradley had always been more like her, Ruby and Zane like their dad.

After a tense silence, Alice spoke up. "It's just for a few more days. And maybe be careful when you're back at home."

Zane had been quiet for too long, like a burning fuse making its way to the bomb. He slammed his hands down on the table.

"So you're telling me that you approve of my life as long as I keep it a secret? Okay." Zane moved, starting to leave the booth.

His mother reached out, trying to calm him down. "Well, if you had told us before the campaign, we could have spun it better." Election day was still more than five months away. This was going to be an eternity.

I grabbed Zane's arm. "I think we've all had a pretty intense morning. How about we table the rest of this conversation and come back when we aren't emotionally exhausted?" I said to everyone.

Andrew, always ready to compromise—which seemed to contradict his success in the business world—said, "I think that would be best." He looked us over like we were still nineteen-year-old kids. "We can catch up with the two of you around dinnertime?"

We took that as our excuse to leave with quiet goodbyes, arms locked at the elbows in solidarity.

Once the forest air hit me, I relaxed a bit. The biggest thing on our shoulders was done. It wasn't exactly how we'd planned, and we still had a way to go before we could live the way we wanted to, but this was progress.

As we walked down the hill toward the guest cabins, I realized I hadn't heard a sound from Zane since we left. I tugged on his arm. "Hey."

The tears streaking down his face told me every emotion I'd been feeling was a thousand times stronger for him. "Come here," I told him, pulling him into a hug. His shoulders slumped against me as I felt the sobs rack through him. "It's okay, babe." I scratched his back, making soothing sounds. He gripped the back of my dress, holding on for dear life.

After several minutes, he let go and stood up straight, looking down at me. "Sorry." He sniffled, wiping his face with his hand. "It was just a lot."

I reached up, wiping away a fat tear as it landed on his cheek. "You did so great in there. It was a difficult conversation to have, and you killed it."

"I know," he said, sucking in a breath. "I just wish Caleb had been there with us."

I squeezed his arm. "Me too. He gets to come to the next one, yeah?"

He gave me one more tight hug. "I should go call him. Let him know what's going on."

"That's a good plan. I'll walk with you to the main office. The service there is okay, but there's a landline you can use if you can't connect."

He smiled through his tears, wiping his face again. "I've been calling him a few times a day in David's cabin. We even had enough bandwidth to FaceTime last night."

I took an enormous step away from him. "Wait. What?"

He had the sensibility to look a little ashamed, but there was a smile hidden there, one that I knew meant that he'd done something sneaky on purpose. "Lizette, I have no idea what you're talking about."

I put my hands on my hips, a gesture I rarely made with him, but I needed him to know I was dead serious. "David's had internet this whole time? I could have been working there every day?"

He reached forward, rubbing his thumb against the skin between my eyes. "You have to watch how hard you scowl. You're going to have some intense wrinkles right here pretty soon." I swatted his hand away, giving him an *I'm being serious* look. "Okay, okay, I'm sorry. But hear me out. If you would have known that we had fast internet in David's place, you wouldn't have left. You wouldn't have ridden horses or come down to the pool." When I started to argue, he pressed on. "And you would have never gotten the balls to talk to Ben . . . let alone sleep with him while your family was at dinner."

He wrapped his arm around my shoulder, guiding me down the trail again. I elbowed him a little before protesting. "You and your sneaky cousins told me I should!"

He laughed, like it had all been part of his plan the entire time. "Yes, but would we have even gotten to have that conversation if you were poring over your precious laptop?"

I wrapped my arm around his waist. It was just the way we'd walked a thousand times before, but this was the most authentic it had ever been. Any anger or irritation I'd had because of his omission washed away. We were two people on the way to being themselves. And that was worth it. "Okay, fine. Maybe you were right."

Chapter Seventeen

I went back to our cabin for a little while, but felt restless. Five minutes of pacing the floor made me realize that I felt more liberated right now than maybe I ever had. I didn't know what to do with myself.

My hands shook at my sides. Is this what being ready for adventure felt like?

I glanced at my laptop sitting on the table and didn't even want to open it. Today, I was going to do things just for myself. Work could wait.

I put on some black leggings and sneakers, deciding I'd hit up a hiking trail I'd seen near the lake.

However, once I was out of the cabin and halfway across the property, I spotted Ben riding in on a horse, a couple of teenage girls and their mother trailing behind him.

I thought about last night. What it would have been like to sleep next to him all night. Regret coursed through me. This morning would have been easier to handle if I'd woken up in his bed. I tried to shake the feeling off. This was supposed to be a fling. Something to help me get my groove back. But there was a pull. A lure I felt around him that I couldn't deny.

Something I had to tell myself wasn't real.

I couldn't be serious with anyone right now, anyway. Stupid politics.

He ran his hands through his hair, laughing at something, and I knew I was in deep. The idea of this being just a vacation fling vaporized in my mind. I couldn't deny that it was more real than anything I'd ever wanted.

As I walked, I watched him say goodbye to his clients, and by the time I'd made my way in front of him, he was putting the horses in the paddock to cool down.

He started brushing down the one he always rode, a giant light brown animal that was much sweeter than I had originally thought, especially since it had been with him when he saved me from my own horse.

Maybe I was going to become a horse girl after this trip, too.

Ben caught my gaze, and I wondered if he was thinking about last night. The smile on his face was a little dark. My skin tingled.

"We told them," I said as I got closer.

He paused his brush strokes, like I'd thrown him off. "Congrats. How did it go?" I must have grimaced, because he laughed a little. "That well?"

"Honestly, the whole situation was a disaster. In a fucked up turn of events, they already knew, so we just confirmed it. And, to make the whole thing worse, they want us to keep it a secret still. At least until Bradley's PR manager can decide how to spin it." I felt the anger from earlier bubbling up. It took me a few seconds to let it go. To come back to this moment.

He swept the brush against the horse's coat a few more times, like he was mulling over the news. Then he turned to me, disappointment in his eyes. "I've got to admit, that last part is a shame. But how are you feeling now that you've come clean?"

I reached up, running my hand across the horse's smooth coat. The sheer size of the animal was still terrifying, but with Ben here, I knew I was safe. I answered honestly. "Kind of free, I think."

"The truth will do that, or so I've heard," he said, chuckling quietly.

His smile and ease, along with the smell of forest and sweat coming from him, scrambled my thoughts. The magnetism between us tugged me closer, giving me a sense of privacy out here in the field. "Anyway, I'd rather talk about something else right now."

"Got something on your mind?" His gaze roved over my leggings and tennis shoes before they landed on my lips.

"I strongly remember a promise of bending me over something today." I was just as shocked that I'd said it as he was, but I was trying this whole empowered woman thing in aspects of my life other than the boardroom. I liked it.

His eyes flickered behind me for just a beat before he

stepped even closer, licking his bottom lip. He grabbed my ass, pulling me against him. "Give me a few minutes to settle the horses and I'll meet you in my office." He glanced over to a door in the barn I hadn't noticed when I was here the other day.

Double-checking that no one was around, I walked to the room tucked into the corner. When I stepped inside, it hit me that this office was more Ben's than the cabin he lived in.

There was a desk that looked to be about a hundred years old, all scratched up and worn, but sturdy and strong. Instead of chairs facing the desk, like in most corporate offices, there was a button-tufted leather couch. I ran my fingers across the upholstery, surprised by how soft it felt. This wasn't just some couch that had been discarded for Ben to put back together. This had been wildly expensive. Probably one of a kind.

The rest of the room was plain, but not in a boring way. It was minimalistic. Low maintenance. It felt like home.

The door behind me opened with a slight creak and I turned to see Ben, an intense look on his face. His eyes were fierce, focused on mine for a moment before flickering to my breasts and then meandering down my legs. He twisted the lock behind him and, within a step, had his arms around me. His lips touched mine briefly before he dragged them down my neck. He gripped my bottom with a force that was on the verge of painful. "I've been thinking about this all fucking day."

I began unbuttoning his shirt, not wanting to wait any

longer. "It's not even lunchtime yet." I moaned quietly as he sucked at the skin below my ear.

He leaned back, eyes dark. "I woke up at five, hard as a rock. Haven't been able to focus on much since then." He pressed into me, the swell in his jeans showing me just how ready he was.

I slid one hand down, grabbing him over the denim, excited by my newfound bravery. It came easily, knowing what kind of pleasure I was about to feel. "Oh, yeah? You weren't able to find relief on your own?"

"I had a feeling you'd be around sooner or later. Didn't want you to miss out on the chance yourself." His hands wandered up my hips. Under my shirt. He slipped it up and over my head in a heartbeat, tossing it away.

"Good thinking," I said, feeling a sweet heaviness between my legs.

He shot me a sly smirk before gripping my hips tightly and spinning me around. "So, you want me to bend you over. Anything else you'd like?" his voice was deeply masculine as it resonated through my body.

"I want you to take me. Just like this." It came out as a whisper. I'd become intoxicated by the moment.

"Hold on," he demanded. I wasn't used to being told what to do, but when Ben did it, I wanted more. I grabbed the upholstery tightly. The freedom of letting him have me fully surged through my veins. The delicate skin between my legs was swollen. I needed him to give me release.

My breath caught in my throat as he pressed his knee between mine, sliding my thighs apart. So much of my life had been me at the helm, making the decisions, taking charge. Giving control over to him filled me with a heady arousal.

He grabbed my breast tightly in one hand, and the other plunged down the front of my leggings. "No panties today, Izzy?" he whispered in my ear as my wetness coated his fingers. A moan escaped my lips as he rubbed his crotch against my ass.

He pinched my nipple through the fabric of my bra, and I yelped. The stimulation shot all the way down my toes like a lightning bolt. I begged him to do it again with a whispered, "Please." His fingers clamped tighter, heightening all of my senses. "My God," I moaned, unable to find other words.

"Oh, you like that?" he growled before pushing the cup of my bra down, releasing my nipple. He rolled it between his fingers, tugging down this time. The sensation continued through my body.

I wanted—no; I needed more. I nodded, and he slid a finger inside of me. Instinctively, I pushed up on my toes, pressing my backside aggressively against the front of his jeans, needing to feel his hardness against me. His finger pumped in and out at a tempo I tried to match with my hips.

More, more, more. I burned for him.

I reached back, unhooking my bra and tossing it to the side before grinding against him harder than before, gripping the couch.

"Is this how you want it?" His voice was dark, like gravel. He added a second finger, stretching me for what was to come. His other hand tugged harder on my sensitive nipple.

"Pull down your leggings, Izzy."

I let go of the couch for a moment and shoved my pants down to my ankles. Being told what to do deepened my need for him. There was a comfort, a trust, in knowing that he was in charge. He could take me to my limit. He knew what he was doing and I could give myself to him fully.

He dragged his fingers from my apex, leaving a trail of wetness up my belly as he pushed me down further into the couch.

"Don't move from that spot."

Then he stepped away, leaving a brush of cold air in his absence. I could move if I wanted to, but something in me knew it would be more fun if I followed his directions.

Looking over my shoulder, I stayed as still as I could while he pulled a condom from his front pocket. My body trembled with the anticipation of what we were about to do. What he was going to do to me.

Ben unbuttoned his jeans, dropping them to the floor. I pressed my face against the couch, stifling a moan from the excitement alone.

Dropping to his knees, he licked me from one end to the other. I'd never felt a sensation like that and wanted to again. My forearms dug into the couch as I leaned further into the soft upholstery, giving him deeper access. His fingers slipped back into my soaked folds with careful precision.

Within seconds, I'd lost all my senses.

"Yes, come for me," he said between my uncontrollable spasms. His tongue exploring all over me was the most exhilarating thing I'd ever felt.

"I need you to fuck me, Ben," I begged into the couch.

With a light slap on my ass, he stood. "Whatever you want, darling."

Before I could take another breath, he entered me, filling me completely. I gripped the leather tighter, not worrying that I'd scratched it when he pulled back and slammed into me again.

His fingers dug into my hips as he took me hard and fast. I felt fully alive as I came over and over, letting go of any restraint I'd had before. He shifted backward slightly, giving me a chance to take a deep breath, but his fingers twined through my hair, pulling me up to stand. I twisted slightly, finding his mouth with mine as his hands roved over my breasts, tugging on my nipples just as I'd learned I liked the most. We both came like this, with his chest pressed tightly against my back.

When we'd been able to breathe again, his touch turned gentle, his fingertips sliding over my skin. "Dammit, Izzy, that was . . ." He didn't finish his thought, but I agreed with him anyway.

He pulled out achingly slow and settled me back on my feet. Fully relaxed, I turned around to face him, with what I was sure was a contented look on my face.

His eyes filled with something like wonder as he ran a hand up my arm, to my neck, then gently rubbed my cheek with his thumb.

"Wow," I whispered.

He grimaced slightly. "Was it too much? I got a little carried away."

I pushed up on my toes, kissing him softly. "Please get

carried away from now on." After another kiss, I added, "Where did you learn . . ." then I stopped myself. "Never mind. What I meant was . . ."

I trailed off again, not sure how to compliment him in this situation.

Laughing quietly, he pressed a sweet kiss to my lips. "Thank you." He took a step back, pulling his pants up to his hips. "Excuse me for just a second."

I leaned against the couch, suddenly aware that my leggings were shoved tightly around my sneakers. His eyes drifted to my throbbing mound and his tongue darted out, tasting his bottom lip. Within a breath, he was against me again, kissing me deeply. His hand reached between my slick thighs like he hadn't gotten enough.

"Sorry." His words were quiet but intent. "I can't keep myself away from you." He'd dropped his jeans and used his free hand to grip my waist, propping me back on the couch. His fingers dove inside me again, his thumb pressing against my clit.

Gripping his shoulders, my fingernails bit into his skin. It only took a few moments for me to let go again.

As I called his name, he gasped for air, like he gained as much pleasure from it as I had.

"God, you're so sexy," he said before taking my mouth with his again.

I opened my mouth to ask him to keep going when there was a knock at the door. We both froze.

"Ben, I need your help with the computer."

Cate. Had she heard us?

He pulled his fingers from me, licking them before calling out, "Hold on! I'm cleaning up after my last ride."

He winked before continuing, "I'll meet you in the main building in five minutes."

I grinned. He pulled up his jeans again and stepped away from me, sliding open a pocket door that led to a small bathroom.

"Give me just a second," he said, closing the door. The toilet flushed, and I realized I was still standing here, virtually naked. I tugged my leggings up as best as I could without making a mess and found my shirt and bra, slipping them on. He emerged just in time, holding a moistened hand towel out for me. His pants were buttoned and his shirt was straight, like he hadn't just fucked me harder than I'd ever had it before.

I peeked into the bathroom behind him. The sink and fixtures were mid-century modern, but in a way that complemented the soft woods of the wainscoting and the natural light coming in through the frosted window. "I love the way you've decorated in here."

"It's the only place on the property that's really mine." He rubbed his hand along the soft leather couch. "I had this shipped from my office in London when I settled in." He shot me that damn smirk again—the one I wanted to kiss every time it graced his face—before whispering in my ear. "Thanks for deflowering it with me."

I held up the towel, stopping myself from begging him to make me come one more time. "I better go clean up."

He pressed a peck to my cheek. "Good plan. I'm going to find Cate before she finds a key." He kissed me again, like he needed me as much as I needed him. "Wait ten minutes, then come get me, okay?"

"See you in ten." I closed myself in the little bathroom to clean up.

The woman in the mirror didn't look like me, with her wild hair and swollen lips. I smiled at her, knowing that she was who I wanted to be when I got back home. The old Lizette was gone, and I was glad to be evolving into whoever the new me was going to be.

Chapter Eighteen

I walked into the main office like I had every day of this vacation so far, but without the intent of getting any work done. I had waited in Ben's office for ten minutes like he'd asked, but it had felt like an eternity.

"Hey Lizette," Cate called from behind the desk. "Where's your laptop?"

Smiling at her, I tried to ignore Ben sitting at his desk, twirling a pen between his fingers. "I'm not working today, Cate. I'm . . ." Shit, I hadn't come up with a reason to be in here. I should have picked up my computer on the way to at least pretend I was going to work.

"She's right on time for our hike." Ben cut in, standing and walking toward the counter. He slung a backpack over his shoulder and picked up a water tumbler from his desk.

"Oh, are you leading a group around the lake?" She sounded interested, like maybe this was something he really enjoyed doing.

"Yes, ma'am." He looked at me, a secret in his eyes.

"Did you tell the rest of the party to meet us at the trailhead?"

I nodded, catching the gleam, and went along with the story. "They're already waiting for us. We should get going before they get restless."

He came around the counter, up to where I stood, and motioned toward the door. "So, how's your day been so far? Anything exciting?"

I had to rub my hands against my thighs to stop myself from reaching for him. Keeping my hands to myself in public was going to be very difficult, especially after what we'd just done in his office. "I just had a pretty fun workout. You know, had to stretch before this hike." Biting my lip for a second, I made a poor attempt at keeping a straight face.

He laughed, shaking his head as he held the door open for me. Over his shoulder he called out, "Hey Cate, this one is probably going to take a few hours. If anyone comes in looking for me, send them to Michelle, please."

I walked next to him on the path as he guided us to the trailhead. For a split second, I worried there might actually be others meeting us on this hike, but when we got to the trail, there was no one nearby.

The walkway was astonishing. The dirt path wandered through a patch of forest, sprinkled with trees and bushes I had no names for. Everywhere was green and lush, with the sprinkling of branches here and there giving us a sense of quiet privacy.

The further we traveled, the closer the lake came into view, but we still seemed like the only two people on the planet.

"You hungry or thirsty?" He asked, pointing a thumb over his shoulder toward his backpack. "I packed us some lunch for when we get to the overlook, but if you want to eat now . . ."

I turned, putting my hand on his arm, about to kiss him for being so thoughtful, but I stopped. This was going to be much harder than I'd anticipated. He smiled like he knew what I'd almost done. "Sorry. I just. Thank you." I crossed my arms, not sure what to do with them. "Let's eat later." I tilted my head, wondering. "How were you able to help Cate and pack your bag in such a short amount of time?"

He huffed out a quiet laugh, one that I was learning meant he thought the situation was a little ridiculous. "I just grabbed some sandwiches from the kitchen. The chef already had them prepped for guests." He started walking up the trail, so I kept pace next to him. "And Cate's computer was unplugged. Apparently, she'd been deep cleaning the office yesterday when she was bored and disconnected everything to untangle the cords."

I laughed. "I could totally see that happening."

He nudged me with his elbow. "So, Lizette."

I looked up at him as we walked. "That's my name."

"I was wondering what Izzy was short for. I just assumed Isabelle."

I smiled. Him thinking about me when we weren't together felt sexy. I hadn't experienced sexy before. Zane had been adorable. Cute, even. But nothing deeper, I'd started to realize. This felt like a warm blossom in my chest.

"My brother called me Izzy from the moment he

could speak, but no one else called me anything other than Lizette." He held back a tree limb so I could continue down the path with him. "And then I met Zane during freshman orientation in college, and he must have overheard Reece call me that when they met. So his family started calling me Izzy, too."

"But that's it?" He seemed genuinely interested, not just asking for the sake of asking.

"Yeah. I'm not really . . ." I had to think about my next words, so I wouldn't come off as cold. "Open with a lot of people. In my kind of work, I often have to remove myself as a person from the situations I handle." His eyebrows furrowed, and I realized that to him I was a real estate agent. The most gregarious people on the planet, so I added, "You know, dealing with banks and all that."

We walked a little while without speaking, the landscape around us taking away our words. The pine trees were tall and thick, but every so often, the lake peeked through, the sun reflecting on the gray-blue surface.

"So, what about you?" I asked. "What's Ben short for? Benvolio?"

"Benevolent, actually." He laughed at the face I gave him. Scratching the back of his neck, he clarified, "Just Benjamin."

"Benjamin Montgomery," I said, trying to copy his slight British lilt as I remembered his last name from the business card in his desk. "Sounds very fancy."

He laughed. "That's what they were going for when they named me. My parents are very . . ." He paused, thinking, "posh."

We continued talking about ourselves, our childhoods and college experiences. He told me about growing up in LA until he was sent away. His parents weren't happy that he preferred reading historical fiction novels more than obsessing over the statistics of his family's company. The only person he had quality time with was his grandmother when he got to come to Michigan for the summers, since his parents were always busy working. After he was sent to boarding school, he only got to visit for Christmas, but stopped coming home once she passed away.

He'd tried to work with his dad for a year, but it ended in disaster and he went back to Europe, hoping to disappear from his relatives completely.

It was interesting how similar our lives had been, even though we had vastly different upbringings. I told him how we moved from place to place every few years, so I never really found a tribe of my own. Even now, all I had were Camilla and Blake, if you didn't count Zane.

Our conversation made me feel special. Like I'd finally found someone like me. Someone who was actually attracted to me, at least.

About half an hour into our hike, we moved into a clearing that overlooked the lake, with the resort behind it. I let out a gasp, covering my mouth. The beauty was unlike anything I'd seen before. The water was a few hundred feet below us, with a sandy beach lining the edges. There were guests down on the beach playing in the water, giggling children chasing each other around, but from up here they looked like dolls.

"Hey ladies." Ben called out behind me, and that's

when my heart sunk. Ruby and Hannah were sitting on a rock, looking over the lake, too. They must not have noticed us either, because they both jumped up, surprised.

"Hey Izzy," Hannah said. When she looked at my companion, her voice dropped salaciously. "Ben."

Ruby had the same shit-eating grin on her face as Hannah as she said, "What are the two of you doing out here?"

Ben answered, not missing a beat. "She wanted to go for a hike. So here we are."

Ruby's eyebrows bounced up and down. "Yeah, you are." She grabbed Hannah by the elbow. "Well, we were just leaving."

They both gave us little waves before passing us on the trail, headed back toward the resort. "Enjoy the view." Hannah called out as they disappeared into the trees.

"Sorry about them," I said as Ben sat on the large flat rock they had just vacated.

"It's okay." He opened his backpack, but paused. "I'm assuming they know about us?"

I turned away, looking toward the lake. Usually, I had a strong ability to keep my face straight, but when I was with him, it was impossible to keep my shields up. It was nice, surprisingly. "They know I was interested in you. That I wanted to spend time with you." After a long pause, I continued. "But I haven't seen them since before dinner last night. Not that it's their business."

He pulled out a small blanket, laying out more than what he could have just grabbed from the café. He unpacked a full picnic right before my eyes.

I sat on the rock on the opposite side. Sandwiches,

cheeses, fruits, and even a bowl of nuts were laid out between us. "Please, dig in," he said, popping a slice of melon into his mouth.

I picked up a sandwich, taking a bite. "Zane knows." I paused. "Everything."

He looked up from his meal. "Oh?"

"Yeah, he caught me coming in last night. Wouldn't let me go to sleep without all the details."

He coughed a little, like he had choked on his food. "Everything?" A few more coughs came out before he pounded on his chest lightly.

I picked up the water tumbler, handing it to him. "Well, not every-everything. But he knows that we . . . hooked up."

"He's not gonna try to kick my ass, is he?" He said with that smile I adored, his eyes crinkling at the sides.

I laughed. The thought of Zane throwing fists at anyone was hysterical. "He was pretty surprised that I went through with it. But he's happy for us. For whatever this is."

I took another bite before I realized that I had made it sound like I was fishing for a label from him. Which I wasn't.

I just didn't know what you called a guy you had planned on sleeping with a couple more times before going back to your real life.

Even if the thought of saying goodbye to him might just crush you.

Thinking about not seeing him after this trip was a stab in my chest. I barely knew him, but in just a couple of days, I'd grown more attached than I'd ever wanted to feel about another person again.

It had to be the mind-blowing sex. All that oxytocin and norepinephrine in my brain that wasn't there before.

Luckily, he didn't seem to catch any of my mental gymnastics, since he had turned, facing the lake below us. "So, how long do we have to keep us a secret?"

Us. What a powerful word.

He'd felt this gravity. It was real to him, too.

I shrugged, trying to play it cooler than the anxiety bubbling in my chest. "Zane's dad mentioned keeping it up for a bit when we're back in California." I popped a ripe strawberry in my mouth, pretending this stupid agreement didn't break something inside me. "So the whole time, is my guess."

"The whole time," he said quietly to himself. His eyes were distant, foggy even.

I waved my hand, protesting. "We can still be affectionate. Just in private." I reached for his hand, tentatively squeezing it. My voice was soft, hoping he could tell how serious I was about us. "When we're out in the middle of nowhere, like this. And in your house. This doesn't have to be the end. At least while I'm here."

He pulled away at my last sentence and I wondered if he picked up on what I didn't have the courage to really say. That whatever this was probably wouldn't work when I was back home.

Part of me filled with grief already, knowing that there was an expiration date hanging over our heads. I imagined a countdown clock in the air and shook my head, trying to think of positives. Like the way Ben's callused hands had felt against my skin earlier today.

After a few moments eating in silence, I started, "It was weird. They knew about it, but were waiting for us to tell them." I filled him in on the details, especially about the private investigator, which was the most infuriating part.

Having my privacy violated so deeply was something I wasn't going to recover from anytime soon, but it was nice having someone to let it all out to.

It was such an off-putting situation. Sure, I was glad that they knew, but not in the way we'd wanted to tell them. And not being able to live our lives because of someone's political career made me feel a little numb.

How many times had I forced someone in my life to conform to something because it was best for my company? I'm sure if I asked my brother right now, he'd have an annotated list.

I'd never go so far to make someone hide who they were. At least I hoped so, anyway.

"That's one of the reasons I had to get out of the city," he said, bringing me back to where we were in this serene moment. Just the two of us. "It has a beauty of its own and I'd love to visit again some day, but I couldn't take having all of my choices made for me anymore."

"Right? I'm a 36-year-old woman who, up until a year ago, had to run anything I did at work by my father —who is not an easy man, by the way. And then trying to keep the failure of my marriage from everyone, to not look vulnerable or weak, took so much effort. But when I think about it, now that I'm kind of on the other side, I feel like I spend so much of my energy being a perfectionist at the office that it stops me from enjoying things. Even if the truth was fully out."

He nodded, finishing the last bite of his sandwich. "When Summer died, it was devastating." He gave me a sideways glance before looking back out at the lake, like he wanted the assurance that I was there with him before opening up. "I was supposed to be in the car with her that night. It should have been me in the driver's seat. But I stayed at the office late and told her I'd meet her at the restaurant instead.

"The emergency responder called me three times before I picked up. I hadn't recognized the number on my cell, so I just kept working." He turned toward me, propping himself on a hand on the rock underneath us. "I know now that it wasn't my fault. That I hadn't given that jackass a bottle of vodka and made him get into his truck. Or that answering the phone on the first call wouldn't have magically saved her life. But it took me years to get here."

He paused, thinking for a second before adding, "I felt like I died that night, with her. Nothing mattered anymore. I didn't leave my bedroom for weeks. Getting dressed was the last thing I wanted to do." He turned back to the water and shrugged like he was unable to sit still. "I've never told any of this to anyone but my therapist." A small smile spread across his lips, "Not even Cate, and she's persistent as hell when she wants to know something."

Having him open up like this, being so raw and honest, filled a gap in my soul I hadn't known was there. It soothed my heart to know that he trusted me, that he valued me enough to share these private thoughts.

He started packing up our trash, putting things back in his backpack in an organized way while he continued telling me the story. "But once I came out of it, once I started feeling like a human again, I knew I didn't want to go back to my old life. That it had been a wake up call for how I wanted to live the second part." He looked down at his hands, stretching them, and balling them up a few times. "Summer wouldn't have wanted me to suffer alone. I'm glad that I found this little place in the middle of nowhere. It brought me back."

I reached up, putting my hand gently on his shoulder. "I can't imagine how you felt, and I'm so sorry. It must have been terrible." I couldn't come up with other words to comfort him, and thankfully, I didn't think that's what he was looking for. He didn't seem upset, just factual, like I needed to know this part of him to fully get him. And I thought I did.

He zipped up his backpack and threw it over his shoulders, chuckling. "Okay, you told me about your divorce on the first date and I'm telling you about the worst moment of my life on this one. We really are doing this in all the wrong ways."

I had to laugh at that. "I think what we've learned through all this is that we get to do things our own way."

He glanced around the clearing before leaning in and kissing me. When he pulled away, his eyes met mine. I should have been worried that someone would find us, but in this moment, the two of us were more important than any bullshit I'd have to explain later. "I'm so glad you showed up in my sanctuary."

I scooted across the rock, grabbing the straps of his backpack, pulling him closer. "I never thought I'd be grateful that some lady stole my suitcase. Or that your resort had shitty internet." I kissed him slowly. "But here we are."

"Here we are," he repeated, his hands skimming my hips as he deepened our kisses. "We shouldn't do this," he mumbled against my lips, not moving away.

"I don't want to stop," I whispered, dragging my fingernails into his hair.

We became a tangle of tongues and hands then, unable to pull away. It was like someone had flipped a light switch in my brain. I'd spent all these years thinking the grindstone was the most important thing for me, but it wasn't what I wanted. Not when something like this, a connection—both in body and soul—was what living felt like.

I'd shifted, moving to straddle him, and his fingertips dug into the back of my leggings. Before we could go any further, though, a coughing noise echoed from the entrance of the clearing. I jumped off Ben, standing a few feet away from him. My heart was absolutely pounding.

"Hi friends," David said. Zane stood next to him, bright red, holding in a laugh. "It's a good thing we got here when we did. It would have been awkward if someone else found the two of you like this."

For the size of this damn resort, the likelihood of my ex-husband showing up was beyond frustrating. "Oh believe me, this is still awkward as hell," I told them, my hands on my hips, trying to look casual, like I wasn't just about to fuck some guy on the side of a hiking trail.

"Is this where I get to say, 'Get your hands off my wife?'" Zane said, chuckling.

I rolled my eyes at him. "You've been dying to use that line, huh?" He nodded, still laughing like it had been the funniest joke in the world. "What are you guys doing here?" Then I threw my hands up, not needing an answer. "Oh, Jesus, the girls sent you, didn't they?"

"I promise we waited until we couldn't resist them begging to come back for you." David said, and I worried about what the girls had told them about Ben and me.

I glanced at Ben. He had a mix of amusement and maybe confusion on his face. Zane must have tracked my gaze since he reached out, patting Ben on the shoulder. "Good job getting her to put down her damn computer. You achieved something that I failed at for decades."

"It was not decades, first of all," I started, but he did that thing with his hand where he pretended his fingers were my mouth and it was just yapping all over the place.

"Can you just take a compliment?" He asked playfully.

I crossed my arms over my chest, trying to be serious. "I seem to recall that you were complementing Ben, not me."

"I would like to stay out of this conversation, please." Ben said, laughter in his voice.

"Anyway," I said loudly. "Thanks for hanging out, but we should get going."

Zane looked down the trail. "Keep an eye out for my

mother when you get back to the cabins. She's handing out jobs to prep for the bonfire tonight."

"Which is really why the two of you are here? Avoiding Alice?" After breakfast, I fully understood why Zane needed some space from his parents.

David nodded and Zane answered, "Yup. Enjoy."

Zane stuck his tongue out playfully, and I turned to Ben. "Guess we should head back?"

"Nice to see you both again," he said to the guys before motioning for me to go ahead of him.

"Sorry about them. Sometimes I wonder how old they actually are, you know?" I said once we were out of earshot.

"They seem pretty cool, though. It's a good situation, being divorced to someone you get along with."

"Yes, but sometimes I feel like we get along too well, you know?"

He laughed, pointing to a bird that landed on a branch nearby and telling me about it. The whole time he spoke, I just stared at his face, memorizing his features. His straight nose, the scruff of his beard, how blue his eyes were. I had to pretend to ooh and ahh because I'd been distracted during his entire bird monologue. He leaned closer, pressing a kiss to my temple, like he'd figured out what I was thinking.

"Where did you learn this from?" I asked, wanting to know more about him.

"My grandmother, the one who lived here in Michigan, used to take me birdwatching. She'd make me get up before the sun so we could find the best spots. I didn't exactly love it then, but now when I see a bird she would have loved, it makes me feel like she's here." He inhaled, his chin resting on the top of my head, and I felt for a moment like we were in absolute paradise.

After a few minutes of shared silence, we continued down the trail, talking about animals and nature and just a little bit of everything. This time I listened intently, and even told him what little I knew about local birds back home, which wasn't much.

It felt so new, breathing fresh air without wondering what I needed to do when I got back to work. I hadn't even thought about The Azure for a while. Not feeling the pressure constantly pressing down on my shoulders was refreshing.

Halfway through the walk, the tips of his fingers brushed against mine. The first couple of times, I figured it was because the trail was narrow, but after a minute I figured out what he was doing, so I reached over with my hand, twining my fingers with his.

It was electrifying, this connection between us. Walking with him like this was more beautiful than all the hills and trees and water around us. I was finally alive. And grateful for the privacy of this trail. A gift from the universe to the two of us.

When we neared the trailhead, he pulled me into a thick copse of trees, kissing me sweetly. "Today was fun."

I thought about what we had done earlier, back in his office, and how it felt to be hand-in-hand with him now. "Yeah. It was nice" I said, but what I'd wanted to say was that it might have been the best day I've ever had. "Thanks for taking me out here. It was gorgeous."

His arms squeezed around me more tightly than

before, like he was also trying to soak this moment in. "I need to get back to work, though. Will I see you later?"

I smiled up at him, not wanting to let him go. "I should probably check in with Alice so I can help with the bonfire. Maybe you could stop by?" A bubble of sadness crept up in my chest. "We can't be like this, but it would be nice to see you."

He nodded, kissing my forehead like he felt the same way. "I'm sure I can find an excuse to stop by for a bit."

Chapter Nineteen

The bonfire the night before had been wildly fun, but as we'd laughed and joked and caught up with each other, I'd wished things were different. Telling stories from the last year would have been easier if we could have shared the real truth, even if part of it stung. I was able to speak to Alice privately, and she assured me that she'd try to convince Bradley to let us live our lives, but she seemed just as stressed over the whole thing as I was. She was stuck in a shitty situation, too.

Understandably, Ben had only stopped by for a few minutes, pretending to check on the fire. When he left, I'd felt so alone, even when surrounded by a crowd of people. I reached for Zane's hand at one point, whispering in his ear that if I felt like this, I hated how he must feel without Caleb.

He'd assured me that it was only for a bit longer, but I caught the sadness in his eyes. We were holding the wrong people's hands on this vacation.

Knowing there was a man less than a quarter mile

away, in his own cabin, hopefully thinking about me was almost too much. And instead of going to him, like a sane woman would, I held Zane's hand, put my hands on Zane's shoulder, and pretended to be in love with Zane.

When that should have been Caleb. He had more of a right to be here than I did, and I was pissed off for him.

The next morning was slow and groggy. Everyone was nursing their hangovers in their own beds, skipping breakfast at the restaurant altogether.

I threw on a dress and my flats, having taken a long shower to get the smell of campfire out of my hair. Zane had been awfully quiet this morning, but if I had to guess, it was because he was missing Caleb something fierce.

The front door opened, and Hannah and Ruby walked in. "Get your bag. We're going to town," Hannah told me, a smile on her face.

"I was thinking about going for a walk down to the lake or something," I lied. I was really hoping to find Ben. To see if he could slip away with me.

"Nope, you don't get to sneak off to make out in the woods with some hottie stranger. You're coming to town with us to tell us all the details," Hannah demanded.

I looked at Zane, begging him to get me out of this, but he just clapped his hands together. "You're not going without me."

Ruby grabbed him by the arm. "Duh. David's already waiting in the car."

We piled into the Escalade, and I felt like a teenage girl, staring out the window, hoping the boy I liked didn't think I'd ditched him for my friends.

Five minutes into the drive, Hannah nudged me with

her elbow. "So, are you gonna tell us what sleeping with Hunky Horse Guy was like or not?"

"I'm not one to kiss and tell," I said, trying to avoid the conversation.

But then Zane called out, "Please! You owe them a story."

I thought for a second, trying to decide how much to tell them. I didn't owe them shit, but I knew they'd drive me crazy until I gave them something.

"Well, the other night Ben cooked me dinner and then we hung out." The rest was between us.

"And just how delicious was dinner?" Hannah asked.

I felt my cheeks turn pink, but I didn't say another word.

"We found them with his hands down her pants in the woods yesterday, so it had to have been good," quipped my sweet ex-husband.

"They weren't down my pants. Just near them," I said, irritated that he was spilling details I wasn't ready to share.

I'd managed to deflect the rest of their questions after that, asking them specific things about their trip. I'd used the tactic thousands of times over the years in the office, especially since the divorce, but I was surprised when it worked so well with this nosy group.

Thirty minutes later, we walked into a nail salon. I was excited to finally get this chip fixed.

The salon, unironically called Hott Stuff, was small, with only two pedicure chairs and two manicure tables. Luckily, we were the only customers here, so there wasn't a wait.

David and Zane took the pedicure chairs, and I'd told the girls to go ahead of me. It had been years since I'd sat in a salon, flipping through a magazine. My usual girl came to the house, or sometimes my office, if I'd had to stay late, but I didn't dare admit it in public. This crew would stop at nothing to tease me about it, especially after our Walmart trip.

There were four employees here, and they seemed like they'd been friends their whole lives. They were all blonde or brunette, with their hair done in elaborate updos and three-inch-long nails. There was even one blowing big bubbles with bright pink bubblegum.

It wasn't a place I would have chosen on my own, but now that we were here, it felt comfortable, cozy even.

I mostly ignored the conversations happening around me, losing myself in whatever drama Robert Downey Jr. was going through that I'm sure the magazine writer had made up themselves.

It was nice to just sit and be for a while. We'd rushed out of the cabin so quickly that I hadn't grabbed my devices. No laptop, no phones. I was completely free.

Ruby nudged into me with her elbow. "Your turn, babe."

I put the magazine down and sat in the chair, telling Rachel, the girl on the other side of the table, what I wanted as she got to work.

"Mister Montgomery is going to love those nails on you. Especially when you drag them down his back later." Hannah said, leaning over my shoulder, a grin on her face.

"Hannah!" I chastised. "I don't know what you're

talking about." We'd been in public for half an hour and she was already blabbing my secret.

The salon ladies looked at each other surreptitiously, but I caught it. So I tried to fix the issue myself. "I'm sure my husband, who is sitting in the room with us, is going to enjoy them."

Hannah rolled her eyes, making her look much younger than she was. "Oh, come on. We're far enough from the rest of the family, to be honest. No one's going to say shit around here." Zane and I both gave her a death-stare.

"I'm going to kick your ass as soon as my feet are dry," Zane hollered at her.

"The hell you are." Hannah stomped over to him, and they started arguing in hushed whispers, probably to stop the spread of our business any more than she already had.

Rachel leaned in closely, inspecting one of my nails much closer than necessary. "Did she just out you for having an affair in front of your husband?"

"No. It's nothing." I failed terribly at keeping my voice level.

The girl sitting next to Rachel blew a big bubble with her gum and popped it loudly. She leaned toward Rachel, who was filing my nails. "Oh my God, imagine if she was sleeping with Ben Montgomery."

I pulled my hand away without thinking and they looked at each other like they'd won the lottery. Rachel gave me a Cheshire-cat smile. "Are you sleeping with Ben Montgomery?"

I squinted my eyes at her, knowing I might be laying

my cards on the table, risking many things I shouldn't be. But I could worry about buying her silence later. I desperately wanted to know what she knew about Ben. "Why?"

"Well, if you're claiming that you've slept with the U.P.'s most eligible bachelor, I've got an awful lot of friends who would like to know how you did it. Many have tried, but all of them have failed." She seemed very intrigued. She took my hand in hers, filing again. I started to worry about how much nail I was going to have left when this conversation was over.

I looked toward the pedicure chairs. Hannah, Zane and David had moved onto another subject, completely ignoring me. Then I looked over my shoulder, finding Ruby's attention glued to her phone.

So I put myself in more potential danger, asking, "What do you mean the most eligible bachelor?" My stomach dipped, wondering how many women around here had slept with him. Sure, she mentioned that her friends had tried, but I couldn't stop from focusing on even the small amount that probably had succeeded.

"As soon as that man showed up and bought the resort from the Bellaire's, we knew he had tons of money. And that face." She whistled, prepping my fingers for paint.

The girl next to her, the one with the bubblegum, added on, "And that voice." She let out a little moan, and I fought the urge to tell her how sexy it was when he whispered in my ear.

Then the rest of what Rachel had said clicked.

"Wait, I'm confused," I cut in before they could say

things I didn't want to hear about the man who had been literally inside of me yesterday. "He bought the resort?"

Rachel cackled. "You claim to be fucking a man who hasn't as much as touched one of us local girls, and you didn't know that he owns the property I'm guessing you're staying at?"

"I doubt she's telling the truth, y'all," came a response from the girl applying a hot towel to David's legs. I hadn't realized she could hear what we'd been talking about, and now I was mortified.

"Forget I said anything. This conversation is over," I said, using my Lizette At The Office voice.

The looks that went through the employees proved that they thought I was being ridiculous. "I think it's time we talk about something else, don't you think?" Zane quipped. He grabbed a magazine next to him and started yammering about Lady Gaga's dress at some awards ceremony.

It seemed to work, since everyone started throwing in their thoughts, but my brain was stuck somewhere else.

Did Ben really own the Lac Brumeux? I'd asked him a couple of times about his position, and he was always pretty vague. Cate also relied on him a lot. So did everyone else I'd come into contact with at the property.

Shit. Had I gone and found the one person in this area who had the same damn job as me?

The rest of the group had moved on to some movie that was coming out soon, something with The Rock in it. I was grateful for the subject change. It was like they'd already forgotten about my drama.

It was difficult for me to track anything. Questions

about who Ben really was raced through my mind. Ruby scrolled on her phone, giggling as she read the worst reviews she could find of the movie they were discussing. It did sound terrible, like it might be a really good guilty-pleasure flick, and I was conflicted about wanting to ask Ben if he'd seen it and being irritated that he'd kept this from me.

The last coat of fire-truck red was going on my fingertips when Ruby launched out of her chair, waving her phone in the air. "Holy fuck. Oh, my God!" I jumped in my seat, causing Rachel to get paint all over my fingers.

"Jesus, Ruby, what is it?" I asked, after apologizing to Rachel and helping her clean up the spill.

"Bradley is going to kill you. And then he's going to kill the rest of us because we didn't stop you," she said, actual terror in her voice.

Zane hopped out of his pedicure chair, which had been drained for several minutes, but had been vibrating pretty drastically, the massage setting cranked to its max. "Give me your phone, Ruby." He snatched it from her and started scrolling. "Oh, Jesus Christ. We're so fucked."

I growled in frustration. "Someone tell me what the hell is going on!"

He laid down the phone in front of me. "This is worse than we could have imagined."

There, on the front page of TMZ was a picture of me leaving Ben's cabin the other night, his hand on my waist and his face nuzzled in my neck. I scrolled down, past the bold headline: **California's Most Popular Senate Candidate Bradley Xu's Sister-in-law Caught Cheating!**

I skimmed the article, but it basically said that while on family vacation with my husband and his family, I'd strayed from my wedding vows, right under my loving husband's nose.

It really painted me as a piece of shit, if I were being honest.

"This is so fucking unfair." Zane bellowed out. "I can't fucking believe this. You did nothing wrong." He was heated. Angrier than I'd ever seen him.

There were two more pictures. One of Ben and me near the barn with his hand on my ass. Another of us holding hands on the trail, coming back from the lake. "Who the fuck took these?" I screamed. There had been no people in the vicinity when we'd done those things.

"Damn. I guess you really did snag Ben Montgomery." Rachel admitted, a proud look on her face, clearly not picking up on how incensed we were. The other women jumped up, attempting to look at the pictures on Ruby's phone. I locked the screen and stood, handing it back to Ruby.

"We have to go. Right now." I couldn't think. Or maybe I'd started thinking too quickly. How would I fix this? What would the family say? I had to breathe, or I was going to throw up. My skin vibrated with nervous energy.

Everyone was going to be so disappointed in me.

Zane put his hands on my shoulders. "Izzy, breathe with me." He inhaled deeply. It took me a few seconds, but I joined him. "No one in this room gives a fuck about this article. We know who we are. We know *what* we are." His fingers squeezed, relaxing my tensed muscles. "Please let Rachel finish your nails. We can't solve any of this right now, anyway."

Rachel took his words seriously and grabbed my hand, wiping off the paint that had smudged over several fingers at this point. I sat, silently letting her do her thing. She really was an artist, especially with my trembling hands making it even harder for her.

Zane looked at David, who was scrolling through his phone, too. "I need you to get ahold of the guy that helped you after you crashed the boat in Ibiza last summer."

"Already on it," he mumbled. "It should be down soon."

I stared at the brush, painting clear over my signature red. "It's over. Bradley's going to lose the election. Because of me." My ribs felt tight, like I couldn't get enough air in my lungs. I couldn't believe that the first time I'd ever done something just for myself, this was the karma I was dealt. No matter how hard I worked, I was the slutty wife who destroyed every life she touched.

I blinked rapidly, holding my head up high. I would not cry. Not yet. Not in front of everyone. The room filled with chatter, everyone talking about how this was going to blow over, how they'd all done worse shit than this. Even the nail salon girls were sharing personal stories that were supposed to make me feel better.

But I wasn't listening. My ears rang, my mind repeating, "you ruined this for everyone," over and over again.

Bradley's career was done. He'd hate both me and Zane because of this.

We had one job. Keep our hands off strangers for a couple of weeks. And I couldn't do it.

Andrew and Alice were going to be so disheartened by me, too. They'd been the only parents that ever gave a shit about me, and the first time they asked me to do something, I fucked it up.

I should have just stayed at home. I should have never taken time away from work.

If this got bad enough, I could lose my seat on my own damn board. I could lose The Azure over this. My company. Because I couldn't keep my hands off someone on vacation.

After deciding my nails were dry enough. I stood, facing Zane. I needed to call the only person that I trusted to talk me off the ledge after this bomb. "I need your phone. I'm calling Reece."

Chapter Twenty

Without a word, Zane unlocked his phone and pulled up Reece's number before handing it over to me. I guess a perk of being married for so long was that he had my brother's number saved, too. "I'm going to step outside. Please give me some space."

Rachel pointed to the back of the salon, her face full of pity. "If you go out that door, you'll have more privacy. Anyone can see you out front."

I thanked her and went out the door to the alleyway behind the salon. There were a few upside-down milk crates just outside the door like it was where the employees of the strip-mall congregated during their breaks.

Plopping down on one, I wondered how the hell life had brought me here. I hit the green button, starting the call, not sure where Reece and his wife, Magdalina were right now. I doubted he'd pick up.

"Yup, hello?" His voice was clipped, like he was right in the middle of something. A guitar went through warm up scales in the background. He must have been at work. He managed a collection of bands and was currently in Europe, something that had been his life's dream that he'd only been able to fulfill pretty recently.

"I'm so sorry. I didn't mean to bug you. I'm not even sure what time it is there." I should have called Camilla. Or maybe no one at all. Another poor decision on my part.

"Lizette?" His voice was suddenly clearer. "Fuck, are Mom and Dad okay?"

"They're fine. I think. I didn't mean to scare you. I mean, I've only heard from him via email about a property I'm trying to buy, but I think he would have told me if they were sick." I rubbed my face with my free hand, knowing I was rambling. "But that's not why I'm calling you." This was a disaster.

There was a rustling sound, like he'd covered the phone with his hand. I heard him whisper, "It's my sister. I'll be right back." There was a feminine voice, then he said, "No, she said Mom and Dad are fine."

"Tell her I said hi," I added. One of my biggest regrets was how mean I'd been to his wife when we first met. I'd been going through a lot—my husband had just moved out. Which wasn't an excuse. I hoped to sit down with her one day and apologize for what I'd put her through.

Reece repeated what I'd said and told her he loved her. After a few moments, I heard a door close behind him. "Izzy, are you okay?"

For some reason, the question was heavy on my heart. I'd always been the one in charge, the one who had everything under control. But right now, it was all being pulled out from under me. "I don't think so." My voice was wobbly, my breaths uneven. I didn't want to cry. Crying was weak and vulnerable. My two least favorite things.

He sounded alarmed, but calm. "Are you somewhere safe? Do you need me to send someone to come get you?"

The first tear fell from my eye and landed on my top lip. That was it, all I needed. I hadn't cried when my grandma died. I didn't even get the sniffles when Zane told me he was leaving me.

Not a tear since I was ten years old when Dad told me that crying would never get me anywhere. *The best way to get shit done was intimidation, not weakness*, he'd said, ice in his voice. And I'd turned that into my whole personality, apparently.

But now it all came rushing out. I hefted deep breaths into my lungs, trying to tamper the emotions spilling out of me. "I'm safe, I'm with Zane. We're in Michigan."

"What are you doing there?" He must have thought I'd gone insane. Maybe I had.

I covered my eyes with my hand. "Oh Reece, it's awful. I really screwed things up."

"Izzy, there's nothing you could have done that we can't fix together. Tell me what's going on." There was a slight smile to his voice, which used to irritate me, but since we'd become closer the last few months, I knew it was because he really was this positive about everything.

"Well, first of all, Zane and I are divorced. And we have been for months." I spat it out like I was a petulant child.

He chuckled a little. "Good. The two of you were terrible."

"What?" I was shocked at his response.

"I mean, you're great people. But together? You were both so caught up in your own lives. It never seemed loving or fun from the outside." He paused, and I heard the muffled sound of a band playing in the background. "I love you both, but you've been miserable for years."

I let out a breath, somehow finding the space to calm down. "You're not upset? Even though you just got married?"

"Is this why you didn't tell me earlier?"

My voice was quiet. "Maybe?"

He laughed. "Look, Iz, Mag and I are solid, but we're also realistic. We know that sometimes marriages end, but we're committed. She knows everything about me. All the darkness. Everything. And I know all about her fears and personal setbacks. It's what makes a marriage worth fighting for."

"Well, I guess that was our problem. We thought we were solid, but there were a lot of secrets."

"So, which one of you cheated?" He laughed, no doubt trying to lighten the mood.

"Neither. He's gay."

"Well, that explains a lot." He didn't seem fazed at all. "No wonder you spend so much time at the office."

I let out a sigh. "As soon as I'd decided to stop working so much, I screwed everything up."

The sound of the band playing was the only noise between us for a few seconds. "Okay, I'm going to need some context."

"You've obviously not seen the internet yet, or you'd know."

"I've been slammed today. Haven't had a chance to look at anything. Let me put you on speakerphone." The sounds in the background made me envision him leaning against a wall in a hallway somewhere, just outside a concert venue. "Can you hear me?"

"Loud and clear." I groaned, running my fingers through my hair nervously. "I'm not sure if I'm ready for you to see pictures of me like this."

"Izzy. I've woken up in a pool of my own vomit after a week-long cocaine bender. There is literally nothing you could do that would make me think you're a shitty person. Ever." Then he paused. "Unless you just murdered Zane's entire family?"

"Just type my name into Google, jackass."

A little while later, he let out a "Hmm," like he wasn't sure what to say. After I thought my heart was going to burst out of my chest, he said, "Good for you, getting back out there, but what are you doing messing around with Jimmy Carlisle?"

"His name is Ben." I dug through the pocket in my jacket, thankful I'd put a napkin in there earlier. As I blew my nose, the name he'd said scratched an itch in the back of my mind. "Wait, what did you say?"

"The dude in this picture with his hand all over your ass is Jimmy Carlisle. As in, The Carlisle Empire. His granddad is the guy Dad wanted to be when he grew up, and his father is . . . well, you know the rest."

"No, his name is Ben. Ben Montgomery. I saw his

business card." My stomach sank. "He owns the resort we had the reunion at, but that's it."

Or was it? He hadn't exactly been truthful about his business. What else had he kept to himself? Had he known who I was? Was I really sleeping with the enemy?

The same kind of anger I'd felt when Zane's parents told us to hide our divorce was rolling to the top of my skin. I didn't like being out of control.

"I'd know this guy anywhere." I heard more tapping on his phone now that I was on speaker. "The first time I met him, I'd just graduated high school, and you were away at college. Dad made me go to this gala that was boring as hell. We sat at the table with the Carlisles to try to get some insider information from one of them. No idea how much Dad bribed the event planner for that one. But this guy, Jimmy—Ben, whatever you want to call him, sat next to me. He seemed pretty nice, but mostly kept to himself. Didn't seem like he wanted to be there, really."

Maybe Reece was wrong. "So you met a tall blond guy once twenty years ago and have him memorized in your brain?"

"You can live in denial all you want, Iz, but I saw him at every event Dad dragged me to while you were at Stanford. I'd know him anywhere." He let out a celebratory yelp. "Here it is. James Benjamin Montgomery-Carlisle the Third. I'll text you this link." I put the phone on speaker so I could see my screen and clicked the link that Reece had just sent. "Scroll to the bottom."

I did what he told me. There, at the bottom of the

page, was an array of people that had worked on whatever project this website was advertising.

And on the top left of the grid was a picture of the man I'd given myself to, with a clean-shaven face and a suit. "Shit. It's really him." I turned off the speaker and put the phone back to my ear, vigorously rubbing my face with my other hand. This was even worse than I'd thought. "Bradley really is going to lose the election because of me."

"Why? Did you sleep with him, too?" Reece asked, and I couldn't tell if he was joking or not.

"No, but I should probably tell you what really happened." I crossed my legs in front of myself, trying to get comfortable in this private alleyway.

I told my brother everything. About my marriage, this trip, my stupid suitcase on the other side of the world, and even what I knew about Bradley's campaign that forced Zane and me to keep up this ruse. At this point, I didn't give a shit if someone had followed me and was recording this conversation from some dumpster. Nothing could make this situation worse.

At the end of it, it felt nice to get everything off my chest. To have no more secrets. But it also felt rotten that the one secret I wasn't supposed to learn, who Ben really was, had been thrown at me because of a stupid TMZ article, and not from the man himself.

"Look, Iz, this isn't as bad as you think it is. I promise. Give yourself some grace and take a step back." He had become so wise since getting clean, I had to give him that.

"Thank you, Reece. For everything." He started to give me a "no problem," but I cut him off. "No. I mean it.

I've underestimated you, and I've been an overbearing nightmare. I wasn't a nice person to you or Maggie. I've been a shit sister for years." Wiping at my eyes again, I hated that I couldn't stop crying. "I'm going to be better. I'm going to pull the stick out of my ass that you've been bitching about for years," I said with a laugh.

"I love you no matter what, Izzy. Now take a deep breath and find out who you really are under that thick armor of yours. I know you can handle this."

"Thank you. I love you, baby brother."

We said our goodbyes, and he told me to call him soon. And I promised myself I'd follow through this time.

Reece was right. I could handle this. Sure, it was still one of the worst moments of my life. To have my sex life out there in the public eye like that. To be labeled as a cheater. Having everyone thinking that I had broken my husband's heart because I couldn't control my lust.

When in fact, Zane pushed me into Ben's arms. It had been his damn idea in the first place.

And to have handed my heart to the one person I shouldn't have. A fucking Carlisle. A man who had the power to crush me professionally. Maybe he'd recognized me somehow and seduced me because he knew I was trying to buy The Azure and he wanted to distract me. It would have been easy for him to read my emails over my shoulder.

Fuck. How was I going to figure out the truth?

The back door of the salon creaked open, and I turned, finding Zane looking more like a nervous lion tamer than an ex-husband-turned-best-friend. "You good? We should get going."

I stood, clearing the emotion from my face like I'd done a thousand times over the years. Vulnerable Lizette was back in her box. Deep, deep inside of me. "Yes. Ready to go."

I tried to hand him his phone, but he stopped, his mouth wide open. "Holy fuck, were you crying?"

I shook my head, wiping at my eyes instinctively. "No."

He wrapped his arms around me. Pulling me in. "Oh, baby. Have I ever seen you cry before?"

He had the audacity to sound joyful. Excited, even. "Fuck off," I mumbled into his shirt.

"I'm so sorry this is happening. I never wanted this for you. It's not fucking fair," he said, squeezing me tighter. Instead of fighting it, I just relaxed, leaning into him.

I really wished he was someone else. Someone a little taller with wider shoulders. Maybe in a flannel shirt that smelled like pine. But that stranger was the wrong guy. Ben didn't exist, not really. "I really liked him," I said quietly. "But none of it was real."

I'd said it. My biggest fear. A fear I hadn't even known was inside me until this moment. I'd opened up, finally, and made the wrong choice.

Zane rubbed circles on my back. "How do you know?"

I pressed my face into his shirt. "Reece knows him. He's a Carlisle."

"Fuck," he said, holding me while I processed what all this meant for me. "It's going to be okay. We'll get through it."

A few moments later, David burst through the door,

causing us to jump away from each other. "Why the fuck aren't the paparazzi here, catching this moment instead?" He yelled angrily, shaking his fists in the air dramatically.

We both laughed, and I hid behind Zane for just a second while I wiped any new moisture from my eyes.

"Did you get it taken care of?" Zane asked his cousin.

"Yeah. It might get expensive. Apparently, the pap who took the shots was paid a pretty penny for them." He shrugged, like this was something he did on the daily. But then his voice dropped an octave. "We do need to find who tipped them off, though. Just because we stop this one doesn't mean new stories won't come out."

Zane stiffened next to me. "I have a theory, but you're not going to like it."

I looked up at him. "You know better than to coddle me."

He ran his hand through his hair. "I think it was Ben."

"What! No! He's a private guy, he wouldn't do that."

Zane and David shared a look like they thought I was insane. David said, "It makes sense. Now that we know he owns the resort—a fact that he kept from you. Why not use a little scandal to drum up business?"

Zane added on, "And now that we know he's related to those bastards, it lines up. You know how many lonely women would swarm here if they knew they had a chance to get mindlessly fucked by a man that wealthy and attractive?"

Those fucking tears began to well in my eyes again, like I couldn't stop them now that I'd let them through once. "That's not what happened between us." There was no conviction in my voice. Part of me believed them.

They both looked at me, in a way that said 'Poor Lizette, she's got no idea what's happening to her.'

Zane cupped my cheek, trying to soothe me. "I'm sorry. I didn't mean to be so harsh. But we've all seen men do this kind of shit before." Zane said.

David added, "Hell, I've done it before."

"Can we just stop talking about this? I need time to think," I said, not sure how I felt about anything. He'd lied about many things. Or at least strategically not told the truth. Anything could be possible at this point

"We do have to go do something really shitty, though." Zane said, leading me through the hallway to the front of the salon.

"What's that?"

"We have to discuss this with my parents. And Bradley."

Chapter Twenty-One

We made it back to the resort, but the whole drive back I'd silently obsessed over my next steps. Hard conversations were about to happen, and I wanted to be ready.

I'd washed my face in the bathroom of the nail salon before getting in the car, but as soon as we pulled up to the cabin, I forced Zane to let me take a shower before we went to talk with his parents. I was not about to go into this conversation with red, puffy eyes.

Hopefully they hadn't seen anything yet, but I wasn't one to bet on that particular four-letter word—hope. Especially after the avalanche the last couple hours had been.

After throwing my wet hair into a ponytail and giving myself a pep talk, I grabbed my personal phone and met Zane in our tiny living room. He told me that the rest of the group was at the big house trying to distract the others before we broke the news. He reached for my hand, and I took it like a lifeline. "Now I get why you wanted me to come on this trip. Why you were worried about all the potential headlines."

He laughed quietly. "It's funny, I'd thought for so long that getting caught was the worst thing that could happen to us." He squeezed my hand as he closed the door behind us. "But it actually feels pretty nice to have the truth out there."

"Umm, first of all, everything feels like garbage. Secondly, the truth is not out there. The whole world thinks I came on a family vacation to cheat on you." This was quite possibly the worst I'd ever felt.

"Well, yeah, it's like this right now. But we'll meet with Bradley's PR team and give them the truth." He glanced down at me as we walked. "The real truth."

"Wouldn't it be easier to just throw me under the bus? Tell them you left me because I'm a harlot with a sex addiction?" It was a strategy I'd seriously been considering. Sure, it would fuck my chances at being on the board anymore if we did buy The Azure. But it could save the campaign.

He shrugged. "I think it's time, Izzy. All those years ago, you and I said vows promising to take care of each other for the rest of our lives."

"Yes, and when we signed the divorce paperwork, we kind of threw those vows out the window."

"No, we didn't. We just modified them. Look at you, here on some insane vacation with me because we love each other. Now I'm going to go into that cabin and tell my brother that his campaign can fuck off and my wife gets to live any life she wants."

His words made me feel brave, like we had an actual

chance at real happiness, regardless of the surrounding fallout. We walked along the trail in silence. But when we got to the large cabin looming in front of us, I stopped. "I'm not ready."

"When have you ever been ready to do anything?"

I thought on it for a few seconds, but before I could answer, the one person I wasn't prepared to speak to came through a trail on the side of the cabin. His soft Henley top and worn jeans were a stark contrast to his picture I had seen an hour ago.

"Listen, James, I'm not in the mood." My voice was full of ice compared to the red hot anger flowing through me. Even if he wasn't the mastermind behind this leak, he'd lied to me.

"Izzy, I need to talk to you." He stopped, blocking me from the walkway in front of the family cabin. "Did you just call me James?" The color drained from his face as he reached up, rubbing his throat.

"Yup. A little interesting, isn't it?" I flipped my ponytail over my shoulder, attempting to show more bravado than I felt. Zane laid his hand on my lower back. It wasn't possessive, but protective.

Ben took a tentative step toward me. "Give me a minute to explain."

I looked up at Zane. "Can you wait by the stairs?" A wordless question flashed in his eyes, making sure it was what I really wanted. "Just one minute, I swear."

He nodded, stepping around me. He stopped next to Ben, whispering something quietly.

I put my hands on my hips, ready for a fight. "Are you going to tell me that you're not James Carlisle? Because that's the only way to undo the lies you fed me." My voice didn't sound like my own as my heart started splintering.

"No." He started to explain himself, but I held up my hand.

"You know what, I don't have the energy to talk to you right now. I have to handle this damn paparazzi issue." He towered over me, but I'd never let that stop me from telling people what to do.

His brow stitched together. "What issue?"

"Oh, so you're going to pretend you don't know about that, either." I clenched my fists, so angry I could scream.

He shook his head slightly. "I don't know what you're talking about."

"You and I are all over TMZ. Making our way through social media, too. We're probably on the front page of Reddit right now. The photographer got some pretty compromising shots of us."

I pulled my phone out of my pocket, hoping we were close enough to wherever the internet was coming from that I could get service. I was right. Pulling up the website, I cringed at the sight of us. I passed it to him, hating that our intimate moments were there for the world to see.

He scanned through the pictures of us, his mouth opening silently. "Fuck. This is bad," Other than when we'd been intimate, I hadn't heard him curse. He gave the phone back to me, stroking a hand down his beard. "We have to fix this."

"We've got a guy that's taking care of it. Worst case he'll spin it so it doesn't look like I was cheating on Zane." I tucked my phone back in my pocket. Hopefully the pictures would be down by the time I had to share the news with Zane's parents.

Ben ran both hands through his hair and turned away from me. "No, Izzy. This is way worse than that." He groaned loudly. "I have to call my father."

"No. The last thing I want involved right now is your company." I'd call my own father before I asked a Carlisle for help. I didn't want them anywhere near this situation. "David's guy should have this scrubbed any minute now. We won't have to call anyone."

Either Ben was one hell of an actor, or he'd really not been involved in the picture leak. He'd turned a shade of green I didn't think was possible. I felt conflicted, but that didn't stop me from being mad as hell. "When were you going to tell me who you really were?"

"I'm not that person anymore." He closed his eyes for a moment. When he opened them he reached for me, but I stepped further away. "Please believe me."

"Who aren't you anymore? James Carlisle, or the person who lied to me about owning this resort?" I wasn't sure I wanted an answer. Would either one make me feel better about this situation?

He cringed. "Can we go somewhere private? I'll tell you everything."

Zane whistled from the deck. "Are you coming or not? I don't want to go in there by myself."

I pointed to the cabin ahead of us. "I need to go do some damage control."

He opened his mouth, and I knew he was going to offer to come help. Tiny cracks formed around my heart, making it hard to breathe.

"Izzy . . ." he whispered. Sorrow gleamed in his eyes.

I wanted to trust him, but I couldn't. "I'm going without you."

His hands curled into fists, like he was trying to stop from reaching out to me. "Okay. But you know where to find me." He looked hurt, but I didn't have the time to handle it. He had lied to me and I had to compartmentalize that to take care of the bigger issue right now.

As I walked away, I had to stuff down the devastation growing inside of me. We hadn't known each other long, but what we did have had been sacred. And it was gone. It took all of my remaining energy not to turn around and check if he was still standing there, watching me.

I stomped up the stairs of the cabin, determined to handle this media shitshow. When I got to the door, Zane was standing on the other side of the deck, out of earshot of my prior conversation. "Let's get this over with," I said to my nervous-looking ex-husband. I knew I was being snappy, but I was really fucking over everything.

Zane knocked, even though we hadn't needed to before. "It's open," came his mother's sweet voice. I knew it wouldn't stay that way for long.

We opened the front door of the cabin and walked in. It was like a vacuum chamber had been emptied out. There was no sound, not even airflow from a fan. It amplified the feelings I was battling inside.

It was just Zane's mom and dad, sitting across from Bradley and Tippy at the kitchen island, but it felt like a deposition.

"Mom, Dad. Can we talk to you? Privately?" Zane said, breaking the heavy silence.

"Anything you are comfortable saying to them, you should be able to say in front of us." Tippy said, the smile on her face was pageant-winner fake. After all, her smiles were rarely genuine.

"I'm sure you've seen the news by now," I said to them, not giving a shit who listened. Zane wanted privacy, but I would let no one shame me for being a single adult who did things under her own volition. Even if they were with a man who hadn't been honest with me. "There was nothing wrong about what I did." I pointed to Zane. "What he talked me into doing, no less." I'd finally gotten everyone's attention—their eyes were glued to me. "I will not apologize for my actions, but I am sorry that whoever the fuck followed me around this property for the past few days has brought drama to our doorstep. I will do what I can to make it right."

Alice stood, motioning for me to take her seat. My hands had been clenched so tightly that they'd imprinted crescents into my palms. I took a breath, trying to relax my hands, and sat on her stool. She leaned her hip against the counter, like she was head of the table at a happy hour. "Sweeties, you're going to have to tell us what's going on."

"You haven't seen?" Zane asked, surprised.

"Seen what?" Andrew seemed truly interested. I wasn't sure what was worse, them finding out on their own, or us having to tell them.

Zane took out his phone, pulled up the news report

still on the TMZ website, and laid it on the table. "Some dirty paparazzi followed Lizette around and took these."

Andrew's jaw dropped to the floor as Alice gasped. They hadn't known.

"Daaaaaaamn," Tippy howled like she was awed by my actions.

Alice spun the phone around, looking at it for longer than was comfortable. "Well," she said before tapping her hot-pink manicured finger against her chin a few times. "There's a couple of ways we can spin this."

"David's guy is already on it." Zane said, his voice a little more positive than the room called for.

But Andrew didn't seem so confident as he rubbed his temples with both hands. "Not the guy who botched the Ibiza coverup?"

Zane looked at me, actual fear in his eyes, before looking back at his dad. "What do you mean he botched it?"

Bradley put his hands flat on the table, letting his breath puff out his cheeks. "Okay, I will take care of this the best I can." His eyes met mine, full of pity. "I don't know if you're going to come out looking great, though. It's getting harder and harder to cover this stuff up anymore."

"Stop talking to me like I'm not an adult." I told him, irritated at his tone.

"Would an adult have made choices that led to this consequence?" He asked, like I was three years old.

No one spoke to me like this. Especially not the man who needed me to keep secrets for his career.

I stood, pulling my shoulders back. "Wow. You know,

you used to be cool." I walked to the door, done with this conversation. "Guess I'll handle this myself, like I usually do." Even if it meant talking to the press. Even if it meant the worst possible thing I could think of . . . calling my father.

Zane didn't follow, but as soon as I left the room, I heard him rip into Bradley. I'd let him handle his brother so I could get started on this scandal.

I walked out to the porch and started down the path that would take me back to our cabin. I'd grab my laptop and go to David's cabin for the fucking Wi-Fi that worked there. I started making a mental list of people I could call that would have contacts at the big television news networks.

My phone rang. I was slightly surprised the call even came through, as far down the path I'd already trudged. I paused in a clearing between some trees in case there was someone following me and pulled it from my pocket. Of course, it was Aniyah, and I panicked.

I answered quickly hoping the board hadn't seen the news. "Is everything okay?"

"Are you fucking ready for what I'm about to tell you?" She asked, her voice was dripping with excitement, something I wasn't used to from her.

"I'm standing in the woods right now, contemplating running away forever. Please let it be good news." I couldn't take anything else today.

"The Azure. The motherfucking Azure."

"Did something happen?" Why was my first thought if it had burned down? Probably because of the fire at The Pacifica being so fresh in my memory.

I needed a nap. Or a real vacation.

"They want to negotiate. Their representative asked to meet as soon as possible so we can talk numbers. It's happening!" She squealed into the phone.

My heart did a little flip in my chest. "Oh, my God. When do they want to talk?"

"They said they can meet at our office the day after tomorrow."

I started walking back to the big cabin. I had to tell Zane that my plans had changed. I had to get back home as soon as possible.

"I have a better idea," I said it as it came to me. "Let's invite them to The Pacifica. They'll see firsthand how well we've taken care of the property next door, which will turn them in our favor when it's time to hand over the keys to us." As dreadful as the rest of my life was in this moment, I was excited by the prospect of getting my hands on this property. I could worry about everything else later. I felt myself slipping into *work* Lizette. Like sliding into a comfortable pair of worn-in heels.

"Brilliant. I'll make sure the meeting room is available for us and take care of the rest of the logistics." As Aniyah shared a few more ideas, I stopped in my tracks.

Ben.

I wasn't ready to say goodbye to him. Sure, I was mad, but I also wanted to give him a chance to tell me the truth. He'd seemed just as upset as me when I showed him the article.

But I thought we'd have more time. Going back to my old life felt like torture. I wanted this whirlwind romance in the woods to last forever. Or at least what we'd had before I found out who he was.

"You know what I mean?" She asked. I hadn't been listening at all.

"Sorry, my phone is cutting out. I've got to go tell Zane. I'll get back to you."

"Perfect. I'll send you flight information as soon as I have it." I could hear her typing in the background.

I hung up, tucking my phone in my pocket and then stopped, stuck between wanting to tell Ben I was leaving and telling Zane I had to get out of here. I'd never planned for either of these options, but I knew I had to get to Santa Barbara before anyone else jumped in with a better offer.

Maybe I could have both. I could go back home for a couple days and then rush back here for the last two days of the reunion. I only really needed to be there for the first couple meetings, anyway.

Spinning around, I headed toward Ben's cabin. All the lights were out, but I banged on the door like a fire marshal even though I knew he wasn't there.

After giving up on that idea, I practically ran to the barn, wondering if he was in his office, but he wasn't there either. "Where the hell are you?" I yelled as I spun around, heading up the hill to the main building.

When I burst in the door, Cate smiled up at me from the desk. I rushed over to the counter, slightly out of breath. I was not in good enough shape to be running through the woods like this. "Where's Ben?" I gasped at her.

She frowned just a little bit. "Sorry, hon. He just took

off in his truck. I could try to call him for you," she offered, and in that moment I realized that I didn't even have a phone number for him.

My phone buzzed in my hand with a text from Aniyah: *Booked you a flight. Commercial was the best I could do. No first-class seats open, but I'm on hold with the airline to upgrade you. Sending you the info now. You'll need to be at the airport in three hours.*

I really hated flying commercial. Especially if it was going to be coach. I sent her a thumbs-up emoji before looking back up at Cate. "Do you know when he'll be back?"

She glanced up at the clock on the wall. "Well, he said he'd be out for a while, but I didn't ask for details or anything."

I thanked her and started to leave, but I stopped. "Can you tell him I said goodbye?"

Her head pulled back slightly in confusion. "Why can't you tell him yourself? Don't you have a few more days before you check out?"

"There's been a sort of emergency . . ." her eyes went wide, so I added, "At work. I have to go take care of some things. But I'm going to try to be back before everyone checks out." Saying it out loud felt like I was willing it into the universe. I was used to getting my way, and I wasn't going to stop now.

She glanced around, like she was about to tell me a secret. "Meeting you was a big deal for him, even if he won't admit it to himself just yet." She tapped her fingernails on the countertop, like she was debating telling me more. "He showed up when this place was falling apart. I've worked here my whole adult life and was terrified about finding a new job. I even had my daughter help me write a resume." She folded her hands together, like she was reminding herself to stay still. "But then he showed up at just the right time and took over. He updated things, spent a year fixing everything that was in disrepair, and even ran ads for the place."

I couldn't stop from asking a burning question. "Do you know why he doesn't like people to know he's the owner?"

She shrugged. "I think he doesn't want people to think of him as some rich city boy who can't be trusted. If he's just the handyman who takes people out on adventures, he can live a quiet life in the wilderness."

I leaned in, wanting this next question to stay between the two of us. "Did you know that he's a Carlisle? Like the hotel chain?"

A sweet grin ran across her face. "He never admitted it, but my daughter found him on the internet once. Neither of us were gutsy enough to ask him about it. He did mention that his grandmother left him an inheritance. She's the only family member he's ever mentioned, and it sounds like they were awfully fond of each other." The door opened behind me and I got a little hopeful that it was Ben, despite how fuming I still felt. "Well, hello! Can I help you?" Cate asked the couple that came up behind me.

Before I left, I reached for her hand. "Thank you. You've been more helpful than you'll ever know."

"I hope you get what you really want," she said with a

small smile before turning her attention to the people who obviously wanted to check in for the night.

I went out the door, wondering if going home right now would stop me from ever getting the truth out of Ben.

The closer I got to my cabin, the faster that imaginary countdown clock ticked down. I packed all my things into the carry-on suitcase I'd bought and made the trek to the big cabin. Carrying the suitcase was a bit of a struggle with my purse overflowing with electronics I haphazardly stuffed inside, but I'd slung it over my shoulder as best I could and went to find a ride.

David and Zane were still there, deep in conversation with Bradley.

"I need someone to drive me to the airport." They'd all turned to me, but no one said a word.

Zane stood, holding his hand out to his cousin. "I'll take her."

I kept my goodbyes short and sweet, promising I'd do my best to be back before the reunion was over. They weren't exactly delighted that I was taking off, especially with Tippy harping about being a united front as a family, but I had to do this.

I just needed a couple of days to finish this deal and then I'd be on the first flight back to Michigan. Hopefully.

The walk to the car was possibly the most awkward moment of my life. From his tense shoulders and tight lips, I had a feeling Zane had a lot to say, but for a very rare minute, he was dead silent. We'd made it to the car, and he grabbed my suitcase out of my hands. "You don't have to do this, you know."

"It's only a couple of days. I'll be back before you miss me."

"And you think now is the best time to leave? When we're supposed to be faking it even harder than before?" His voice was uneven. Angry. Which made me angrier.

"This is my career, Zane. Besides, the damage has already been done. If Bradley's going to lose the campaign over this, it's already over." I wondered if his anger was really with his brother, but he was taking it out on me.

He blocked me from reaching for the passenger door of the Escalade. "How many properties do you even need, Iz?"

Suddenly, I was pissed. This was not like him at all. He, of all people, knew how important this was to me. "It's not like that. You know The Azure has been the goal for a long time."

He put his free hand on his hip. "And you can't let your team handle this? You just started letting things go."

I took a step back. "This is my project. This is my dream." He knew what this property meant.

"You do know throwing yourself into this isn't going to make your dad love you more."

I audibly gasped. "Asshole," I said, reaching for my suitcase. "It's not even about my dad."

"Please, you're only doing this because of him. When are you going to live for yourself?" I'd never seen his face so red before. This was absolutely because of the pressure from his family, but I wasn't about to give him an inch.

"Zane. You understand how important family legacy

is. You dragged me out here because of yours. This is mine."

"You're being ridiculous. You can't even take a fucking vacation without caring more about your business than your family. Maybe you're more like him than you think," he spat out.

I took a step toward him, about to tell him how he could take his family bullshit and shove it up his ass, but I was interrupted.

"Excuse me?" came a voice behind me. Ben. He wasn't gone. But he'd chosen the absolute worst time to show up. "What did you just say to her?" The initial relief of him being here was overshadowed by the fury in his eyes.

"This is not a conversation for you, Carlisle," Zane said to him as he finally opened the passenger door for me, trying to usher me in.

Ben took a few steps toward us. "Oh, it's just a conversation for someone who strung her along for a decade before breaking her heart?"

I tried to jump in, telling him that's not how it was, but Zane stepped in front of me, blocking me from Ben. "I'm sorry, you've known her for what? A week? And that makes you the expert?"

"Guys, please," I begged, grabbing Zane's arm, but they ignored me. I was angry at both of them. Needed answers from both of them. But this wasn't the way to do it.

"In the week that I've known her, we've had a deeper connection than you ever did. If you weren't so wrapped up in using your secrets to control her, you'd never put her down like that."

"Oh, so my secrets are poison. Good one." Zane set down my suitcase and pushed the sleeves of his sweater up to his elbows like they were about to go to blows. Before either of them could start swinging, I put two of my fingers in my mouth and whistled loudly.

"Cut it out. Both of you," I yelled. Their hands dropped to their sides, but they continued arguing.

"Where did you get those pictures from, anyway?" Zane demanded.

Ben's eyes flew open wide, his mouth dropping in shock. "Are you accusing me of hiring a paparazzo to come to my property and follow me around?"

"Who the fuck else would it be?" Zane roared. "Sure would bring in some business, huh? To have the owner of your rival company in your bed?"

It only took a split second to see that Ben wasn't surprised. "That's not how it is between us. I didn't want that from her."

I cleared my throat. "You knew who I was?" I was about to fall apart again, the tears welling in my eyes.

He looked at me, heartbreak showing through his eyes. "Izzy."

I took a step back, covering my own shattering heart with my hands. "How? Did someone tell you? Did you . . ." I felt a tear drip down my cheek.

He reached for my hand, but I stepped away again. "Izzy," he repeated. "It's not what you think."

My head shook involuntarily as I looked up at him,

trying to stop myself from crying further. "Did you know the whole time?"

"Yes." He closed his eyes for a second. "I recognized you when I saw you in your room that first day, but not because of who you are." He paused, digging through his front pocket.

Before he could continue, Ruby came running up the path, looking like she'd been out for a jog around the property. "Is everyone okay? I heard a lot of yelling."

I barked out a humorless laugh, hardly believing the twists and turns of the last half hour. Leave it to Zane's family to interrupt every time I needed clarity.

Zane began filling her in on what was happening at the same time my phone vibrated in my pocket. I knew it would be Aniyah, so I pulled it out, checking. Her text read: *Got you a first-class seat, but it's on a different flight. Your boarding pass should be in your email. Get your ass to the airport ASAP.*

I looked at Zane. Guess I wouldn't be getting any answers before my trip home. "I'm leaving. Now." Then I turned to Ruby, eyeing her up and down as she caught her breath. "Are you sober?"

Her brows bunched together. "Yeah, I was going to have a cocktail after my run, but . . ."

I stopped her with my hand. "I want you to give me a ride to the airport."

"Sure thing." She grabbed the keys from her brother.

Ben stepped toward me again. His hand had come out of his pocket, but it was empty. "The airport? Why?" His eyes scanned mine, concern running deep.

Ruby mumbled something about getting her purse and rushed to the big cabin.

I held my hand up, stopping Ben while I grabbed my suitcase. I stared at my ex-husband, who'd finally chosen to tell me how he really felt about my own family issues. "You stepped out of line and you know it. We'll talk about this when we're home, because apparently there's a lot we need to unpack."

"I didn't mean it," he admitted, holding his hands out earnestly. "I got caught up in my anger about Bradley and the campaign. I'm sorry."

"Well, you said it, so there's some truth in there you've been harboring." I shook my head at him. "At least I learned something from those therapy sessions we went to."

He opened his mouth to speak, but I cut him off. "Later. Once we've been home for a few days. We'll be okay."

Then I looked at Ben. "And you." I fought the urge to reach up and brush my fingertips across his stubble. God, I hated that even if I was angry, I still wanted him. I needed more of the truth, more explanation. There wasn't a doubt in my mind that we'd made it past a fling and had a real connection. But I didn't have time to hear him out. "We could have been something really special, you know, but we didn't get to start." I had to blink a few times, clearing my eyes. "Did you know I was a Howell the whole time?"

"No." He rubbed his forehead. "I mean, kind of." He let out a groan. "It's a bit of a long story."

I lifted my suitcase a few inches. "I have to catch a

flight." Turning to Ruby, who almost slammed into me when she came running with her purse over her shoulder, I asked, "Are you ready?"

I looked at Ben one more time. It would have been so easy to push up on my toes and kiss him. But I didn't know what he really wanted from me. Or whether he'd used me this whole time. I was finally ready to move on with my life, but doing that with someone I couldn't trust wasn't an option. Either we were fully honest with each other, or we were destined to be strangers.

"I have to go, too," he practically whispered. Sure, I didn't know him well at all, but there seemed to be something deeper in his words. Something I couldn't quite put my finger on. As he turned away and walked up the path, a chasm opened in my heart, taking all the oxygen from my lungs.

"Come on. I don't have much time." Suddenly bone-tired, I opened the back door, slipping my suitcase inside. I couldn't control much in the next twenty-four hours, but I would sure as hell try.

Chapter Twenty-Two

The town car Aniyah had sent dropped me off in front of my house. It felt dark, despite the bright white of the modern stucco and the landscaping lights, which usually felt fresh and clean. Tonight they made the place feel more like a mausoleum than a home.

I tossed my bags on the floor right inside the front door while kicking my shoes off. I'd had a fitful nap on the plane and was now battling a splitting headache. Hopefully I could fall asleep quickly and wake up more like myself in the morning.

Everything in this house was pristine. Not a thing out of place. Usually I came home and felt relaxed that I lived in a beautiful house that, thanks to my phenomenal cleaning lady, was perpetually spotless, but just like outside, the inside felt cold and sterile.

I crept up the stairs to my bedroom, feeling more like a visitor in an Airbnb than a person in her own home. Who the fuck was the woman who lived here? Had I really been her before my trip to Michigan?

The bedroom felt just as bad as the rest of the house. Cold. Colorless. Lonely.

I undressed, slipping into bed, feeling the shock of the icy sheets against my skin.

Sleep came quickly, but I must have tossed and turned. I woke up to the sun shining in my eyes and my sleep mask just out of reach. Confusion filled me as I looked around the room. Why was I at home?

I should be waking up in a wooden bed, with barely enough space to move around. Not this giant monstrosity. It was a catacomb, not a sanctuary.

I could do this. The plan was to be here for two days, and then I could think about how to fix everything.

Today we'd meet at our central office so our team could finish building our bid package for The Azure. And then tomorrow would be the negotiation at The Pacifica. If it went well, I could rush back to the family reunion. If not . . . I didn't even want to think about it. Failure was not an option.

I stared at the ceiling for a few minutes. Had the last week even happened? Based on my surroundings, it had been a fever dream.

The heat drained from my bare feet when they touched the floor, but I made my way to the bathroom to start my day, anyway.

As soon as I finished getting ready, I went downstairs, realizing I hadn't checked my phone since getting in the car last night. Guess I'd gotten used to not having any service.

Dozens of notifications glared on my screen. People asking if I'd seen the news, people asking me about the hottie from Michigan, but the most important one was from my brother, asking if I was okay.

I texted Reece back: *Home safe, sorry I didn't check in earlier. Passed out as soon as I got in the door. Headed into the office to figure things out. Thanks for talking yesterday.*

His reply came almost immediately: *Thanks for letting me know. I was going to wait one more hour before making Sal go bang on your front door. Which one of us is the crazy sibling now?*

Then he sent: *Just remember, you're Lizette Howell and you don't take shit from anyone!*

I tugged on the hem of my blazer, straightening any errant wrinkles. He was right. I didn't take shit from anyone.

The next string of texts I checked was from my group chat with Camilla and Blake.

Camilla: *WTF you're home and you didn't tell us?*

Blake: *I got a call from Aniyah saying there was a team coming to The Pacifica and to have the meeting room ready, and then THE NEWS of all places said you were in town. Call us.*

Those had come in about an hour after I'd gone to bed. But there were more from this morning.

Camilla: *Lizette, did you make it home? Should we panic? They haven't shown any footage other than your front door. POSITIVE SIGNS OF LIFE PLEASE.*

I wondered what she meant about footage, but read the next text, hoping it would offer insight.

Blake: *If we don't hear from her by 9, I'm sending Sal to knock down her front door.*

I laughed, thankful that two people I loved dearly would send Blake's boyfriend to make sure I was alive. It was also nice to know that people worried about me, despite being the ice queen I thought no one cared about.

I replied: *Home. Left my phone downstairs all night, sorry! Really long story, but I promise to catch you up soon. What footage are you talking about?*

Blake replied: *Have you not looked outside? There's a camera pointed directly at your house. The morning show is hoping to catch you leaving today.*

I walked over to my front door and moved the curtain over just an inch. Three photographers perched at the end of my walkway. My stomach flipped as both anger and panic filled me.

I replied: *Fuck. This is terrible. I have to get to the office.*

I looked around, making sure I had everything I'd need for the day. If I rushed out to my detached garage, they couldn't get too many pictures of me before I left.

Then I got a text from Aniyah: *Bad news. Jerry called in sick. Apparently, something is going around. We'll make it work, but I wanted you to know before you got here.*

I checked my ruby-red lipstick in the mirror in my foyer, wondering how the fuck we were going to build this bid without our lawyer at the table while I was also being stalked by America itself.

But then I remembered, I had a lawyer at my fingertips. I sent another text to my girls' group: *Camilla, do you think I could steal you from your company for the day? I'll give you more than your hourly rate. Please say yes.*

She told me she was free and agreed to meet at my office in an hour.

Now there really was no way we could fail.

I finished going through texts, replying to Ruby and

Hannah, promising that I'd rush back to Michigan as soon as I could. Even though I doubted I'd be welcome there anymore.

I tried not to dwell on the one person in particular I wished I'd heard from.

Ben . . . or James . . . whoever he was. Missing him as hard as I did right now felt pathetic. But I was a Capulet, and he was a Montague. Our families were sworn enemies. Could I leave him as a notch on my headboard and move on?

I paced across the kitchen, dragging my fingernails through my hair. It had only been a few days. I shouldn't have such an attachment to him.

But I did. And I hated it.

I looked across my empty house.

If I could be in one place in the whole world, it wouldn't be here. It would be on a leather couch in a barn office, with a gorgeous man's arms wrapped around me. Even if he'd hidden his real identity from me.

But on the other hand, if he really was involved in his family's company, there's no way he'd let me buy The Azure. He'd be thinking of ways to crush our bid into the ground.

Maybe he didn't hire the paparazzi. But I'd be willing to bet that once he'd known who I really was, he'd told his father. And I wouldn't put it past that jackass to cause this turmoil.

Especially after Ben had mentioned calling him when I told him about the news.

I really was going to have to let him go. So much for

getting my groove back . . . not that I really had one to begin with.

And now that I'd had time to dwell on what Zane said, I knew he was at least a little right. I'd really just up and ran as soon as a business deal fell into my lap. I was a grown woman who only cared about living up to my daddy's expectations.

Coffee. That's what I needed to get focused for my day. I set the machine up and started my brew. I couldn't stop worrying about the cameras sitting out front, though, so while I waited for it, I turned on the TV in the living room, even though I knew it was a bad idea.

The television was Zane's, really. He just hadn't taken it to his new place when he left. Caleb probably had a bigger one, anyway.

I only used it to check the news and the weather in the morning. Other than that, it didn't get much quality time with me.

Which was another thing I told myself I could change. How many movies or shows had I skipped because I felt like I had to work? I could have been included in years of jokes about Ted Lasso.

Why had I let it get this bad?

I flipped through channels, looking for something that wasn't a commercial, when I stopped dead on the morning show. Two women in brightly colored outfits were having a cup of coffee, laughing at something hilarious.

My coffee maker finished just as the screen changed, and I realized the women were making fun of someone.

They were making fun of me.

My face popped up on the screen, a headshot that I'd taken for the company a few years ago. Then another picture came up, me coming out of Ben's house, his hands on my hips. "These two have the power to make the wealthiest babies on earth," one of the hosts said before the camera went back to just the two of them.

The one on the left, a blonde in a lime green dress, leaned against the arm of her chair. "I feel like we need a name for them. What do you all think?" She asked the camera.

The other one giggled a little. "It's hard with names like theirs. We have Lizette and James." She tapped her fingers against the little table between their chairs. "Lames sounds too mean . . . and Jizette." She gasped, covering her mouth, "Can I even say that on TV?"

"Fuck," I whispered to myself.

"What do you think this is going to do to Bradley Xu's campaign? I mean, he can't possibly think the American people will have any respect for his family anymore, right?" Green Dress asked.

The one who couldn't stop giggling straightened her face. "I agree. If he was okay with this going on under his nose, what else is he okay with? He might as well pull out at this point."

Clicking to another channel, I found another set of talking heads commentating whether Ben and I had been faking this to drum up business, since it certainly wasn't helping get votes for my brother-in-law.

Disgusting.

A third news channel was just live helicopter footage of the Lac Brumeux Resort. The newscaster was talking about how they had contacted both of our companies for comments, but that they hadn't heard from either of us. And that the campaign had been eerily silent, too. All I could think about was how horrible it must be for all the guests, being trapped inside their own cabins to avoid being shown on a national news channel.

They went on about how historically mine and Ben's families have not gotten along, how it's caused tension in many real estate deals and how both of the heads of our families have been stubborn in their dislike of one another. They started speculating about what started the rift, and I hit the mute button.

I scooped up my phone, sending a text to Zane: *What the fuck, I thought this shit was supposed to be fixed by now?*

He texted right back, probably hanging out in David's cabin: *OMG! David's guy promised he would handle it, but we think he took money from someone else to blow it up worse. Dad called his guy right after you left, and he said he's having a hard time clearing things up. We haven't been able to go outside all day. These journalists are like cockroaches.*

Great. All the work I'd done to keep my life private had blown up in my face. The TV showed even more images of Ben and I together. Someone had followed us much longer than we thought they had.

Finally, the screen showed a video of Bradley. And just like that, our biggest fear was real. The ticker at the bottom was spewing garbage about him not only being a nepo-baby but also keeping secrets about his family from his constituents. "Xu Campaign in Shambles" flashed in bright red letters above his head.

So far, there was nothing about Zane and nothing

about our divorce. Apparently, the reporters hadn't started digging deep, but it was only a matter of time before the whole world knew those secrets, too.

I sent another text to Zane: *Look, we need to do something. I can draft a statement this evening.*

Zane: *No need. Bradley's campaign manager showed up an hour ago. He's going through some ideas with my brother, and when they have the script ready, they'll let us know.* He added an eyeroll emoji at the end, which was exactly how I felt, too.

For a fleeting second, I wished Ben was here. The Ben I was getting to know before this disaster. I wished he'd been honest with me and we'd been able to talk about this, to fix this together. I was so upset that my little bubble had been popped. All because of a couple reckless nights and an asshole photographer.

I knew I shouldn't, but I sent: *Have you seen Ben? I hope he's okay . . .*

Zane replied: *You mean Mr. Carlisle himself? He can kiss all of our asses.*

So I replied: *I was just wondering. You don't have to be best friends with him, but I never wanted it to end up like this.*

I felt the sarcasm in his reply: *He's a rebound, Izzy. He'll be fine.*

I chose to ignore his words. Ben didn't feel like a rebound. Our connection was stronger than what I'd had with Zane for years. I wondered what Zane would say if I called Caleb a rebound, but I held my tongue.

Stuffing my phone in my purse without replying was the only thing I could do. Zane and I would air our grievances later. For now, I had to get to work.

I turned off the TV and poured coffee into my

favorite tumbler before grabbing my purse. Hoping the paparazzi camped outside would let me out without a struggle, I snatched my big floppy hat and went out the front door, ready to deal with the jerks out front as I walked confidently to my detached garage. I wasn't going to let them see me shake.

As inhumane as paparazzi are, they were surprisingly quiet. They even moved out of the way as I backed my Bentley out into the street. The lenses pointed at me, however, made me wonder just who had tipped them off that I'd be home. It's not like I was a fashionista or an influencer with a huge social media following. I was just a lady who owned a company. A very successful company, sure. But I wasn't anyone special.

I headed to the office, which was only a twenty-minute drive, thank goodness. And it didn't look like anyone was following me.

Three minutes in, my phone rang.

It was my father.

I knew if I avoided him, he would make it worse, so I hit the button on my display, answering the call. "Hello," I said, not sure how to greet him.

"Are you trying to give me a heart attack?" He sounded angry. In that quiet way that most people missed. But I knew him too well.

"My day is going just fine. Thanks for asking. I hope you and Mom are well."

"Cut it out, Lizette. What were you thinking?"

I paused, focusing on the traffic in front of me. "I'm headed to the office right now to work on negotiations to buy The Azure. In case you were wondering."

"So you opened your legs for the son of James Carlisle and now he's helping you get the property we always wanted? I should have thought of that a decade ago."

Pompous ass.

"It wasn't like that." My voice cracked. He had hit a nerve, which was his specialty.

"Oh please. I know you better than that. Everything you do is for the sake of our company." This hurt even more. It was true.

But I didn't do it just for me like he always had. I wanted everyone at my company to be successful. This was my corporation, not his anymore. "I have a heart, Dad."

He laughed. "You and I are the same person, my dear. Now do me a favor and call the number I'm about to send you. We need to get a statement to the press immediately."

"You know what? No," I said, shocked at the determination in my voice.

"What did you just say?" His voice was like ice. I'd never said no to him before.

"This is my company. You trusted me enough to let me take it over, so you need to trust me now."

He growled into the phone. "What has gotten into you, girl?"

"I'm a grown woman, father." I took a few breaths while I waited at a stop sign. "Now if you'll excuse me, I'm about to go meet with the board to review our bid for The Azure. You know, the one property you weren't able to get your hands on in the decades that you tried." I tapped the screen, hanging up before he could say another word.

Once I pulled into my parking space, I wondered if I'd burned one bridge I might need after this meeting was over, but it was too late now.

I went inside and started working with my team. Camilla joined us right on time, helping us write a proposal that it would be stupid for The Azure to reject.

Several hours later, we'd sent everything to the sellers, crossing our fingers they'd agree to finalize negotiations at The Pacifica like we'd offered. If our plan worked, they'd be more willing to let us take over their property after seeing how great The Pacifica was doing.

As we waited for the reply, it hit me. I'd had fun doing this. Writing this bid, coming up with this business plan, brought me joy. Yes, I'd spent so much of my life giving so much of myself to this company, but at the end of the day, working on a project I'd wanted for so long was exhilarating.

I was married to my job. But maybe I just needed a break every so often, not a full separation.

Fifteen minutes later, my email inbox dinged with a response.

That's all it took to get a reply.

They agreed to meet at The Pacifica, but "Wanted to keep negotiations fully open," whatever the fuck that meant.

This business ordeal was something I could easily handle. I'd get my hands on The Azure and head back to Michigan. I was a real estate goddess, and maybe one day I could have it all.

"You kicked ass today," Camilla said as we walked to our cars in the parking lot.

"All in a day's work." I wasn't sure I was ready to talk about my personal stuff yet, but I wanted her to know how grateful I was. "Thanks for coming. I hate to ask for help, but—"

"But I'm the best at what I do," she said, smiling. "I know you're going through some shit, and we can go talk about it if you want, but I want you to know I've got your back no matter what."

Staring up at the sky, I mulled over my words. "I want to talk. I really do. But I'm exhausted."

She held her arms out, hugging me. "Jet lag's a bitch, I get it." She pulled away, holding my arms. "Tomorrow? We'll get together with Blake and get it all out, yeah?"

"I would like that," I told her.

After leaving the office, I went straight home, only finding a handful of photographers at the edge of my property, and ordered takeout from my favorite Chinese place down the road.

Did I turn on the TV and absorb whatever the media had dug up about me and my family?

Yes.

Did I lie on the couch and scroll through social media to the same effect?

Also yes. Like some masochistic idiot.

I even texted Zane, asking if we were allowed to speak to the media yet. He only sent two stupid words: *Not yet.*

Mentally, I gave him another twelve hours, then I'd walk right up to whatever photographer was closest to me and tell them . . . well, I'd figure that out later.

When my brain had turned to mush, I went upstairs, drew a bath, and grabbed a paperback I'd been wanting to read for months. It started out fine, but the further I got into the romcom in my hands, the more I missed Ben.

Even if he was James.

Even if I had been raised to think he was the son of the devil himself.

He was the first man that had ever made me feel seen. That had ever made me feel wanted.

And it was over.

I lost track of the words on the page as I wondered what he was doing. If he even missed me at all. Maybe it was his thing, making women on vacation feel like they'd fallen in love with him. Maybe I'd been a big catch he'd been trying to get.

I shut the book and smelled the spine. Nope, I was not in love with a man I'd barely even met.

Lust, maybe. Deep affection, yes.

I tossed the book onto the little table next to my tub and dunked my head under the water. There were eight billion people on earth. Surely there would be another one that was meant for me. One that would give me the butterflies just by looking at me.

Who would be okay with me not wanting to dance at the bar, even if it was his favorite song playing on the juke box.

Even if I'd regretted not dancing with him later on.

I came out of the water, inhaling deeply. A voice of protest inside me said I didn't want some random stranger. I wanted the man who had taken my breath away as he stood on the top of his ladder. I wanted the man with stubble I could scratch my nails through and bright blue eyes that looked like the clear lake he lived next to.

But that dream couldn't come true. Especially if I wanted to buy this property. It was a conflict of interest. I could either have Ben or The Azure. And since I'd told my father what my endgame was before telling him off, I knew I'd already chosen the property.

I got out of the tub, dried off, and wrapped my hair in a towel. As I applied my night cream and moisturizer, thankful that I was back home for my cosmetics alone, I couldn't help but dwell on how free I'd felt back in Michigan.

I plugged my phone in, laying it on my nightstand, and crawled into bed, slipping on my sleep mask. The bed felt emptier than it ever had before, and when I grabbed the spare pillow, pulling it close, I was disappointed that it didn't smell like the forest.

Chapter Twenty-Three

The next morning, all I wanted was to get this deal over with. As much as I loved what I did for a living, I wanted to be somewhere far away from sunny California.

I'd slept fitfully, dreaming of swimming in a pool, surrounded by faceless people. The pool became too crowded, and I didn't have any space to tread water. When I couldn't swim anymore, my head went under and I woke up, gasping for air.

I'd gotten dressed in my favorite Chanel suit, but it felt more like a Halloween costume than an outfit I'd worn to the office several times.

When I went downstairs to make my coffee, I turned on the TV, even though I knew I shouldn't.

The damn morning show hosts had taken a picture of me and one of Ben and merged them together to see what our possible baby would look like.

They'd used a picture of Ben with a shaved face which gave our imaginary baby really adorable cheeks, but it was still wrong.

Even though the whole stupid thing made me miss him more. Our lives were so different. But that didn't mean there wasn't some way to work it out.

Maybe I'd buy the news station and shut it down, just to spite them.

It was surprising to me, however, how quickly the two of us had become so internationally famous. For having spent our whole lives trying to stay out of the public spotlight, this was one hell of a way to be thrown into the country's zeitgeist. It was also slightly depressing how soon they'd moved on from trashing Bradley's campaign, instead focusing all of their energy on my sex life.

So much for the fixers Zane and his dad had called so far. My bet was that someone was actively working against us, paying their own people to blast my face to the world. For what reason, I wasn't sure of yet.

There were pictures of me and Ben from our high school yearbooks, from family vacations all over the world, and even one of him very young that looked familiar somehow. Probably from that stupid baby mashup picture. I would never tell a soul that I'd snapped a picture of it with my phone just in case I ever used the eggs I froze ten years ago and wanted to compare my real baby to this imaginary one.

I might as well get to keep something for myself from this disaster.

After slipping past the photographers still camped outside my house, I drove to The Pacifica, where Blake had assured me the meeting room was set up for the negotiation. I was so glad I had her to lean on.

Whatever happened next was what the universe

wanted for me, which made it even harder for me to get Ben out of my head.

Because of what the newscasters had said about the two of us. Not because I'd missed him. Or because I'd regretted not staying to hear his side of the story.

We had about an hour before the team from The Azure arrived, so I went looking for Blake.

Lucky for me, she was standing on the far side of the lobby, helping an elderly woman read a map of the resort.

When she was free, she looked up at me. "Lizette, hi. Everything the way you wanted it?"

Bless her for knowing that my first thought would be making sure the team was ready. "I'm sure it's perfect, as always. Thank you." I knew I could trust Blake with anything.

A screech echoed across the foyer, and I spun around. Camilla threw her hands up in the air. "My best friends, together again!" she yelled.

"Camilla, we are at work. And I saw you yesterday." My tone was lower than I'd anticipated. I really was nervous.

"Yes, but yesterday you were all stuffy and focused on numbers," she said with a giggle.

"And today I'm trying to buy the resort next door for millions of dollars." My palms were sweatier than they'd been in a long time.

Camilla pulled me into a bone-crushing hug. "Please, it's already in the bag." Needing no invitation, she walked around the concierge desk and through the door marked 'staff only.' "Come on, ladies, we have to catch up," she ordered as she motioned for me and Blake to follow her.

Blake checked her watch as she entered the hall. "Let's go talk in my office."

I followed, wondering if I should be spending this time double-checking numbers or ensuring the flowers in the hallways were fresh, but I needed to let some things go. Loosen up on the micromanaging.

I sank into the barrel-shaped chair as Blake sat behind her desk and Camilla took the seat next to me. Before they could speak, I felt my bottom lip vibrate, as my eyes went glossy. I thought I had myself under control, but now that we were alone, the dam was breaking.

"Honey. It's okay." Camilla's voice was calming, like she was talking to a small child.

I took a few deep breaths, trying to stop myself from ugly crying. After a few moments, Blake asked, "You alright?" She sounded frightened. Which was understandable for somewhat of a newer friend watching me melt down.

I grabbed a handful of tissues from the box on her desk, blowing my nose. Their faces would have been comical if I wasn't living through the worst event of my life.

The concerned eyes and pursed lips made me wonder if that's what I'd looked like when they'd cried in front of me before. I would much rather be on their end than mine. "I can't believe this is happening," I mumbled.

Blake cracked a smile. "At least he's cute as hell."

The two of them looked at each other and grinned. Just bright joy coming off both of their faces. It worried me to death. "Why are you not freaking out? You said you saw the news."

Cami spoke first. "Well, we love you and we know the real truth."

And then Blake added, "And you've needed this for like, I don't know, forever?"

I felt a little defensive. "What are you saying?"

They both laughed and Camilla said, "Someone to dust off the cobwebs."

I gasped, remembering Ruby saying something similar before this mess was something I'd ever thought I'd find myself at the center of.

"But what am I going to do? What about Bradley's campaign?"

Camilla's face went serious. "You're going to hire a fixer. They'll spin the story and everything will be right in the world again."

Blake's forehead scrunched up. "Wait, those exist? Like Olivia Pope from Scandal?"

Camilla turned to her, a roll in her shoulder. "Of course they do! Were you not curious when you googled that perfect boyfriend of yours and found nothing but positive things?"

Her eyes sparkled when she thought of Sal. It was a little weird that Blake was living with Camilla's brother, but they made it work somehow. "It's because he's perfect," she said wistfully, like a woman newly in love.

Camilla cackled. "No, ding-dong, it's because our parents had things cleaned up when he fucked around and found out." Then she looked at me again. "Do you need a phone number? I've got a guy that does great work."

A smile tugged at my lips. "Zane's family is already on

it, but I think their guy is an idiot. I'd love to get ahold of whoever cleaned up Sal's bullshit."

She picked up her phone, tapping a few things before looking back at me. "Okay, so here's the big question we're both wondering." She glanced at Blake for a second before putting her hands on my knees. "Why are you here and not underneath that fox of a man in the middle of the forest?"

I sighed. "Because The Azure is a big deal."

"And you have the best team in the business. You could have stayed," Blake admitted.

Then the truth finally clicked. It should have been obvious, but I was just figuring it out for myself. "Because I like chasing the deal." It wasn't because of my father. It wasn't because of anyone but *me*. What I loved doing. This was my passion, and I had the right to pursue it without shame. The joy that filled me when I made a business deal come to fruition was worth all the hours. All the hard work I put into it. It was part of my identity, and I was proud of it.

Both of my friends smiled brightly again. "There's our girl," Cami said. Zero judgment. Zero pressure. Just understanding.

Then she tacked on, "Why are we talking about work? We need to know more about James." She leaned back, tucking her hands into her lap. "Please."

I let out a sigh, not sure where to start.

"His name is Ben. I don't know him as James, anyway." I closed my eyes for a few seconds before spilling my frustration. "It's terrible. Never in a million years would I have guessed he was a Carlisle. And now the news is just blasting it everywhere. I'm such a fool."

"Those motherfuuuuckers." Blake stretched the word dramatically, which made me feel a little better. For a minute, I'd worried I was overreacting.

"And to make it worse, he didn't even tell me who he was. I had to find out from my brother," I added, feeling the heartbreak all over again. "And he owns the resort we were staying at."

"So he really is just the boy version of you." Blake said.

Cami patted the arm of my chair. "Tell us what makes him perfect until we have to leave for the meeting. Is he really that hot in person?"

Heat pooled in my face. I wasn't sure I wanted to share anything with these ladies while we were sober. "Well, he's really kind. And we're a lot like each other, obviously." And as much as I tried telling myself that he was just a fling while I was on this trip, I found myself thinking just how much I really, really liked him. That if our circumstances were different, we could be together.

Blake stuck out her tongue. "That's not what we care about."

"Yeah, how big is his dick?" Cami asked. Blake cackled with laughter.

I rubbed my face. "Why did I even tell you anything?"

"Because of our ability to give undying love and support when you need it most?" Blake answered, not missing a beat. "And also, we can't talk about my boyfriend like this, so we need to talk about yours."

"You gonna answer the question or what?" Cami asked.

Did Blake just call Ben my boyfriend? I had to admit; it sounded nice. Even though it wasn't true. Especially since I knew who he really was now.

"You have to tell us one thing." Cami asked, her tone serious. "Even with this drama, was it worth it?"

I chewed on my cheek for a second. "I'm not sure. Had he told me who he was in the first place, it would be so different right now." I thought about it. "And now that I'm home, I don't think it would work. We're at different places right now." Literally and figuratively.

Blake tapped her finger against her chin for a few seconds. "It's so weird to me. He meets you, Lizette Mother-Fucking Howell-Xu, and then hides his identity. Sounds sketchy." She paused, looking up at the ceiling for a second. "Do you think he was intimidated?"

I started to answer, but stopped. "I don't know. He mentioned right there at the end that he knew who I really was the whole time. So what if he was using me?"

"Wait." Camilla put her hand on my arm. "Go back for a second." I should have known the lawyer would hang on every little detail.

I thought about how to explain the interaction better. "Right before I left for the airport, he said, 'It's not what you think,' after I confronted him."

She waved her hand. "No, dummy. You said Ben knew who you were the whole time. Why wouldn't he know?"

Blake looked a Cami, concern painted across her face as she whispered, "Did you just call her a dummy?"

I opened my mouth to speak, but no noise came out.

"Oh, my God, Lizette, did you lie about your identity?" Blake had the audacity to look excited.

"It wasn't like that. Zane's sister told everyone I was in real estate and I just went with it." As soon as I'd said it, I realized I'd been a total hypocrite.

I thought back to our hike when Ben called me Lizette. Had he been giving me the opportunity to come clean, and I totally missed it? "Dammit." Covering my face with my hands, I inhaled deeply. "I wish I'd had more time." I looked back at my best friends, who were just sitting there, smiling like a couple of assholes.

"Maybe his reasons were similar to yours." Camilla said, a little hope in her voice.

I slammed my fists down on my chair. "Fuck all of this. I hate it." I didn't like feeling out of control. "Why can't things be smooth? Easy?"

Cami looked at Blake. "Aww, our girl is figuring out how hard it is to be open and vulnerable."

"It's adorable, really," Blake responded.

There was a knock at the door, and we all turned, looking at the intruder. It was Aniyah, a clipboard in one hand and a walkie-talkie in the other. "Sorry to interrupt, Lizette. But they're here. We should get settled if you want to be there when I walk them in."

I thanked her, adding, "I'll head that way in just a minute."

"I should get back to work, anyway." Blake stood up, holding the door for us.

I followed Camilla, but stopped when I heard a

familiar voice coming from the front desk. Like a moth to a flame, I traveled toward him.

At first I thought I'd imagined it, but as he stepped away from the counter and checked his watch, I knew exactly who'd just strolled into my resort. My mouth became impossibly dry.

"Why is he here?" I whispered to myself. This wasn't the plan. He was supposed to be in Michigan grooming horses and setting up bonfires. Not here, in my resort, about to take The Azure away from me.

He'd shaved his face and gotten a haircut, but standing there in his navy suit, I'd known his body just as well as I knew my own. My heart was torn. I wanted to go to him, to make him tell me everything. To burrow into his chest while he wrapped his strong arms around me.

But I also knew he was here to negotiate for the property I'd spent my whole adult life preparing to buy. He was the enemy.

Thankfully, he hadn't seen me yet, but Camilla had to give a low whistle and finished it with, "Damn, he's even cuter in person."

His eyes met mine then, and a lightning bolt shot through me. "Izzy," he said, breathlessly.

"James." I wasn't sure why I'd called him that, but I felt both pride and sadness when he winced.

"I know there's no time to talk." He reached into his pocket like he'd done the other day, but this time, he had something in his palm. "But I need you to have this before we meet with the negotiation team." He laid whatever it was on the counter, and I left my friends in the doorway to go up to the concierge desk, looking at what lay between us.

As soon as I recognized it, I gasped.

It was my bracelet. From when I was twelve years old.

My eyes darted to his as the puzzle pieces slipped into place.

Ben had been the boy. From the coatroom.

I scooped the bracelet into my hand, taking a closer look. It had aged since I'd seen it last, but I would have recognized it anywhere. Some of the beads were missing paint, and the little dangling flowers were chipped, like it had been carried around for years.

Like he'd carried *me* around for years.

This was why his pictures on the news looked so familiar. I'd met him that night at the gala. When I'd been hiding from the world.

He'd been hiding, too.

Feeling a little dizzy, I slipped the bracelet on my wrist. It was a little tight but still fit.

"How?" I whispered, looking up toward him. But he was gone.

Aniyah's voice called out from behind me. "Lizette. We really have to get going."

There were too many emotions flooding through me. I wanted to see him. I'd missed him even more than I thought. And I needed to know why he'd held onto this treasure for all these years.

Tears strained at my eyes, begging to be released.

But I was at work. I was a representative of my entire corporation, and couldn't look weak. Not now, when so much was on the line.

This was the worst possible moment he could have dropped this bomb on me. It was going to be difficult to compartmentalize during our meeting.

Mindlessly, I made it to the conference room. When I pushed the door open, I remembered the first time I'd been here. I'd been so horrible to my now sister-in-law because I was going through such a miserable time in my life. All I felt was regret. I'd been rude to her, and I'd let my team be terrible, too.

How she and my brother were able to forgive me, I'll never know. But I was glad they had.

As I scanned the faces of the people already sitting down, I remembered to give myself grace, as the therapist had encouraged me to do while Zane and I were at rock bottom.

I sat next to Aniyah. She slipped a folder in front of me, like she always did at the beginning of negotiations. It took me a bit to get back into work mode, to clear my mind and focus on the numbers ahead of us. Which wasn't like me at all.

All I could feel was the bracelet squeezing against my wrist.

After a few minutes of uncomfortable silence, the representative of The Azure walked in, along with Ben and a woman I didn't recognize. She was whispering in his ear, and he looked like he was trying to lean down and listen while also walking into the room confidently. I fidgeted with the beads of my bracelet, itching to ask him about it right here at the negotiation table.

I had to admit, he filled out a suit nicely. It wasn't as attractive as his soft jeans, but there was something about seeing him so . . . professional, that just did it for me.

"Thank you for meeting with me today," the woman from The Azure said, commanding the room the way I usually did. Except today I didn't want to be here. I twisted the little flower bead between my fingers, wondering if I even wanted this resort.

What was the purpose of all this? Why was I here when I could be lying at the beach, watching the family that cared for me play on Jet-Skis or paddle boats?

Apparently, I'd zoned out during introductions, as everyone was staring at me. I sat up straighter. "I'm Lizette Howell, representing The Howell Group."

Aniyah leaned in, whispering as Camilla introduced herself as our lawyer. "The rep from The Azure is Judith. Then there's James Carlisle and Angela Jones from The Carlisle Corporation."

"I'm sorry," I cut in, looking at Judith. "I thought you were here to negotiate with us. Why is The Carlisle Corporation here?"

She looked confused for a split second. "Oh, I thought we'd all agreed that an open negotiation was best for our property. Our goal is to be as transparent as possible with the sale of The Azure."

I nodded, not loving this situation, but without the ability to control anything in my personal life, I figured I might as well let my professional life spiral in front of me, too.

Aniyah took the lead, sliding a folder to Judith, telling her what we were offering. I sat, looking down at my fingernails. The chip had been fixed, but it felt like it was still there. The crack was on the inside, traveling through my whole body.

As Angela passed their folder forward, Ben put his hand over it, stopping her. He looked at Judith. "Wait."

Time stopped as everyone turned to him. He dragged the folder to the space in front of him, and I wondered what was happening. His eyes met mine, and it felt exactly as it had when he was on top of me. Inside of me.

I had to force myself to breathe. The chemistry between us was undeniable. I couldn't lie to myself about my feelings any longer, but I also couldn't be with someone who was working against me, who didn't support me.

He cleared his throat, still covering the folder. "We're willing to offer a dollar less than The Howell Group."

Judith's brows scrunched together. "Do you mean a dollar more?"

He looked at me and everyone else in the room disappeared. "No. I meant what I said. We don't want it." He shoved the folder to the middle of the table, discarding it.

My heart stopped. He was a Carlisle. He was supposed to steal this property out from under me. Bowing out from this negotiation went against every action our families had taken for decades.

I leaned forward in my seat, jamming my finger against their folder. "Absolutely not. We want to bid a dollar less than they do." My eyes stayed locked with Ben's. "We don't want it, either."

Aniyah jumped in, surprised. "Wait, we don't?"

I turned to her, wondering if the shock on her face

was mirrored in my own. "I don't know if we do. I have to think about it."

Judith scooped up the folders from both companies and tapped them against the table, aligning them in her hands. "Well, this was a massive waste of my time. Reach out to me when either of you are actually willing to negotiate." She was up and out of the room quickly, leaving us in her wake.

"Well, that was awkward," Camilla said to the table. "Thanks for inviting me." She was the only person in the room with a smile on her face. She stood, reaching her hand out to Ben. "I'm her best friend, by the way, and I'm wildly prepared to crush your balls if you hurt her."

"Nice to meet you, too," he said, warily shaking her hand.

She spun on her heel, turning toward me. "I'm going to go to my real job, since we're obviously done here, but you need to call me later. There are things," she glanced quickly at Ben, "we need to discuss." She waved at the rest of the room and left.

Shortly thereafter, Aniyah asked Angela if she wanted any coffee and the two of them left the room like Ben and I had the plague.

So there we sat. Complete silence and the entire world between the two of us.

Chapter Twenty-Four

We sat, staring at each other from across the table for a few moments.

"I hate your haircut," I finally said.

He laughed quietly. "Thanks. I hate it, too."

"And your face," I said, my bottom lip quivering. I knew he caught the lie in my wavering voice. "Your beard's gone." I forced my lungs to take in air. "You look like a different person."

He propped his elbows on the table, leaning forward. "I'm not, though. It's still just me." His tone was somber.

"Why are you here?" I asked, not sure if I wanted to know the answer.

"My father refused to call his fixer unless I agreed to come here and . . ." He paused, like he was remembering what had been said. "Clean up my mess." When I didn't say anything, he said, "The pictures. They weren't from me. I still don't know who hired them, but I'm going to find out."

I blinked slowly, somehow knowing he was being

completely honest. "There's so much more than that going on between us."

He blew out a breath. "I'm sorry I kept the truth from you. I didn't mean to hurt you or hide anything. But you didn't exactly tell me who you were, either."

He'd known. And had the balls to call me out. I'd give him kudos for it if I wasn't filled with shame. "At the time, I didn't think it was important. I never would have guessed you'd be a Carlisle."

"I know. And I didn't think my family history would matter at first. I knew from the moment you walked in that you were in the industry somehow." That threw me back a little. "But not because we work for rival companies. Because I remembered you from when we were teenagers. It wasn't until I spoke with your father-in-law that I learned you were running your family's company."

"So why didn't you tell me you owned the resort when you found out who I was?" I asked, gently touching the bracelet at my wrist.

"It's complicated," he said, rubbing his face, like his beard was still there.

"So un-complicate it." Sitting here in the meeting room gave me more confidence than I felt.

"I fell in love with the resort in Michigan the moment I saw it. But I didn't have access to my inheritance. I won't until I'm 40." He sighed, leaning back in his chair. "At the time, I'd been running our European offices and had just told my father I wanted to leave the company. I'd said I needed to get out, that the work was killing me." He paused, crossing his arms. "He made it very clear that it was unacceptable to take a step back. 'Carlisles don't quit,' he barked at me. So I told him I didn't want to be a Carlisle anymore, that I was going to start using my mother's maiden name, Montgomery." A sad smile crossed his face. "But then he reminded me that I had no money. My house belonged to the company. So did my car. I'd been making a salary, but what I'd had saved was only enough for a down payment on the Lac Brumeux. And knowing how much work the property needed to be up to par, well, I knew the bank would take it before I got to make it my own."

"So you asked him for help?" I asked, more to myself than to him. A tumultuous storm raged in my chest. I wanted him. I wanted him so badly. But now that he was here, close enough to touch, I started to doubt the logistics of it all. The Lac Brumeux was his home. His sanctuary. And mine was here.

He nodded. "I asked him for just enough to get by for the first five years, but he refused to help unless I mortgaged the resort." He looked down at the table. "So technically, the resort belongs to The Carlisle Corporation. Until I can pull money from my trust fund in two years." His eyes met mine. "He's been holding it over my head ever since then. Threatening to sell it out from under me if I don't do little jobs for him every once in a while." He tapped his knuckles against the table. "If I didn't show up here to negotiate against you."

"Which you did a brilliant job at, might I add," I said, smiling despite the ridiculous show we'd given the rest of the team.

"I've been saving as much as possible, hoping to pay

the mortgage off before my trust is available. I want to be just Ben Montgomery." He reached for a pen that had gone untouched during our meeting. Laying it on the table, he rolled it back and forth. I understood exactly how he felt. I also wanted to be just myself more than ever. Not anyone's legacy.

"So you didn't tell anyone you were a Carlisle, so you could do it on your own?" When he nodded again, I added, "No wonder your father and mine hate each other. They're the same brand of asshole."

"So many people in this industry are. They are unfeeling and rigid, and I just didn't want to be like that. I felt myself turning into him, and I couldn't do it." He spoke to the pen more than to me. Cold flashed through my body. I was the unfeeling and rigid person who'd run my corporation to financial greatness. I was the person in the industry he hated.

It took me a few seconds to realize he was tinkering with the pen because the table wasn't level, which made me think of his desk back in Michigan. He really was meant to work with his hands. Not to be trapped in a boardroom. I wondered if he was even aware of what he was doing.

"The first year, he made me come to a few meetings, to remind me of his power, I think. But since then it's been pretty quiet, just a random virtual check-in with board members every few months. And then the worst thing happened." He looked up at me, his eyes earnest. "I fell in love with the resort. I love every single day up there. Waking up every morning excited for the adventure and the challenges makes me so happy."

I knew how he felt. The entire time Blake and I worked on the renovation plans for The Pacifica was so fulfilling, in a challenging kind of way. Even the last two days building a bid for a new company. Making something mine brought me the most joy.

He spoke again, bringing me out of my head. "But then the pictures were leaked, and I knew I couldn't hide in the woods anymore. He called me, raging that I'd been with you—a Howell, of all people. He accused me of doing this to him on purpose to stop him from getting his hands on the property next to yours, like he had some master plan to take your company down with it."

My heart rate sped up, his words echoing my worst nightmare. "Would you let him do that?"

"Never." He tugged at the lapel of his blazer. "This isn't me, Izzy. I don't give a shit about negotiations. I don't want to do this. I want to live in the woods and ride horses and take walks with the woman I could see myself falling in love with." He ran his fingers through his hair and let out a growl, unable to grab any of it now that it was neatly trimmed. "I want a life. I want to be free."

I folded my arms, fighting the urge to stand and go to him. Especially at his admission. It sounded like a dream. But was it sustainable?

I played with the dangling flower on my wrist again, not sure what to say.

"I didn't want it to be like this." He broke the silence quietly.

I pulled the bracelet off, laying it on the table between us. "You held on to this all these years?"

He reached for it, but didn't quite touch it. "I was

thirteen years old and had just been told they were sending me to England, where I wouldn't know anyone. I'd heard horror stories of boarding school and knew that my life was over at best, and about to become a living hell at worst. And then they made me go to that stupid party even though I was leaving in two days. I didn't even get to say goodbye to my friends." His eyes met mine as he inhaled, his eyes foggy from the past. "When it got to be too much, I hid in the coat closet. I wanted to melt into the background. To disappear."

His finger grazed the dangling charm as he continued his story. "And then you were there," he said with absolute certainty.

"I'd been hiding that night, too." It came back so clearly in my mind.

He pulled his hand back, folding his arms again. "We were just kids, but I knew you were something special. So I kept the bracelet, thinking I'd find you one day. I even came home one summer and went to every damn event with my father, hoping I'd find you. But you weren't there, so I moved on. You became a ghost."

I picked up the bracelet, rolling the plastic beads between my fingers. "But you still kept it with you?"

"Not exactly." He shook his head, his eyes tracing the ceiling. "I loved Summer. With every single part of me, I loved her. I'd put the bracelet in a drawer before I met her, and I'd mostly forgotten about it." He watched me lay the bracelet on the table again, and it looked like he was itching to pick it up. "But when I asked her to marry me, I had this fear that one day, the girl in the coatroom would show up and I'd have to tell her I let her go." He leaned back in his chair, like he couldn't stay still. "And then . . . after the accident, I packed up everything that was important to me in my suitcase and there it was, in the back of my dresser. I couldn't get rid of it, so I brought it with me."

He'd held on to this tiny piece of me for half of our lives. He'd held out hope for me. For us. For a relationship that never got a chance.

I wondered how different my life would have been if it had been him I met in college instead of Zane. But the truth rang true in my heart. I would have devoted my time to my work. I would have let him down. He would have left me, too.

He took a deep breath, and I knew he wasn't done speaking. After a moment, he went on, "And then you walked out of that room with your hair all messy and those damn legs and you took my breath away. I even asked Cate to find your name on the reservation, but only Zane was on it."

"So you didn't know who I really was when I came out of that bedroom?" My words were apprehensive.

"Not until later, no." He'd laid it all on the table, and I knew he was telling the truth. That he hadn't done anything to purposely hurt me.

He hadn't known I was his adversary. I was just the coatroom girl all grown up. And I'd lied to him about who I was. If anyone should be mad, it was him.

This was all so heavy. I felt honored, even a little excited that he remembered that night from so many years ago, but there was no way I could live up to what he'd imagined since then. There was no way our current lives would fit together.

The woman he wanted didn't exist. I was a workaholic without a romantic bone in my body.

Could his passionate heart be enough for both of us?

Probably not.

"Why didn't you say anything when you learned who my father was? That I'm the daughter of your family's largest competitor?" I almost didn't want the truth. I knew myself. I knew that I was incapable of healthy relationships. His answer wouldn't matter in the long run, anyway.

He ran his thumb along the edge of the table. "I was afraid if you found out who I really was, you'd hate me."

I laughed, knowing he was right. But in the few moments I had to think about the two of us—what it would really look like to be a couple—I drew a blank. "We can't possibly be together. It won't work." Saying it out loud felt like shoving a knife in my own chest. But I knew it had to be like this. Regardless of how much I wanted him, or how long he'd been pining for me, our lives were too different. *We* were too different.

He stared at the small piece of jewelry, his eyes dull, before looking up at me. "Yes, we can. I want this. More than I've ever wanted anything."

The distance between us grew larger with every beat of my heart. "We live in two different worlds, Ben. Maybe if we were still those kids, hiding in the coatroom, we'd have a chance." I motioned around the room. "But I have an empire to run, and you . . ." I bit my cheek to keep from crying. "You have a whole existence that I don't fit into."

"Lizette, please." His breath hitched. "You don't even want to try?"

I pushed the bracelet toward him, standing up. I wanted to try more than anything in the world. But I knew I would fail. And failure was not something I could handle again. "Here's what would happen. We'd make it work long distance for a few months. Maybe see each other on weekends and holidays. You'd hate being in California, and I'd be too busy to move to Michigan. It would be miserable for us both." His eyes were turning red, like I'd hit him right where it hurt the most. Lord knew I felt the acute pain between my own ribs. "I'd like to have children one day. Would we raise them separately?"

"We can figure all that out. We have time." His pleading almost broke me.

"No, we don't." I stepped back, pushing in my chair. "You know I'm not good at relationships, anyway. You'd begin resenting me and I'd just pour myself harder into work to avoid talking about it. We'd end up alone. Again."

I had to do this. I had to break his heart along with my own. I'd started to feel those first sparks of love with him, too, and I couldn't let that vulnerability—that risk of losing him years down the road—win. This was for the best.

He started to speak, but I held up my hand. "We have to let each other go."

I walked out of the room, terrified to look behind me,

to see if he'd followed. Counting my breaths so I wouldn't break down, I somehow made it down the hallway. Blake stood ten feet away, wringing her hands together nervously. "Need a hug?" I nodded, but kept walking.

I made it to her office, opened the door, and dropped into the chair facing her desk. As soon as the door closed and locked behind her, I let it out.

I covered my face with my hands, crying into them, losing all control. She rubbed my back, making soothing noises, and even reached over, handing me the box of tissues. But she let me cry, and I loved her for it. It was a small kindness, and I was glad that she knew exactly what I needed.

After a few minutes, I calmed down, and the sobs turned into a whimper. Blake finally sat in the other barrel-chair, turning it toward me. "I'm not gonna lie. You're the most formidable woman in my life, but seeing you cry is downright terrifying."

I laughed at that, as I'm sure she had wanted, but she just sat there, waiting for me to speak.

"I'm such a fucking idiot," I admitted.

"What happened in there?" Her voice was calm and collected, even though I was falling apart.

"He tried to let me buy The Azure. Without a fight."

"Wait, isn't that what you wanted?"

"No." I paused, blowing my nose into a clean tissue. "I mean, yes, it was. But not anymore."

"Since when?" She sounded like she didn't believe a word I'd said.

I pursed my lips together. "Since he sat down at the table in the conference room." I inhaled through my mouth, wiping my face with another tissue. "I saw him there, miserable, with his terrible hair and that ridiculous suit and he looked so much like . . ." I blew my nose again, unable to stop. "He looked so much like me. In my overpriced outfits that shield my real self. Perfectly curated for the office."

Wiping my eyes one more time, I looked up at her. "But it wouldn't work. My life is here, in California. And he's in love with Michigan." Tears pooled in my eyes again, so I forced myself to count to ten.

"I'm pretty sure he's in love with you," she said, pulling another tissue out of the box and waving it at me.

I grabbed it, sniffling pathetically. "No. He's in love with some memory from a hundred years ago."

"Why can't you have both?" She scooted her chair closer to me. "Couldn't you work remotely part of the year?" I started to argue, but she stopped me. "Seriously. Did you not offer to finance my wildest dream recently without hesitation? Wouldn't you want the same for yourself?"

"But I have to keep it all running. Everyone's depending on me."

"Are they, though?" She leaned back, looking skeptical.

"What would happen to the corporation if I took a step back?"

She smiled, tucking her legs under herself like we were just casually hanging out in here and I wasn't having the biggest crisis of my life. "People would continue living. They'd figure it out. Someone might even fill the vacuum."

I attempted a smile. Maybe if I faked it, I would feel it. "I want to believe you."

"Go home. Sleep on it. Tomorrow will bring some clarity." She really sounded like she knew what she was talking about. I felt guilty for not letting her know about all of my problems much, much earlier.

There was a knock on the door. Aniyah called out, "It's me. Can I come in?"

Blake got up, unlocked the door, and let her in. She closed it as soon as Aniyah was inside, protecting my privacy.

She held the clipboard she always had, but had something cupped in her palm. "This was on the table when you left. I was going to throw it away, but it looks really old." I held out my hand, and she dropped the bracelet into it. Clutching it to my heart, I started crying all over again.

"Holy shit," she whispered, looking at Blake with panic in her eyes. "Is she okay?"

Blake opened the door, rushing her out. "She will be. I promise."

When it was locked behind her again, she turned to me. "You're going to be fine. It doesn't feel like it right now. But after you have a bath and maybe a nap, you're going to feel better."

I had a feeling she was full of shit, but I was determined to do what she said. She was way better at this relationship stuff than I was. I slipped the bracelet on my wrist and inhaled deeply. "I hate everything."

"I know, love. I've been there, too."

Chapter Twenty-Five

I woke up the next morning groggy as hell. I'd come home, soaked in the tub like Blake advised me to, and gone to bed.

Well, after watching half an hour of the entertainment channel, which had pictures of both Ben and I walking into The Pacifica yesterday along with all kinds of comments about how we'd arrived and left separately. They'd even zoomed in on his face to discuss whether or not I'd crushed his soul while he'd been in there.

No one zoomed on my face or worried about my emotions. Not that I was complaining.

Where the hell was Bradley with his statement? The news kept reporting that neither of our camps had said anything other than "No comment." If we were being smart, we could twist this any way we wanted. I sent a text to Zane telling him we needed to call the media, with or without his brother, but all he sent was: *I'm trying. Give me a few hours.*

After waiting a bit, I sent an email to the contact Camilla'd sent me. I didn't want to divulge too much without knowing them, but I was becoming desperate to solve this problem.

So here I stood in front of my coffee machine, dressed in my robe and house slippers, begging for it to hurry up. It was still dripping when the doorbell rang.

Without thinking, I went straight to the door, swinging it open. Seeing the single paparazzi standing at the end of my walkway made me groan, but the delivery man had a bright smile as he handed me his electronic pad. "Sign here, please."

I looked down, wondering what I'd ordered, and saw my missing suitcase. "Oh my God, I could kiss you!" I squealed as I signed my name.

I grabbed the handle, dragging it inside, wondering just what the pap would tell his handler about me.

My coffee smelled divine, but I ignored it to look at my luggage. How different would the last week of my life have been if this thing would have stayed with me? Would I have gotten the courage to go out with Ben? Would I have turned down the purchase of the one resort that was supposed to make me happy?

Then it hit me square in the chest. My first thought when I had what I'd been waiting for was what my heart really wanted.

I should be in Michigan. With Ben.

Not being afraid of all the what-ifs that the future held.

I knew I'd been stupid the moment I walked out of that meeting room. I'd told him we couldn't be together, but it was because I was terrified. I was afraid that once he got to know me, he would reject me. Or that he would get sick of me after a while and I'd be alone again.

But I wasn't scared when it came to business, so why would I be like that in a relationship?

Yes, we lived in different worlds. But at the end of the day, we were cut from the same cloth. He'd seen my workaholic ways, and he hadn't judged me for it.

And yes, my marriage with Zane had ended. But was it a failure? My instinct told me no, it was just a situation that helped two people grow into who we were meant to be.

Now that I'd had Ben's whole story and a night to sleep on it, I wondered if we could make it work. If he'd still have me. If I let go of my fear of letting everyone down and just tried, maybe we could have something beautiful.

But first, I needed to fix things. As much as I'd loved seeing him yesterday, I hated that he'd been forced to come. That he'd had to sit at the negotiation table in the first place.

There had to be a way for me to make life better for Ben. Even if our lives couldn't meld, I wanted him to have freedom from his father.

Grabbing my phone, I made my decision. I was the boss of The Howell Group. I could use my connections for more than just myself.

I dialed Zane's number, hoping he was somewhere within cell range.

"Hey, how'd the meeting go?" He asked as soon as he picked up.

"Terrible. The representative for The Azure walked right out of the room." It sounded worse now that I'd said it out loud.

"Jesus. Are you okay?" He sounded more concerned than he had two days ago.

"No," I said, laughing a little at my own honesty. "Anyway, that's not why I called. I need to talk to your dad."

"Izzy, we need to talk. I need to apologize." His voice was full of emotion.

"I know, and we will. But I have to do something first. Please let me talk to your dad." I tried to sound lighthearted, but I was worried my plan had too many moving parts.

He put Andrew on the phone, and I laid out my idea. It was a long shot, but if the Xu International Bank held the mortgage for the Lac Brumeux, I could move some money around and give Ben the freedom from his father that he really wanted. I could use my wealth to untie him from the life he wasn't in love with.

Now I just needed to get back to Michigan and tell him what I'd done.

After rushing up the stairs, I got ready for the day, manifesting my future. I sent a text to Aniyah as I brushed my teeth: *Not going to make it to the office today. I'll catch up with you soon.*

The words I'd said to Ben rang through my ears as I slipped my bracelet on my wrist. Yes, our lives seemed incompatible. But were we really that different?

Maybe we could split our time together. Or work out

a schedule for me to work from home part of the year, like Blake had suggested.

He'd come all the way here and laid it all on the line for me. Why couldn't I do that for him, too?

I started opening drawers after I'd gotten dressed, thinking about what I needed to pack, and then it hit me. I already had a suitcase ready and waiting for me downstairs.

Half an hour later, I was in the car, driving to the airport. I'd booked a commercial flight—I had to fly coach . . . which was a sacrifice in itself—to Michigan. It was going to take me two layovers to get to the Upper Peninsula, but I'd do it. I'd even rented a car to drive to the resort when I got there.

Once I'd checked my suitcase in at the airline, I sent a text to Camilla and Blake—on the only phone I'd brought with me: *Going back to Michigan. I made a huge mistake and have to talk to Ben. I promise I'll call soon.*

I put my phone on airplane mode, and worried for the first time that this might be a terrible decision. I had no proof that Ben was back in Michigan. For all I knew, he'd let his dad take the property I'd just paid off and went back to Europe.

The thought made me want to throw up in one of those paper envelopes in the airplane pocket. But I had to push through. This was the only place I knew where to find him. And I'd wait however long I needed to.

This was the first time I'd ever done something because I wanted to do it, not because I was trying to please my father or show the men in my industry that women really could have it all.

My heart had chosen Ben. If he'd still have me.

I had to try.

I'd thought the flights were going to drain all my energy, since I didn't have my laptop, but I blew through the paperback I'd tried to read the other night, not wanting to put it down when I switched planes for my layovers. It turned out to be hilarious and adorable and all I wanted in a firefighter romance.

I'd made it to the last plane, the small one that would take me to the final airport. Hoping and praying that my luggage was with me, too, I was glad I'd stuffed an extra set of clothes in my purse, just in case. If this went south, it's all I'd need.

And if it worked out, well, I wouldn't be too worried about clothes, either.

After I landed, I found my bag on the carousel. I even waved at the security guard I'd met the first time I was here.

The shuttle bus took me to the rental car pickup, which was an adventure in itself, but soon I was in my own little car with my trusty luggage as my companion.

As I drove down the quiet highway, it hit me. This was what it was like to be an adult. To make decisions for myself. I was thirty-six years old, and for the first time in my life, I was actually living. I wasn't going to let fear of the future guide my decisions like I'd been doing for so long. I was going to have faith that I could be successful in more than just the boardroom.

Turning up the radio, I drove to the resort, hoping that Ben had decided to come home after our meeting. I guessed I could have called the front desk, but I didn't want him to know I was on the way, in case he couldn't forgive me.

After parking in front of the main building, I took a few calming breaths before going inside. I'd left my suitcase in the car, but crossed my fingers that there was still room for me here.

Cate was standing behind the counter, a huge smile on her face. "Lizette, you made it back." She seemed genuinely happy to see me.

A little breathless, I said, "It's nice to see you, too. Is Ben here?"

She looked confused. "I thought he went after you in California?" She covered her mouth in shock. "You didn't come all the way back here without him, did you?"

I wasn't sure what to say. "Maybe?" I whispered.

She grimaced. "I doubt I'm allowed to tell you this, but . . ." she leaned forward, telling me the secret, "He said he was going to stay in Santa Barbara until he won you over."

I sucked in a breath. "No. That's why I came back. I need him here, now."

She waved her hands. "Everyone from your party is still here. You go get settled and I'll call him. I'll let him know you're here." She held her hands together like a prayer. "We'll get him home."

Oh, I was fucked. I'd assumed he'd come back after our meeting. I never would have guessed he'd stay in California waiting for me.

I got back in the car and drove to the little cabin I'd shared with Zane, wondering if the actual man I'd wanted to be with would show up anytime soon.

Chapter Twenty-Six

I typed in the code to unlock the door to the cabin. The place was a mess, clothing tossed everywhere, and the shower was running. It was four in the afternoon, so I assumed Zane had been at the lake or something and was rinsing off.

"I'm back!" I called out, but he must not have heard me. So I opened the bathroom door. "Hey, I'm back for the night, not sure how long—"

My explanation was cut off by a blood-curdling scream. The curtain pulled open slightly, revealing a man that was very much not my ex-husband.

"Fuck, Caleb, I'm so sorry." I wanted to laugh, but he looked so frightened, I thought better of it.

"Thank God it's you, Lizette. I was afraid I was going to have to murder someone in the woods while wearing a shower curtain I'd tied into a toga." The soap on his head made him look more like a cartoon character than a man.

That had me actually laughing so hard that I snorted a little. "That's wildly specific."

He shrugged a shoulder, which was coated in bubbles. "I have very specific fears."

I pointed to the door. "I'm gonna go."

"No, stay." He paused, glancing down at his bottom half, which was thankfully covered by the curtain he had clutched in his hands. "Not like, in here. I'll be out in a minute. But have a seat on the couch, please. I'd like to talk."

I gave him a very awkward thumbs-up and closed the door behind me. This place had turned into a disaster, and I'd only been gone for two and a half days. I started picking up clothes and folding them on the couch, keeping myself busy. Once it was all tidy in here, I sat down on the couch, trying to relax.

Waiting to hang out with my ex-husband's boyfriend while he finished his shower had not been on my bingo card for the day.

Caleb stepped out of the bathroom in sweatpants and a white t-shirt. I thanked my lucky stars that he'd had clothes in there with him. His body was ripped, being a personal trainer, and I didn't need to feel any more self-conscious about being replaced by him than I already did.

"When did you get here?" We both asked in stereo.

We shared a smile, and I continued, "You first."

"He called me right after you left. He was really upset, and I knew I couldn't stay away any longer. So I booked a flight and came straightaway." He sat on the couch next to me. "I'd seen you all over the news and figured what the hell, if they see Zane and I together, it's not gonna make anything worse than it already is."

I agreed with his thoughts, but I wondered if my ex-husband did. "How did Zane feel about that?"

He smiled, those damn dimples on his cheeks making me want to pinch them. It was impossible to ignore how adorable he was. Like a golden retriever. "He was so surprised, he kissed me in front of his dad."

"Wow!" I was really happy for the two of them. Even though I was unsure of my personal relationship, or whatever we could call it, I was happy that Zane had found his person.

"I know!" He said, before turning serious. "How did you make it in here without the news crews following you?"

I looked toward the window, which had the curtain pulled across it. "I didn't see a single reporter."

"Crap. That probably means they're at the big cabin. The resort's been full of them since you left. Reporters jumping out of trees and everything." He stood up, peeking through the curtain. "I wonder if Bradley's giving his statement."

I felt guilty. I hadn't wanted the media to take over this beautiful haven. "Should we go talk to Alice and Andrew?" I wasn't sure if I was ready, but I knew it needed to be done.

"Yeah. Let me find my shoes." He looked around before turning to me again. "Did you come in here and clean?"

"Nervous habit," I said, smiling.

"Maybe we do need you to live with us," he joked.

I put on my floppy hat and sunglasses before we walked down the trail to Zane's parents.

There was a big commotion right outside the big cabin. Reporters covered the porch like a colony of ants. We slipped into the trees to avoid being spotted and headed toward David's cabin instead.

Caleb knocked three times and called out, "Strawberry Cheesecake." I looked at him questioningly and he whispered, "It's our secret password. With all the photographers in the last twenty-four hours, we had to come up with a way to know it was safe."

The door opened, and David waved us in frantically. "Hurry up, it's starting."

Ruby, Hannah, Zane and David were lying on the floor in front of the tv, making them look like kids watching cartoons. The screen showed the news, with a "Breaking News: Bradley Xu Press Conference" ribbon across the bottom.

Bradley's face came into view in front of the big cabin. "It is with great regret and sorrow that I need to suspend my campaign for senator of the great state of California. My family needs me at this time, and I feel that it is best to put my energy elsewhere. I still love our state and all of its people, but as you know, my family is the most important thing in my life."

A journalist pushed forward, a microphone in her hand. "Mr. Xu, there have been critics saying that you hired the investigators to follow your sister-in-law during your family vacation and they in turn sold the photographs to the media. Do you care to comment?"

"I have no comments regarding this, nor will I in the future. Thank you for your time." He nodded his head and turned around, walking back through the front door of the big cabin.

"That was the statement that took two days to write?" I asked the screen, shocked at what my former brother-in-law had said . . . and didn't say.

The screen went back to the newscasters, but Zane exploded. "Oh my God, I know that look on his stupid face!" He stood up, shaking his fists. "It was Bradley, and he's full of shit! He fucking hired those photographers." Filled with rage, he leaped for the door. "I'm going to kill him."

All the muscles in my body went weak. Complete shock filled my every pore. Bradley had done this to us.

The only thing I could do was follow Zane out the door.

He was a man on a mission and didn't stop, even when the reporters recognized him, and then they identified me, even though I had my hat on.

Someone grabbed Zane by the hem of his shirt as he walked by and he spun around, pointing at the reporters. "Shame on you. On all of you!" He yelled. "Lizette and I are private people and are allowed to have private lives." He stepped forward, towering over the cameraman. "If you'd bothered to do your damn research, you'd know that we've been happily divorced for months."

It took him a second, but I think he registered what he'd just told the whole world before grabbing my hand. "And no, we won't be commenting any further, either." He dragged me up the stairs and through the front door of the big cabin where the rest of the family had been hiding.

"Where is he?" His voice bellowed. It was the angriest I'd ever seen him. My shoulders tightened, worried he was going to hit his brother.

Tippy came running toward us, putting her hand on Zane's chest. "He didn't mean it. We promise."

Zane brushed her aside, still holding onto me. We managed to find him in a bedroom in the back of the house, alone. I closed the door behind us, stopping anyone from joining, including Bradley's wife.

It must have been some sort of trauma response—fight or flight taking over my brain—but I felt suspiciously calm in this moment. "Boys, we need to keep this civil," I reminded them before pulling out of Zane's grip and putting my hands on my hips. "But I need to know everything."

Bradley sat on the edge of the bed, cupping his face with his hands. "It was me. I had it planned the whole time." I wasn't sure who gasped louder, me or Zane. He looked up at both of us, guilt-stricken. "I didn't want to be a senator. I don't even think I wanted to be a lawyer. But suddenly I blinked and my life was here." He sat up, clutching his hands together. "Tippy kept pushing me to keep going. And I appreciate her, I do. But we got to a point where I was living her dream, not mine."

He paused, but neither Zane nor I were willing to speak just yet. He finally went on, "Blowing up your scandal was the only way I could suspend the campaign without looking like a loser."

"So that's why none of the fixers were able to do their damn jobs." My voice was quieter than I thought it'd be. I was struggling with the disbelief that someone we trusted would do this to us.

He shook his head. "My team counteracted all of the attempts you made to bury the story."

"You motherfucker." Zane whispered, his body practically vibrating.

"I get it," I said, quietly. Zane looked at me, his mouth wide open. I waved my hands to tell him I wasn't done. "I'm still pissed. There's a lot of people that were hurt by your stupid plan, but I understand. I just blew off the purchase of a resort I'd wanted because I'm not living my life for me, either."

"You did what?" Zane asked, ignoring his brother altogether.

I shrugged at him, frowning. "I'll tell you the whole story later."

"I'm so sorry, you guys. I thought it was going to be a quick scandal. The private investigator didn't discover that it was James Carlisle until we'd already sent the first pictures to the media." I had to admit, he sounded honest, which made me feel for him more than I should have.

"But you had no problem fucking over Lizette and me?" Zane's anger escalated even higher than before.

"You'd shared that you were divorced already. And I made damn sure that nothing about your sexual identity came out."

"Yes, some things are sacred." Zane's sarcasm was palpable.

I cut them both off, knowing this conversation needed to be between the two of them. Privately. The cat was out of the bag and there wasn't a damn thing I could do about it. "Look, I have something I need to handle. Promise you won't kill each other if I leave?"

They both murmured their agreements, and I left the room. I walked through the house, saying hello, promising to tell everyone what happened in California as soon as I was done with a few things, and slipped into the woods, hoping none of the reporters that were packing up their gear saw me.

Back at the main building, I found Cate behind the counter, a welcoming smile on her face, as usual. "Did you hear from him?" I'd blurted out without pretense.

"I left a message on his phone, but he hasn't called me back." Her smile was definitely strained. "He's really good at checking voicemails, so I'm sure he'll book a flight soon." She tapped her fingernails on the countertop nervously.

"I need to book a room," I said, knowing that I was going to stay for however long I needed to make things right with Ben, but I also didn't want to share a tiny cabin with Zane and Caleb.

The cringe on her face terrified me. "Oh, honey, we don't have anything open. With the rest of your family and the reporters in town, we're fully booked."

"I guess I could find something in town," I said, more to myself than to her.

"You won't. I know everyone in this town. Everyone's full."

"Fuck," I whispered. "I guess I can go ask my sister-in-law if I could stay with her."

Her eyes lit up. "I have an idea, but you might not like

it," she said with a private smile. When I took a step closer to the counter, she went on, "Stay in Ben's cabin. You could watch some TV or make dinner while you wait. If he's already on his way home, he'll be back in a few hours."

This was the worst plan I'd ever heard in my life.

But it's not like it would be weird. I'd been stark naked in there before. Plus, our relationship was all over the news, so if anyone saw me going in there, they wouldn't be surprised.

I hesitated. It would be just as easy to stay with Ruby and Hannah or any of the other aunts and uncles.

But I missed Ben. I wanted him to know that what I felt for him was strong. Maybe not love just yet, but the seed had been planted. Something was sprouting. "Okay. I'll do it," I said, like she'd asked me to ride a canoe down a white water rapid.

She grabbed a key she'd already laid on her desk and handed it to me. "I think you're making the right choice."

Chapter Twenty-Seven

I'd hefted my suitcase out of my rental car and rolled it down the dirt path, wondering if there was anyone in the woods taking pictures of me entering Ben's cabin.

Not that it mattered. They knew who we were already, and I wasn't doing anything I needed to hide, anyway.

The house smelled just like him. I knew it wasn't his style, but it felt more like home than my own house had. Everything was soft. Comforting. An actual sanctuary. It was hard not to want to stay here forever.

I pulled my phone out of my purse, finally switching off airplane mode, and a barrage of texts came through.

Aniyah wanted to know if we were going to buy The Azure or not. I told her to hold on, I'd figure that out in the morning. It felt exhilarating to be so cavalier about work. This place really had changed me.

Reece had stayed up all night watching the news, wondering which things they'd said about me were true. By the end of his thread, I worried he was going to get on a plane and come punch the reporters in their faces, so I told him I was safe and didn't need support just yet, but I'd keep him in mind if something else happened. It was a relief that he'd forgiven me so quickly, even though I'd been a pain in his ass for years.

Camilla and Blake had also asked how I was, so I let them know I wasn't sure, but would report back with complete honesty in twenty-four hours. I wished they were here, but I knew if I told them that, they'd book the next flight, too, and I didn't need more people witnessing what was most likely going to fall apart.

After I finished replying to the people who cared about me, I stood up, hungrier than I thought I'd be. Feeling a bit like Goldilocks when she breaks into the bears' house, I opened the fridge, wondering what I could snack on.

There was a plastic container with a single-sized serving of the roast Ben had made earlier this week. I usually threw away takeout that was more than three days old, but I couldn't stop myself. I put it on a plate, warmed it up in the microwave, then ate the whole thing in just a few minutes.

It was just as good this time, if not better. But it made me miss Ben even harder. I missed the love and attention he put into this meal. I hoped he hadn't been looking forward to eating it.

After cleaning up, I went back to the living room and stood in front of the couch. All I could think about was the last time we were here together. It hurt, thinking that there was a huge possibility I was going to lose him. That what we'd had, the beginning of a love story here in this room, was coming to an end.

I couldn't handle being in here any longer, but I didn't want to leave. Even if Ben got on a plane at the exact moment Cate called him, he wouldn't be here for several hours. I looked down at the purse I'd set on the coffee table and knew there was only one thing for me to do.

I grabbed a paperback I'd bought at the airport—one with a floral design on the cover that Blake had said was smutty as hell—and decided it was time to dive in.

The couch didn't seem like the right place for this, since it made me remember all the ways he'd touched me, but there weren't a lot of options in this tiny house. I finally decided on the bed, but I propped the pillows up so I wouldn't be tempted to cuddle up, smelling Ben all around me.

Trying to ignore how much this house felt like a home, I began reading. I made it through a few chapters, excited to find out which of the two lovers the main character would pick in the end. The soreness in my cheeks, the smile on my face, was surprising. I was actually having fun. Like real fun that didn't require anything but the pages in front of me.

I must have fallen asleep somewhere around the halfway point. The bed shifted under me and the book flew into the air. I gasped, my mouth dry from being open too long.

When I finally registered what was going on, I covered my face, worried I'd been drooling. "Ben. What are you doing here?"

He smiled from where he sat next to me on the edge of the bed. "You're inside my house."

"I'm sorry. There wasn't anywhere else for me to go."

He laughed. "According to Cate, huh? And you believed her?" He picked up my book, careful not to lose my place. "She reads more of these than you do." He grabbed a bookmark from his nightstand and tucked it in, laying it next to one of his own. "We should talk."

I moved to sit up straighter, giving him more space. "Or we could kiss?"

He laughed. "You didn't just fly across the country after telling me we could never be together so we could make out one last time, did you?"

I shrugged. "It was worth a try." I'd gone through so many scenarios in my head over the past twelve hours, trying to figure out how to tell him what I'd done for him. I wanted him to know that I wasn't doing this so he'd be with me. I wanted him, but I wanted him to feel like he was free from his father more than anything. "I paid off the resort."

His brow furrowed. "The Azure? I thought they were going to renegotiate later?"

I reached for his hand but stopped myself. This wasn't about us. It was just for him. "No, this one. Lac Brumeux."

He shifted, like he wasn't following where I was going. "You did what?"

"I used my connections at the bank to find out how much was owed on the mortgage." He knew who my connections were, but the less he knew about what I'd done, the better. I had to move around a lot of money, but luckily it was all mine, not my company's, so there would be minimal repercussions.

"Hold on. How many laws did you break in doing this?"

I laughed, knowing he would be concerned. "Listen, Martha only got five months for insider trading. All I did was pull some money out of a few accounts and use it on something important."

He pulled away a fraction of an inch. "And your expectations?"

"That's exactly why I did it. I don't have expectations. And I don't want anyone else having them, either."

His eyes were guarded, his brows pulling in deep. "But I can't pay you back. Not until my trust is available."

"Then I guess you're stuck with me for another two years." Relief brushed across his face, but I wanted to clarify my intentions. "I'm kidding. It's yours. It's not about the money." I looked around the room. "You love it here. This is your home. I didn't want anyone to have control over that ever again."

"But why?" he asked, wonder in his eyes.

"Because I couldn't stand someone taking your happiness ever again."

"Thank you." His words were quiet, but powerful. "I'd tell you I couldn't accept it, but I've seen you negotiate." He laughed. "I'm not telling you no."

We sat for a few moments in awkward silence. When I was ready to break the tension, I pulled the bracelet off my wrist and handed it to him. "Also, I had to bring this back to you."

He looked at it, small in his palm. "But it's yours."

I shook my head, taking his hand and wrapping his fingers around the piece of costume jewelry that had become worth more than my entire wardrobe. Than my empire. "I never forgot about you, either. Maybe it's why I married someone safe, someone who didn't set my heart on fire. Because I had to wait until the time was right for us."

His voice was deeper than usual. "What you said in California was right, though. We have a lot of hurdles to jump over if we're going to do this." He pursed his lips momentarily. "Maybe too many."

I squeezed his fist. "I was scared, and I pushed you away. But as soon as I walked away, I knew it was a huge mistake. I shouldn't have let fear drive me." Scanning his eyes, I felt more open than I'd ever been before. "I realized, in this ridiculous adventure, that I want a partner. I want someone who will love me for who I am. Who will put up with me when I work too late, but not hate me for being driven." I inhaled deeply, about to jump off the cliff. "And I want that person to be you. If you'll have me."

His eyes focused intently on mine. "You were wrong."

I let go of his hands, wondering if he really didn't want this thing that was growing between us. "About what?"

"I'm not going to hate living in California. We'll go wherever you want. Wherever makes you happy."

I sat back, not sure how to take in his words. "But this is your home."

He opened his hand, looking down at the bracelet one more time before putting it on top of my book on the nightstand. "Home isn't a place. Home is who makes you happy." He leaned toward me, propping himself up on his fists. "And I think that person is going to be you."

I reached up then, pulling him in for a kiss. When our lips met, I knew that wherever he was, was exactly where I needed to be, too.

～

After we talked, and left his bed completely disheveled, we ate and slept. Then I remembered this was the last day of the reunion and everyone knew I was here, waiting for me to come by.

So of course we got dressed, but stopped to make love on the couch one more time before actually trying to get out of the house.

It was refreshing, having someone who couldn't keep his hands off me. But it was also new and invigorating to have a man I couldn't get enough of, either. His haircut was growing on me, even though it was more difficult to hold on to when his face was tucked between my thighs.

This thing between us was new. It was fragile. But we both wanted it. We deserved to give it a chance and see what would happen.

Assuming it had been enough time for the reporters to leave, eager for their next story, we took a nice quiet walk to Zane's family's cabin.

I reached for the doorknob of the big cabin, but shifted on my heels slightly before opening it. Squeezing Ben's hand reassured me in a way I never thought I'd needed before.

As soon as we walked in, Ruby came running over to

us, squealing. "We wondered if the two of you would get off each other long enough to come say hi." The house was packed, like it always was the last night of these reunions. One last chance for everyone to talk and joke before the rental cars had to be returned and we went back to our real lives.

I looked at Ben, wondering what he was thinking, but he just extended his hand to Ruby, thanking her for welcoming us to the party. We chatted for a few minutes, and he seemed to relax. I hadn't yet, but as long as he felt calm, I wasn't afraid.

The room seemed to part dramatically as Zane came up to us. "Can we talk?" He asked me quietly.

Ben stiffened beside me. The last time we'd both been with my ex-husband, it hadn't been pleasant. "We don't have to do this right now," I said, trying to keep my voice even, so no one picked up on the tension between us.

"I can't, Izzy." He looked devastated. Eyes red, shoulders slumped. "I didn't mean any of it."

I held up my hand, cutting him off. "No, you were right. I spoke to my dad. He's not in charge of my company or my life."

Both men pulled back slightly, like they weren't expecting to hear that from me. I huffed out a laugh. "I wasn't a fan of your delivery, but you put a lot into perspective."

"I'm so fucking sorry. I was such an asshole." He sounded miserable, which I had to admit made me feel a lot better.

I grabbed his upper arm. "It's okay, Zane. I promise." And I meant it.

Zane then turned to Ben, offering his hand. "I also owe you an apology, man." They shook, and Ben shrugged a shoulder slightly. "I shouldn't have discounted your relationship or assumed you were trying to screw her over. I just got protective and said a lot of shit I didn't mean."

Ben looked down at me. "I don't know. I think she does pretty well protecting herself." I felt my smile grow, looking up at him, knowing that he saw me fully. That he was aware of my faults and was here for them.

Zane must have noticed the look we shared, because he groaned playfully. "I'm gonna leave you two to catch up. I should probably find my boyfriend, anyway."

It wasn't the full closure I wanted from our previous conversation, but this wasn't the time or the place. We would work through this part of our relationship, just like we'd worked through the last.

But now I had a man by my side that wanted me. Truly, deeply. Who understood my loss and wanted me to be the best version of myself regardless of his position in my life. Ben must have read my mind, because he leaned down and pressed a kiss to my lips.

I wrapped my arms around him, pulling him in tightly. Sure, it was new, but it felt more real than anything I'd ever felt before. I was falling hard and fast for him.

A throat cleared next to us, and I stepped back from Ben, finding Alice and Andrew smiling like a bunch of meddling parents about to drill into their daughter's new man. Without a word, Alice wrapped her arms around Ben so tightly that I thought he was going to turn blue.

When she let go of him, she looked me in the eye. "I know we can't talk right now, but I'd like to sit down with you soon. To apologize for the way we handled this situation. We messed up, and I hope you can forgive us."

My biggest fear this whole time had been that I'd be sent away. That I wouldn't be part of this family anymore. And in a heartbeat, I discovered that it didn't matter. That I belonged to them, and they belonged to me, whether I was married to their son or not. Whether their other son would actually be elected or not. They saw the real me, and that's why they loved me. Something else to unpack when I went back to therapy, but at least for the time being, I felt secure.

I reached for her hand briefly. "I'd like that a lot, actually."

She squeezed her palm in mine. "You'll always be our daughter. Even if you're not with our son anymore."

Ben looked down at me, slight panic in his eyes. I patted him on the shoulder. "Don't worry, I think you're one of us now." We were surrounded by people who loved me, so I knew they'd love him, too.

The rest of the night followed just like that. Everyone was kind and welcoming. Loving and understanding.

Bradley and Tippy had apparently packed up and caught the next flight home, with their proverbial tails between their legs.

Hours after the sun tucked itself behind the mountain, our small group sat on the porch. Ruby, Hannah, David, Zane, Caleb, and me, with Ben's fingers twined through mine. We'd run out of things to share an hour ago, but we stayed, just sitting in the moment, loving our lives together.

And when it was time for us to go, Ben walked me to his cabin, his arm around my shoulder. "I think this was the most fun I've ever had on a date before," he said, kissing the top of my head.

"Well, next year you'll get to come to the whole thing."

He squeezed me tighter against him. "I'd like that."

Stopping, I looked up at him. "I'm serious. I want this. And if that means stepping back from my responsibilities at The Howell Group or moving my headquarters here, I want to give us what we deserve. I don't want to be the partner that works all the time."

His smile was so bright, so beautiful, when he said, "I think I have an idea." He kissed me, holding me close, and then shared what he'd been thinking on the way back to his cabin.

Epilogue

Seven years later

My hands were full, but the sand between my toes made it all worth it. "Are you sure you can't carry this bag?" I asked, shifting it on my shoulder. "It's too heavy.

Ben turned around, carrying a huge umbrella and a couple of lawn chairs. My husband looked just as delicious today as he had the day I'd met him, just up the trail from where we currently stood.

We'd made it work, this insane schedule he'd put together all those years ago. We lived here in Michigan during the summer, but spent the rest of the year in California, running The Azure together.

We'd gotten married at the courthouse in Santa Barbara, much to our families' chagrin. Both of us had already had big fancy weddings and even fancier prenups, so this time we did it small, intimate. Just for us.

And it worked.

"Give it here," he replied, his voice still making my

heart flutter even after five years of marriage, "but I'll need help with that thing once we find everyone." He pointed to the cooler twenty feet behind us, which had been left there, the wheels stuck in the trail.

I winked at him. "I bet you have a thing I can help you with."

He rolled his eyes, leaning down to kiss me. "Christ, woman. You are insatiable."

He pulled my bag off my shoulder like it weighed nothing. "Jeez, Izzy, what's in here?"

I blushed a little. "Books." I reached up on my toes, pecking him on the cheek. "But to be fair, half of them are yours."

He looked in the bag, confirming what I'd said and laughed. "Okay, fine, I'll give you that."

"Over here!" A voice called out from a few hundred feet down the lakeshore. Ben grinned, even more excited to see Zane than I was. The two of them had become close since Ben moved to Santa Barbara. At first, it was because he didn't have any friends in town, but now the two of them were a lot like brothers. It should feel weird to me, my husband being best friends with my ex, but nothing about us was normal, so it didn't bother me one bit.

"Get over here and help!" Ben called out. "The cooler is stuck in the sand."

Zane jogged over to us, ready to help. "Really Izzy, the tequila shirt? How is it still in one piece?" He asked, tugging at my threadbare shirt.

I swatted him away. "It's the most comfortable thing that fits right now."

Leaving the two of them to figure out the cooler issue, I walked further toward our family, who were mostly set up for the first day of the reunion. When we were about twenty feet away, Ruby leaped from her beach towel, running toward me. "Oh my God, Izzy, you're absolutely massive!" Her hands were on my belly, and she leaned down, already giving a baby-talk monologue about waiting to come out on her birthday instead of my due date, which was two weeks later.

My brother, who lay on a giant beach blanket next to his wife, spoke up. "Ruby, you're not supposed to tell pregnant women how large they are. Believe me, I learned the hard way." He let out a yelp when Magdalina kicked him in the shin playfully. The baby dozing on her chest didn't even flinch.

"It's true, though," I told them, rubbing my lower back. "I wasn't even this big with the twins. This guy is going to be huge." Then I looked up, scanning the gaggle of children playing in the sand. "Speaking of the girls, did they make it here? They took off before we'd finished unloading the car."

A fit of giggles cut me off, and Jamey and Lilly jumped out of a hole that had been dug in the dirt, apparently for the sole purpose of jumping out at me. I pretended to be scared, throwing my hands in the air. Our three-and-a-half-year-olds fell over each other, laughing uncontrollably.

"You really got me!" I said, so damn happy that our kids got to spend this time every summer with all their cousins. Caleb grabbed the shovel and whistled, getting all the kids' attention. "Okay, it worked on Auntie Izzy, but I think if we make it wider, we can really scare Grammy and Grampy!"

Little hands grabbed sand, tossing it out of the hole, all except for Allister, Zane and Caleb's two-year-old, who'd decided to eat his. I was reaching down, helping remove the dirt from his fist, when someone shouted behind me.

"Sorry we're late. We had to stop for more snacks because someone ate them on the plane." Blake looked adorable in a pink one-piece swimsuit with a yellow sarong tied around her waist.

Her boyfriend Sal, dressed in all black, grumbled behind her. "It was half a bag of gummy bears." Their matching floral tattoo sleeves were the only indication that they had anything in common if you didn't know them personally. Her bright colors always contrasted his dark denim and motorcycle boots—which he was even wearing here at the lake.

She tossed her ponytail over her shoulder before pushing her finger against his chest playfully. "Listen, Salami, I don't want to hear it."

He was a giant of a man, broad-shouldered and tall, but the smile that blossomed across his face made it obvious that he'd eaten more than he was admitting to the crowd. "Oh, you're going to hear it," he said before grabbing her by the waist, tickling her until she screamed.

The rest of their group reached us: Camilla and her husband, as well as Blake and Magdalina's best friend Valerie and her husband.

Reece's daughter Zinnia, the oldest of all the kids,

climbed out of the hole construction zone, rushing to give the newcomers hugs and kisses, too.

Our crowd had easily doubled in size here on the lake, which didn't include the majority of Zane's family yet. Two people had somehow managed to get out of every reunion for the past several years, not that we missed Bradley or his wife. In fact, we hadn't seen them since that insane reunion all those years ago.

It was amazing, the unconventional family we'd built on our own. Full of love and laughter. Everything I hadn't had as a kid that I wanted my own children to have.

Ben found me, pointing to the chair he'd set up under the umbrella. "I got you the perfect spot," he said, taking my hand and twirling me in a circle before dipping me and planting a kiss on my neck. He was always affectionate. Always handsy, if I were being honest. My favorite dance partner.

"This might be our biggest reunion yet," I told him, settling into my chair.

He sat next to me, taking my hand in his own. "I think so, too." He looked out across the lake, inhaling deeply. Absolute joy spread across his face when he looked back at me. "Happy anniversary." He pulled our joined hands to his lips, kissing them. "I love you more and more every day."

"I love you too," I replied. Not for the first time, and not for the last. But right now, I was the happiest I'd ever been.

Acknowledgments

I'm so grateful that you came on Lizette's journey with me. From the moment I envisioned her as Reece's overbearing sister in *A Liar and a Thief*, I knew she would get a "get your groove back" kind of story. I didn't know when I'd write it, but as I wrote *Love and Reservations* and she softened through Blake's friendship, I knew she absolutely had to be my next great love.

It was important to me while developing this story to take common tropes and flip them on their heads. Marriage of convenience, only one bed, enemies to lovers, friends to lovers (in this case lovers to friends), second chance romance (but in a secret way) . . . as many of them as I could fit. I thought it would be fun to break out of the norm—since Lizette and her love story was nothing close to normal.

So, first and foremost, I want to thank YOU for being here. For taking a chance on this story that has lived inside my heart for so long. I am so honored that you gave your time to my little piece of art in the world, and I hope the time you spent with my words will encourage you to do the hard things, even if they terrify you.

I want to thank my family, for being okay with all the hours I spent holed up with my laptop, pretending to live in an imaginary resort in Michigan. For acting like you actually cared when I freaked out over a plot hole, or when I got excited about a new idea and talked so fast you couldn't track what I was saying, but went with it anyway.

For my mom, who reads more books than I do and recommends the ones she loves, and also reads all the smutty ones I recommend without any judgment. For my dad, who is also working on a manuscript, so I finally have someone to share what I've learned with, but was interested in the craft well before it was something you wanted for yourself. For my mother-in-law, who will sit with me for hours and talk about a little bit of everything and a little bit of nothing. Those are my favorite days. I'm also so eternally grateful for my father-in-law (who hopefully will never actually read my books, because . . . well, you know) for planning elaborate family reunions that gave me the idea for having an adventure in tiny cabins in the woods in Lizette's love story. I can't wait for the next one!

I'm so grateful for my friends, old and new, for letting me throw ideas around with them and for always having a shoulder to lean on.

For Alexandra, for answering every single question I could think of regarding the Upper Peninsula of Michigan, and even giving me some specific ideas to sprinkle into the story. Anything I got wrong about this beautiful location is because of me, because your knowledge has been beyond helpful in every moment of this project. Thank you for being a friend I can be myself around, even if that self is a complete weirdo.

I'm thankful for my local writers' groups for support

and encouragement. I tried a lot of scary things this year, and I couldn't have done it without the members of all the groups I've shown up to and read pages with.

To the ladies in my online communities, for reminding me that I need to rest and celebrate small victories, which has been the hardest thing to do for myself.

This story wouldn't be what it is without help from my amazing alpha/beta team: Catie, Bethany, Wendy, and Brennan. And to my resident bravery-encouragers, Michelle and AJ. Thanks for making it feel like I really can do the hard things. And thank you Clara, for taking this massive pile of words and finding every single comma that I misplaced (or at last doing the best you could do with this heap of comma splices).

I'm so grateful for Jennifer J. Williams. My 'does this even make sense' sounding board friend. The woman who reminds me that freaking out is absolutely normal, but that I can also use that energy to turn my dreams into reality. You're a North Star and I'm so glad I get to orbit you (and also read your books).

Catie O'Neill. Thank you for being my totally legitimate twin sister that is from the other side of the country and also a year younger than me but is actually my twin in any other sense than genetics. Because, what does science even mean anyway? Thank you for all the support and jokes and just . . . everything. I am so grateful that you're in my life. I would link this page to a spreadsheet listing the many ways you have shown up and supported me, but it would bore the hell out of anyone except the two of us.

And then there's Tamara Rene. My Fairy

Bookmother. This story wouldn't be here without your commitment, compassion, and advocacy. You literally stopped me from deleting this entire manuscript when I was grieving so many things and didn't think I could keep writing. You read this story almost as many times as I have. You've been pulling for Ben since he first showed up as a spark in my imagination, even though we both struggle with blond men. You guys… Tamara taught me what a Chesterfield was only after I used it as a person's name without knowing it and then . . . well, you know what happened to the Chesterfield sofa if you've made it this far. I literally would not be the writer I am without you. Or maybe even a writer at all anymore.

To ZJ . . . throwing around story ideas when we drive to school is one of my greatest treasures. Having a kid who loves storytelling as much as I do has made me so proud. One day you're going to take over the world and I hope you know I'm here for it, one hundred percent of the way.

And finally. To my hot husband. The answer to all of my hopes and dreams. The man who tells me he got so lucky every time he looks at me, even when I haven't showered for days and am wearing sweatpants and a messy bun, and probably have pizza stains all down my shirt. I am the luckiest person because you exist. Thank you for always supporting me, even if my ideas are probably insane.

I love every single one of you. Thank you for being exactly who you are.

FOLLOW THE AUTHOR

Instagram | Facebook
DeeRollingsBooks.com

Join my Newsletter to access exclusive content, news, and get access to bonus scenes coming soon!

BOOKS BY DEE ROLLINGS

Discordant Memories

The Pacifica Resort series:

A Liar and a Thief

Love and Reservations

First Loves and Last Resorts

He's her Mr. Wrong . . . and her new roommate.

Resort manager Blake Thomas has no patience for weddings — she's seen far too many lovestruck couples pass through her doors. She'd rather pursue her "weird" hobby of geocaching than try to find The One.

But when a last-minute eviction notice turns her life upside down, Blake is forced to move in with a man she'd rather keep tucked away in her past. And Sal has one condition in exchange for free rent: he needs a fake girlfriend to impress his estranged parents.

Determined to avoid reawakening painful memories, Blake avoids her new "boyfriend" by throwing herself into house-hunting, her best friend's wedding, and an offer for a major promotion.

But as long-buried sparks ignite, she begins to realize that their scheme is becoming all too real. And Sal is hiding more secrets than Blake ever imagined . . . .

*A sweet and steamy, first person POV contemporary romance, the second novel of **The Pacifica Resort, Love and Reservations** will have your heart fluttering from beginning to end.*

A car accident, amnesia, two supposed lovers, and many dark secrets. In a race against time, who will come out on top?

Catrina Banks wakes up with bruises on her body and no memories from the last six months. An illustrious painter, she feels as though someone has stolen the colors from her canvas.

Under the teeming hospital lights and white coats crowding around her, Catrina faces questions she has no answers to. How did she end up in a city far from home? What was she doing there? Where is her phone, her ID, and most of all: *Who assaulted her?*

Struggling with intermittent flashbacks, Catrina tries to piece her life together. Cradling a gray hoodie and wedding bands she has no memory of, Cat returns home with her boyfriend Danny.

Even after she's safe at home, she can't shake the weird feeling that something is *off*, nor can she ignore the haunting glimpses she gets of a different life with another man.

Discordant Memories *is a **gripping romantic thriller** that will have you on the edge of your seat, desperate to flip the pages to find out what happens next.*

About the Author

Dee Rollings was born and raised in the big city, but her heart lives in the forest. She does her best writing on the porch of her tiny house in the woods when she's not wrangling her kid or her dogs and having one-sided conversations with chipmunks.

She's a multi-genre author, penning both romantic thrillers and romantic comedies, but there is one thing for sure about all of her books—they'll make you think a little differently about society and the world, exploring topics such as addiction, grief, womanhood, and self-worth.